Stormy weather . . .

Jules glanced up to note that clouds, dark and menacing, had gathered to the west. "I believe your father may have had the right of it after all. Look at those clouds." He took the opportunity to tuck her arm more firmly close to him, then turned back toward the house.

Before they reached the tables, rain began to fall. He virtually carried her up to the shelter of the rear entry to the house. "There; little damage done."

But the rain had dampened her gown, allowing it to cling enticingly to her figure. Jules thought he had better get her inside and dry before he betrayed his attraction more than he had already. He wanted to kiss her and never let go. He couldn't imagine what she might do in the event he gave way to his impulse. . . .

The Rake's Revenge

Emily Hendrickson

A SIGNET BOOK

SIGNET
Published by New American Library, a division of
Penguin Putnam Inc., 375 Hudson Street,
New York, New York 10014, U.S.A.
Penguin Books Ltd, 27 Wrights Lane,
London W8 5TZ, England
Penguin Books Australia Ltd, Ringwood,
Victoria, Australia
Penguin Books Canada Ltd, 10 Alcorn Avenue,
Toronto, Ontario, Canada M4V 3B2
Penguin Books (N.Z.) Ltd, 182–190 Wairau Road,
Auckland 10, New Zealand

Penguin Books Ltd, Registered Offices:
Harmondsworth, Middlesex, England

First published by Signet, an imprint of New American Library,
a division of Penguin Putnam Inc.

First Printing, March 2001
10 9 8 7 6 5 4 3 2 1

REGISTERED TRADEMARK—MARCA REGISTRADA

Printed in the United States of America

PUBLISHER'S NOTE
This is a work of fiction. Names, characters, places, and incidents either are
the product of the author's imagination or are used fictitiously, and any
resemblance to actual persons, living or dead, business establishments, events,
or locales is entirely coincidental.

*I dedicate this book to Sherrie Holmes,
that witty and wonderful friend from Olalla.*

Chapter One

The early-morning May sun gilded the still figure of a woman seated near the waters of the Serpentine, picking out golden highlights in her dark russet hair. The haze that had drifted over the park at dawn had thinned, allowing shafts of sunlight to accent the woman so deeply in thought.

A viewer would have called her a lovely creature, a young lady of refinement. The pensive expression she wore somehow added to her beauty. She tossed a pebble into the water, a vehement splash that sent water arching.

Plainly, matters were not to her liking.

Regina stirred slightly. It was so blessedly peaceful here, so removed from the problems that beset her. What to do? How? She could see no way out of her dilemma.

A duck settled noisily in the water, splashing and quacking loudly. It was a beautiful sight, but, as she well knew, beauty was no guarantee of happiness.

How foolish she had been, to think that finding a husband would be a simple matter. She wasn't a diamond of the first water, true, but she was accounted a beauty—or so she'd often been told—with odes to her charming face, her glorious hair, and elegant style heaped at her feet. Her dowry was more than respectable, and her parents both descended from the most impeccable lineage. However, she had not calculated on the vagaries of Society, nor had she contemplated how devastating gossip could be—spiteful and contemptible.

Could she remain in London? Never in her life had she been so unhappy. She had tried hard to be proper, to do all that Society deemed correct, to stifle her natural spontaneity.

Her upright posture, always so admired, drooped with her dejection. A bit of help would be nice. Alas, there was no one she might turn to for advice. Her father pooh-poohed her worries as nonsense, claiming that a good man would see the gossip for the malicious tittle-tattle that it was. Her mother knew well how difficult life was at present for her elder daughter, but Mama's health was delicate.

Regina had tried to shield her younger sister, Pamela, from the barbs of gossip that had been aimed at Regina, and she thought she had succeeded there. It was her only achievement to date in an otherwise dismal time.

She had not the least notion how to combat the snide remarks, the evil little darts of verbal poison that stung along with the insincere smiles of commiseration. Surprisingly, women were not the only ones to scorn her. So far she had received a great number of speculative looks from so-called gentlemen and one less than respectable offer.

What to do? Who could help? She wanted to fight! She braced herself as though preparing for battle.

From a distance Jules, Lord St. Aubyn studied the figure sitting in solitude, obviously wishing to be alone. Society being a small world, he well knew what caused her unhappiness. Miss Hawthorne did not look as though she was contemplating the cold waters as the solution to her predicament, but he decided to intrude anyway. One never knew. He rode closer to where she sat in silent contemplation.

"It is not the end of the world, you *must* know. Although I suspect you believe it to be at this moment." His voice broke into her reverie, startling her, as he had hoped it might.

She stiffened, rising to stare as he dismounted, looped his horse's reins over a stout branch, and then strode across the lawn to face her.

"Obviously, you have not only read the papers but you were also at the Oldershaws' ball last evening." Her mocking look dared him to offer pity. He admired her for that. Only a closer look at her blue eyes revealed the depths of her distress.

"You had expectations?" His remark was somewhere between a question and a statement. He suspected she had anticipated an offer from Torrington, but he didn't know if she was in love with the man. Had her heart been broken? He well knew what a shattering effect such an emotion could have for a woman.

"You must know I did. It seems everyone else in London had the same notion." Her words were understandably tinged with bitterness, but her smile was heartbreakingly valiant. Jules wondered just how much of her heart had been engaged. He met her gaze with a steady one of his own, catching her curiosity and holding it.

"I *know* only that you have received particular attention from Lord Torrington and it was expected among some of the Society gossips that you would eventually make a match of it." He kept his voice carefully neutral, almost sympathetic.

"My Lord St. Aubyn, then you know as much as I do. I daresay you read in the papers that a wedding is to take place between Lord Torrington and Katherine Talbot. I thought he had broken with her, lost interest in her. After he danced attendance on me, I naturally had expectations. Obviously I was wrong." The bitterness was clear now, her voice ringing with anger and frustration.

She turned away from him, most likely to conceal tears. Whether they derived from hurt or regret, he couldn't know. He offered a square of white linen without saying anything and was pleased when she wiped her eyes, blew her nose, then crumpled the handkerchief into a ball, as though by doing so she could dispose of the hateful gossip.

"Yes, I heard the whispers last evening." *Rejected Re-*

gina, they had called her. "Not the nicest, I must confess." Jules gave her a half smile and took a step closer.

Her beauty had a haunting quality as she turned back to him, particularly her eyes. Delicate rose tinged her pale cheeks, and violet shadows made her troubled eyes seem even bluer. Her courageous stance seemed poignant.

"Already I have received an offer from one labeled a gentleman. Needless to say, it is not a proposition I shall accept." She gave a short laugh, a mere catch of sound. "I never in my life thought to be offered a slip on the shoulder."

"I saw you when you entered the ballroom with your parents and your sister." He took another step forward, wanting to extend consolation, comfort, and not sure how to do so.

She looked away from him with a shrug of slim shoulders covered by a smoky-blue wool riding habit that reflected her eyes and flattered the russet glory of her hair. "The evening was not far advanced before I became aware of women who were only too delighted to see my situation. I had not thought their smug satisfaction could be so hard to endure."

"Satisfaction?" Jules frowned as he recalled some of what he had heard. Well, it was a far cry from sympathy, that was true. They both knew how catty some women could be. He didn't know Miss Hawthorne well—they had danced, talked, but never been close. Society didn't often permit that. After all, a few dances and a chap could find himself engaged!

"Glee, perhaps?" She exhaled deeply. "I do not see how I am to come about from this, for I sense those spiteful women will not permit such a splendid morsel to die a quiet death. 'Rejected Regina' will perhaps be my epithet for as long as I remain in the City. What gentleman will make an honorable offer for a woman so publicly rejected? I do *not* fear becoming a spinster. I *do* dread what might happen to my younger sister. She must not pay for any folly of mine."

"It isn't your folly," he objected. She was being very candid. Perhaps the bitter indignity of the previous evening had removed her caution. Or perhaps she thought him a safe repository for her thoughts—which surprised him a bit.

Her impatient hand waved his protest aside. "How silly of me to think that the Marquis of Torrington had any lasting interest in me." Her words snapped out, sharp and curt.

"It was beyond your control. Besides, it was not unreasonable for you to believe he intended to offer marriage." His voice proffered consolation, but it seemed she was not to be comforted, at least not by him. Jules wanted to ask her if she had cared deeply for Torrington, but such a question was not to be raised. He knew her slightly, and he had his reasons for extending pity, but would she understand?

She abruptly turned away from him toward her docile mare, which waited patiently not far away. "You are too kind, sir, to listen to my woes. I must go before someone sees us and leaps to strange conclusions. You might find yourself in the peculiar situation of having offered to make me your mistress." She glanced back, her smile brave and slightly mocking.

Jules gave her full marks for pluck. His estimation of the beautiful Miss Hawthorne had risen considerably in the past few minutes. She was not one of the empty-headed society misses. There was a depth to her he had not seen in other young women, certainly not in the blond beauty ranked as this Season's incomparable.

Jules stepped to Miss Hawthorne's side, tossing her up into the saddle with ease. "No one would dare to say such a thing of you or me."

"Lord St. Aubyn, you forget—someone already has invited me to assume such a situation. Strangely enough, he was a man I had considered a possible suitor, at the very least a friend. How lowering." Her face grew scornful, an expression that sat ill with her beauty.

Jules studied the exquisite face beneath the clever rid-

ing hat with its blue plume trailing along the tender line
of her jaw. He looked away for a moment, thinking fast.
"I would help you." How, he didn't know at the moment.
"May I come to call on you later—this afternoon,
perhaps?"

"I would be pleased. Heaven knows I have no notion
as to how best to proceed. 'Chin up, shoulders back,' as
my father urges, does not quite do it, you know." Her
gallant grin wobbled a bit.

"I admire your bravery, Miss Hawthorne. I am glad
to see you are not about to seek oblivion in the lake."

"As I said, I do not fear being a spinster. And I am
not about to take a coward's way out of my dilemma."

"You think suicide a coward's path?" He gave her a
curious look, taking a step away from her.

"It would seem so to me." She glanced behind him,
seeing what he heard—approaching riders. "Until later,
my lord." Within seconds she was but a beautiful
memory.

Jules had no desire for company at present, and so he
swiftly mounted to ride in the opposite direction as
quickly as possible, not casting any glances toward the
riders, lest he feel compelled to join them.

And then he wondered what in the world had possessed him to offer his help. What could he as a single
man, and one with a reputation—carefully cultivated, to
be sure—of a rake at that, do to assist a young woman
in regaining her reputation? It was near laughable when
he considered the matter. Yet he also remembered what
one whom he held dear had suffered.

He cantered out of the park, going straight to the
mews where he stabled his mount. From there he sought
a change of clothes before heading to White's. If he was
to learn the latest gossip, that was a good place to begin.

Regina handed her mare to the groom, then made her
way into the house, using the convenient back entrance.
Taking the back stairs at a thoughtful pace, she mulled
over the encounter in the park. Would he truly come to

see her this afternoon? She hoped he might. He had offered sensible words, a reasonable attitude, and kindness.

"Dearest, is that you? You went riding so early." Lady Hawthorne approached her elder daughter along the dim hallway, a worried expression on her face. Regina was glad when people said she resembled her mother; she could think of no nicer accolade.

"Indeed, Mama. I had an agreeable ride this morning. It is rather nice to be out and about before the rest of the world." She reached out to pat her mother's shoulder, and the handkerchief she had balled up in her hand fell to the floor. Swift as she was to scoop it up, her mother noted the size of the linen square.

"That is not, I think, one of yours."

"True. A kind gentleman I met while near the Serpentine loaned it to me. I must have it washed to return it to him promptly." She evaded her mother's probing gaze.

"Gentleman? And who might that be?"

Regina gave a sudden grin. "Perhaps one of the few in London—Lord St. Aubyn!"

"Heavens, Regina! He has a scandalous reputation." Lady Hawthorne placed an arm about her daughter, drawing her along to Regina's room. Lady Hawthorne's curiosity fairly bubbled.

"Well, it would seem that we are two of a kind in that event. You must know that after last evening and that item in the papers I have acquired a similar standing." Regina raised her chin, giving her mother an impudent smile.

"Oh, my dear girl! What are we to do?"

"Lord St. Aubyn has offered to help me. What he might be able to do is more than I can think. However, I shall not turn away from any assistance offered, especially when it seems to be offered in a spirit of genuine concern."

"Indeed," Lady Hawthorne said briskly. "This Season is a far cry from what I hoped it would be. You know, I recall something about his family from two years past, but being so ill and deep in the country, I fear the details have escaped me."

Regina nodded, then slipped out of her riding habit to change into a highly respectable round gown of white muslin decorated with delicate blue embroidery. If Lord St. Aubyn actually did come later this day, Regina intended to look the part of a virtuous miss. If he came.

Jules sauntered to his club, considering the problem of gossip. How many young women in past years had been devastated by Society tattlemongers spewing their malicious words? The harm done by these insensitive females to the young ladies making a come-out into Society was incalculable. One sneering look, one cut direct, and the damage began.

He well knew the effects of such words. It seemed to him that all that was needed after that was a few whispered sentences, scornful looks, snide little laughs, and the deed was accomplished. How could a young woman counter the whispers, the looks, the cuts? It took a brave girl to face them down. Few did. They usually fled London, finding relief one way or another—as he had reason to know.

Jules entered White's, tossed his hat toward the porter, then climbed the stairs with ears attuned to catch any conversation that might be going.

What he discovered while playing at cards in the hours that followed did not please him. Men, he decided, were just as vicious as women when it came to shredding the character of another, even a young woman of undisputed innocence like Regina Hawthorne, the baron's eldest child.

"Dashed pretty filly," Sir William Snyde exclaimed when another chap brought up Regina's name. "Heard that Wrexham made her an offer."

"Which she rejected!" Percy Botham slapped his friend on his shoulder in amusement. "Poor old Wrexham was fair annoyed, too. Thought he would get there first, you know."

"Just because Torrington returned to his first love doesn't make Miss Hawthorne less desirable, does it?" Jules inserted casually, while studying the cards he held in his hands. "He may have been trying to make up his mind, and concluded that Miss Talbot suited him the best. It does not follow that Miss Hawthorne should be rejected by others because of his choice."

" 'Course it does!" Percy bestowed a scornful look on Jules. "But then, you are hardly acquainted with proper females, are you?" He guffawed at his witticism.

"Perhaps I have been missing something." Jules gave Percy a lazy grin, biting back his anger at the fool. "I just may have to rectify that omission."

"I suspect Lady Monceux wouldn't take such action kindly." Sir William studied Jules with curious eyes, as though wondering how serious he might be.

"Her ladyship and I have not met recently. I have no idea as to what she might or might not think." Jules was far too polite to reveal that he had found Lady Monceux totally lacking when it came to anything other than romantic dalliance. She might be clever in her own way, but she bored him beyond tolerance in spite of her luscious charms. Once he had reached that conclusion, his removal as her admirer was immediate.

"Oho!" Sir William said with glee. "The Monceux is on the prowl for a new, er, friend, is that it?"

"She might be. I have no idea." Jules tried to keep the distaste he felt from coloring his expression or words. He had never been one to flaunt his conquests before others. And if he intended to help Miss Hawthorne, he had better figure a means of doing so properly—without destroying her in the process.

"So, tell us who is now to be the recipient of your attention, St. Aubyn?" Percy Botham grinned, quite as though he had placed Jules in an uncomfortable position.

Jules returned the grin with effort. "You will have to wait to discover that, my friend. Surely you do not expect me to reveal her identity to the lot of you?"

Sir William chuckled. "All the young bucks in town

would flock to her door at that. Likely beat you to it, if gossip travels as fast as I believe it does."

Jules gave Sir William a speculative look, wondering on which side of the fence he sat. Would he cheerfully mince Regina's reputation should Jules pay her any attention—as he now fully intended to do?

"Well, there are enough young women in the matrimonial bazaar this Season. You will have your pick, if I make no mistake." Sir William gave Jules a half smile that revealed none of his thoughts.

"Ha!" Percy retorted. "What fond mama is going to allow a gentleman of St. Aubyn's reputation near her little ewe lamb?" At Jules's hostile look he added, "Beg pardon, but you must know how you are viewed amongst Society."

"Perhaps that is why I ought to do something different," Jules countered. "Maybe I ought to flirt with one of the incomparables or perhaps a fledgling?"

"That will be the day," Sir William muttered quietly.

Jules decided he'd had quite enough and rose to leave. "I am off to discover new fields of, er, interest, gentlemen." He gave them a mocking salute. "Wish me well."

"Wrexham won't," Sir William concluded thoughtfully.

Jules carried those words with him as he left the club. Miles, Lord Wrexham was a man he would rather not cross. Yet if he were the one who had offered Regina a slip on the shoulder, it would seem that such a confrontation might be forthcoming. Jules was not a coward, but he didn't go looking for trouble, either.

Late that afternoon, almost at the end of the proper time when people paid calls on others, the butler announced Lord St. Aubyn. There was a general shifting, and uneasy glances were exchanged among those few gentlemen who graced the Hawthorne drawing room— who were likely appearing there out of curiosity, Regina decided. The women, nosy to a fault, stirred with obvious interest.

Firm footsteps on the stairs were followed by the appearance of St. Aubyn in the doorway. His dress was understated, with a simple but elegant cravat tied above a corbeau waistcoat having the cut of a renowned tailor. His gray coat became him, accenting his dark hair and dark brown eyes nicely, while biscuit pantaloons molded thighs that needed no padding.

Regina studied his modish appearance and smiled. He eclipsed all the others completely. She had hoped he would. Why she pinned so much faith on this man she wasn't sure. Decisive, dashing, debonair—all fit him. He possessed that air of one who could do anything, and often did.

Her mother bestowed a pleased smile on him, quite as though she didn't know his reputation. But then, she could scarcely cast slurs at Lord St. Aubyn, considering the pickle in which Regina had been placed.

Scandal was so delicious. Society fed upon it. Even now, the matrons present who were well aware of St. Aubyn's history were speculating on his appearance in this charming gold-and-blue drawing room.

"Welcome, Lord St. Aubyn. This is indeed a surprise," Lady Hawthorne said, a firmly fixed smile on her face. With a gracious gesture to the sofa upon which she sat, she urged, "Please join me."

After a quick glance about the room, Lord St. Aubyn did as requested. "Lovely day." He settled upon the sofa with a masculine grace that Regina could but admire.

Priscilla Carvil giggled; her mother looked mortified and pinched her arm. They rose, intent upon leaving.

The Honorable Olivia Russell smirked, clearing her throat rather loudly as though to draw his lordship's attention to her. Her mother pulled her to her feet and hastily murmured something about having to be on their way and what an interesting chat they had enjoyed.

It seemed that with the advent of Lord St. Aubyn most ladies felt it time to depart. A few curious gentlemen remained, desirous of learning what had brought the celebrated St. Aubyn to this house. Regina knew he had never before been known to dangle after a miss making her come-out. In fact, she'd learned he usually confined his attentions to well-endowed widows or other fair charmers not likely to seek a permanent attachment, like marriage. She could imagine the speculation that would follow his call on the Hawthornes.

"How is your dear mother?" Lady Hawthorne said into the awkward silence of the room.

"Fine. You know her?" St. Aubyn seemed surprised.

Well, wasn't that a wonder, Regina thought, for Mama said Lady St. Aubyn rarely came to Town, and then only for a brief time to visit her mantua-maker and do a bit of shopping.

"We went to school together. Henrietta and I were dear friends in our girlhood. I've not seen her in years. I fear I am a bit of a recluse now because of my health."

"Mama," Regina whispered, "you are not overly tired?" To St. Aubyn she added, "It is a pity that the influenza taxed Mama so terribly."

"I would know something of my dear friend's son, Regina." She smiled at St. Aubyn. "If you are at all like your father, you are much sought after. I recall him so well. He was a dashing and kind gentleman."

Evidently deciding they were in for a rather boring time, the two remaining gentlemen took their leave, offering Regina significant looks and what almost amounted to flirtation right under her mother's nose.

Regina seethed beneath her calm demeanor, but she said her farewells with a graciousness that the nodcocks did not deserve.

When all were gone—even the pushing Mrs. Dudley, whose nose fairly quivered with curiosity and a desire for a tidbit of gossip—St. Aubyn rose from his place beside Lady Hawthorne to take a turn about the room.

"How long has this been going on?" He gestured to the chair that Mrs. Dudley had at last vacated.

Not misunderstanding him in the least, Regina spoke before her mother could reply. "This is but the second day of such intense curiosity. If I did not know the cause I should be flattered. Do you not agree?"

"True." He gave her a wry grimace before pacing about in front of the fireplace, now devoid of any warmth. "However, since we know differently, we must do something to alter the circumstances."

Regina rose, clasping her hands before her, and went to the window to peer down at the street below. "They have all gone. I wish they might all stay away from here. I am quite sick of the lot of them."

"I can hardly argue with that assessment." Lord St. Aubyn crossed the room to take one of her hands in both of his. "There must be something, some way of halting this gossip."

"Well," Lady Hawthorne inserted, "my mother once said the best way to end one bit of gossip was to replace it with another."

"But what?" Regina looked first at her mother, then to Lord. St. Aubyn. At last realizing that he held her hand in his, she reluctantly withdrew hers from his surprisingly comforting clasp.

"I have considered this at some length," he said. "Lady Hawthorne is correct. We need to substitute some audacious tittle-tattle for the present item regarding Torrington. May I offer my services as an escort, beginning with the soiree this evening at the Beachams'? We shall stir the pot before bringing it to a boil."

"Oh, dear." Regina gave him a worried look, then turned to face her mother. "What do you think, Mama? It sounds a trifle risky to me. Not that you are not the crème de la crème, sir," she hastily added to St. Aubyn. "Any young lady should be pleased to have your escort."

He looked amused rather than offended, as he might well have been. He rubbed his chin, seeming speculative. "And I believe that we should attend that wedding. They are calling it the wedding of the year. Would it not set the cat among the pigeons were we to go together, arm in arm? It would make the gossip regarding you and Torrington seem rather foolish."

"I suspect that restoring Regina's good name will not be quite so simple a matter," Lady Hawthorne said dryly.

"Far be it from me to prevent you from trying, however. You do realize that you may be creating a hornet's nest of your own?"

"I cannot see that at all. Why, it is a simple matter of escorting Miss Hawthorne to a party, then the wedding. Perhaps a few drives in the park to top it all off? What do you think?" He made it sound like a picnic.

Lady Hawthorne smiled, albeit with seeming reluctance. She shrugged, then nodded. "Very well. It would seem the scheme has merit. I certainly cannot think of anything that is any better than what you propose." If she wondered at the reason for his assistance, she didn't ask.

Regina gave Lord St. Aubyn a dubious look. Was he truly offering his escort, willing to shepherd her through the coming days? She wasn't certain it would work. On the other hand, it certainly ought to stir the pot, as he put it. Causing that pot to boil was a different matter entirely.

"What do you say, Miss Hawthorne?" His lordship again took one of her hands in a light clasp, his intent gaze fixed on her face. It wasn't as though he was asking her to wed him or anything like that. Goodness, he was merely offering help.

"Well, I cannot see that it will make matters any worse than they are now." She turned to her mother to add an observation. "His lordship is highly regarded in Society, Mama. I cannot think of any gentleman who would elevate me in better style than he."

Lord St. Aubyn cleared his throat, then smiled persuasively at Lady Hawthorne. She rose to join them.

This time her smile bloomed in full force. "High praise, indeed." She bestowed a fond glance on her daughter, then offered the freshly laundered handkerchief to his lordship, who promptly tucked it into a pocket. "I believe that belongs to you, sir. I thank you for what comfort you offered my daughter and commend you for the help you have now offered. It remains to be seen how it goes off."

"Mama!" Regina gave her mother a shocked look, then turned to St. Aubyn. "Sir, if you have any misgivings do not hesitate to reveal them now."

Put thus on his mettle, St. Aubyn stood a trifle straighter and bowed to Lady Hawthorne before capturing both of Regina's hands in his. "What color do you wear this evening? I would have us be a foil for each other."

Regina gave her mother a look of disquiet, then mentally went through her wardrobe. "I intended to wear a gown of white satin with an overskirt of spangled gauze."

He nodded with apparent satisfaction. "Fine. I cannot wait to see it." He released Regina's hands, then bowed to both ladies. "Until this evening—say at eight?"

"Indeed." Regina gave him a faint smile, then listened to his footsteps going down the stairs and to the door closing behind him.

"I hope the ruse works," Lady Hawthorne murmured as Regina supported her in her walk to her room.

Regina could only nod, while thinking that something was bound to go wrong. Everything else had. "I hope he won't regret this."

Chapter Two

Regina examined the reflection in her looking glass, tweaking a russet curl piled high atop her head. Her maid had created a pretty arrangement of curls gathered with a silver ribbon, allowing the hair to cascade nicely down the back with just a curl or two by her ears. A single pearl in each earlobe and a strand of pearls at her neck were her only adornments. Pamela had peeked in while the maid was at work, declaring that Regina looked perfection. Pity she didn't feel that way.

It was time to go down. She far preferred to remain here, safe in a cocoon of family affection, but she had never been one to yield to defeat. Was she brave or merely foolhardy? She made a face at her looking glass, then left.

Each step down the stairs brought greater reluctance to face the evening ahead. When she entered the drawing room, she knew a strong urge to escape before the sharp tongues and insinuating looks could reach her. Yet she also knew that unless she overcame this situation, she was likely doomed to spinsterhood, and possibly her darling Pamela would have difficulty in making a good match.

The blue-damask-covered chairs and sofas were old, but Regina liked their contrast to the gold silk-hung walls. It was an appealing room, one with comfort as well as luxury. She glanced at the looking glass over the fireplace to assure herself that she appeared composed.

"I think you'll do very well, dearest." Her mother's soft voice startled her, coming from the depths of a wing chair not far from the fireplace where tonight a cheerful fire glowed.

"I am surprised, Mama. You are dressed to go out. Surely you do not feel strong enough to go with us?" Regina didn't want her mother to witness the snubs she was certain to receive if tonight was anything like last evening. "Pamela will be with me, and since Lord St. Aubyn has offered to escort us, there should be little problem." Ha! A fairy tale if ever there was one. She needed her mother, but had not dared ask for her help, given her fragile health. Lady Hawthorne had never been strong, and that bout of flu had nearly taken her from them.

"I am feeling remarkably well this evening, and I would see for myself how you go on. Lord St. Aubyn will agree, I feel sure." Her manner brooked no dispute.

Regina was about to argue with this bit of nonsense nevertheless, but Norton came to the doorway to announce their guest. "Lord St. Aubyn, my lady."

St. Aubyn entered immediately, crossing the room to where the women awaited him, offering a courtly bow to each.

"Good evening, ladies. I shall be the most favored of escorts this evening." He looked at Lady Hawthorne. "I am pleased to see that you join us, my lady."

He turned his attention to Regina. She thought his smile encouraging. "I believe you can fend off any unpleasantness—you look like an angel." Garbed in black and white, he was a perfect foil for Regina's silver gauze and white satin.

She gave him an answering smile, but when she spoke her words were wry. "We can but hope the evening will not prove to be a disaster. I would have spared Mama."

"However," the earl interjected, "your mother lends not only her support. She will be able to hear what we do not—namely, the direction the gossip is taking."

"Ah, yes, I forget. 'What dreadful thing did Miss Hawthorne do to give the marquis a disgust of her?'" Regina turned away from St. Aubyn, the ghosts of overheard conversations returning to haunt her. "It disturbs them that no one appears to know. Never could it be that he merely decided he preferred her to me." She snapped a stick of the fan she carried, then discarded it with a rueful grimace, annoyed with herself for giving way to anger.

She avoided meeting Lord St. Aubyn's gaze after her display of temper, small as it was. What would she see there? Could *he* guess her failure? Heaven knew she had tried over and over again to find her fatal flaw, the trait that had turned the marquis to another woman.

"We must be prepared for anything. My good friends will rally around us. Your friends as well, I daresay. With their help we ought to be able to see the evening through. Come, now, it shouldn't be too difficult."

Regina gave him a hesitant smile. Her appearance was her armor, but she feared she made a poor knight. When, she wondered, would Lord St. Aubyn realize that he had a battle on his hands? Or would it be a tourney, with foe after foe to unhorse? She almost smiled at the notion.

Lady Hawthorne rose from her chair as Pamela entered the room, dressed in pale rose muslin. Like her father's, her hair was brown and her eyes clear blue. A pretty girl, with a nice smile and pleasant voice, she showed promise to become a beauty in time. Her ladyship's gown of dark-blue satin rustled as she joined her younger daughter. "We may as well depart. Anticipation is often the worst, like going to a tooth-drawer."

"You go with us, Mama? Oh, good! You will be the prettiest mother there." Pamela blushed when she looked at Lord St. Aubyn. "That is, so many of the mothers are old and fat." She stopped and looked embarrassed. "Well, you must know what I mean, even if I can't say it properly."

Lady Hawthorne sighed, took Pamela's arm, and led the way out of the room.

"You look splendid, you know." St. Aubyn's softly spoken words soothed a few of Regina's fears.

"Thank you for that, and for what you do. I trust you

will not regret this evening." She followed her mother and sister, grateful for his lordship's touch at her waist.

Jules saw the women settled, then sat back against the plush seat of his town coach with an inner sigh. He had more than a few misgivings about the coming evening. Percy Botham had gleefully informed him that Lady Monceux was expected to attend the party. There might also be others besides her who had reason to wish him ill. He feared his offer to help Regina Hawthorne might be foolhardy. What if he made matters worse for her, rather than eliminate the nasty gossip?

Jules and Torrington had had a slight rivalry, but then so many men of the *ton* sought to challenge him. It would be interesting to take Regina to that wedding, show her off. He did wonder what had made Torrington choose Katherine Talbot over Miss Hawthorne. Katherine was a nice, quiet girl, but she didn't sparkle as did Regina, nor did her smile charm, or her voice have the musical lilt that Regina's did.

Since Torrington was safely engaged and out of the picture now, no rivalry existed between them anymore. Competition would come from other quarters. Not that he intended to compete for Regina Hawthorne. He was merely helping her through a bad patch.

Lady Hawthorne interrupted his musing. "I hope it will be an agreeable evening. There are certain to be ladies I have not seen for a time. Being ill is so tiresome, you know. It quite takes one out of the scene." She grasped the conversation firmly in her capable hands, confining her remarks to the most soothing of topics—the sort to calm jittery nerves.

The Beacham residence was not quite palatial, but it was certainly larger than the average London house. Guests trod upon red carpet up the steps to the door, which was opened by a footman in dark gray livery. The butler could take honors for stuffiness, Jules decided. But then, he was required by his employers to set the correct tone.

At first it seemed as though their fears were for

naught. Certainly the host and hostess were as gracious as they might wish, greeting the Hawthornes with smiles.

Jules glanced down at the young woman so silent at his side. He could feel her tremble, although none would have known it from her serene smile and proper posture. He'd wager she'd had a stern nanny when she was a little girl.

Percy Botham stepped forward to greet them, giving Regina a speculative look before he caught Jules's narrow gaze upon him. "Miss Hawthorne, could I claim a dance?"

"Indeed, sir. The third?" She replied in a somewhat hesitant manner, giving Jules a glance before turning to say something to her mother.

Several of his friends came to ask Regina to dance, earning smiles of appreciation from Jules. He claimed the first dance, leading her out while catching a glimpse of fans suddenly employed, no doubt to serve as a screen to mask the gossip going on behind them.

It appeared to Jules that they had few worries. He peered about the ballroom with a satisfied feeling.

And then he spotted Lady Monceux drifting across the ballroom in their direction, and he noted the expression on her face. Clearly, he was in for trouble. Did she think he had a new interest in Miss Hawthorne and seek to kill it?

When the dance concluded, he handed Regina to her next partner, then set off to deflect Beatrice, Lady Monceux before she might do any damage. She likely thought she had reason to be spiteful.

"Jules," she cried softly. "It has been an age. How are you, sir?" She flicked open an exquisite sandalwood fan, one he had given her some months before, and waved it slowly before her.

"I have been busy, my lady. And you?" His manner was as distant as he could manage. He could see Regina from the corner of his eye. She was talking with one of his friends, preparing to dance. "The music begins. May I claim this dance with you?"

"I would talk, but perhaps we can find a few moments to exchange words." Her face was a polite mask.

Jules did not trust her an inch. He knew her well enough to guess that anything she said would be unpleasant.

The pattern of the dance did not permit conversation at first. Then, when they had to wait for the other couple in their set to perform part of the pattern, she had her chance.

"What are you about, Jules? Playing nursemaid to a girl making her come-out, and at that, one who is the talk of the town?" She raised her fan, her manner intimate.

"If she is indeed the talk of the town, as you say, it is through no fault of her own. She is a delightful young lady." At the slight alteration of her ladyship's features, Jules guessed he had not helped matters by mentioning that Regina was young. Beatrice was quite aware that she was no longer youthful, although she did her best to counter the aging process and kept the candlelight in her rooms to a minimum come evening. Soft candlelight was so kind to a woman, particularly one on the wrong side of thirty. She took a deep breath, her admittedly impressive bosom enticingly displayed as a result. He might not like her, but she was striking.

"She is so young and beautiful with a splendid dowry, yet she was rejected. One must ask . . . why?" Her limpid gaze could have fooled anyone but Jules. She had no compassion for anyone, least of all Regina. "Ah, Jules, my love, I believe you are championing one who cannot win." Lady Monceux's voice held a trace of spite. Her eyes narrowed like a cat's, and she tilted her head in a challenging way. "I never knew you to back a certain loser."

"Since when was I your love, Lady Monceux?" Jules took her hand in the pattern of the dance, offering her a harsh look. When close enough to speak again, he continued, "What I do and whom I befriend surely can be of no interest to you."

Her eyes flashed with the fire of her displeasure. "You

assume too much, sirrah." The moment the dance concluded, she turned away to greet Lord Wrexham, who was providentially close by.

Jules gave them a mistrustful look, then retired to the side of the room and joined Lady Hawthorne where she sat observing the dancers. "How does it go, my lady?" He bent over, speaking low so that no one else could hear his words.

"I believe that things go about the way we expected, my lord. It is so lovely to see so many friends and such attractive gowns. I have missed a great deal by being so tediously ill. It is vexing to be out of touch with the latest happenings. Of course, there is always someone willing to bring one up to date." She turned to bestow a slight smile on a woman sitting nearby.

Jules pulled up a chair so that he might be closer to her. "And someone has so kindly done just that?"

"Indeed. I learned about your, er, friendship with Lady Monceux, as well as the ill-advised attention paid by Lord Wrexham toward my daughter." Lady Hawthorne fixed her gaze on the figures of Lady Monceux and Lord Wrexham as they chatted while going down the line of a country dance.

"Regina told me what he offered." Jules met Lady Hawthorne's gaze to find her eyes glittering with anger.

"Since she obviously spurned any attentions he might have wished to give her, that *ought* to be the end of it." Her voice betrayed her skepticism as to Lord Wrexham's nobility. "But if he dared to suggest such a path to a girl of decent birth and fortune, would he give up easily?"

"You have doubts as to his future goals?" Jules considered Lord Wrexham. He was handsome and wealthy, indeed, all a mother might ask for in a suitor. How he dared suggest an improper relationship to Regina—with her ancestry and dowry—was beyond Jules.

"We shall see how matters progress. I do not like what I sense, however. And my instincts are seldom wrong." Lady Hawthorne smiled, her face revealing nothing of the inner misgivings she must be feeling. Indeed, she appeared to be discussing nothing more earthshaking than the weather or the color of a gown.

Jules didn't like what his intuition sensed either, but he remained silent. He turned his attention to Regina, who was taking part in a country dance, performing the allemande with exceptional style. Sir William partnered her, and Jules wondered what that gentleman had said to bring flags of color to Regina's cheeks.

"You are very graceful, Miss Hawthorne." Sir William said, oozing charm. "All other dancers pale by comparison. A nymph could take lessons from you, I feel sure." He studied her as though he intended to buy her.

Regina felt much like a mare on the block. "You are too kind, sir. I fear my talent is quite ordinary, although I confess I do enjoy dancing." Regina gave him a determined smile, wishing she could escape. If the others were anything like Sir William, she would find the evening heavy weather.

When the dance at last ended, she discovered they stood near to the exquisite Lady Monceux. Not having been privy to the conversation her mother had endured, she knew nothing of the closeness between the widow and the earl. Not acquainted, Regina merely nodded, then turned away.

"Miss Hawthorne, how do you do?" When she chose, Lady Monceux could effectively reach any distance with her voice, and Regina was close.

Turning back to face the woman she had never met, Regina gave her a polite, if blank, look. "I am quite well. And you?" One was civil to a beautiful woman, for one never knew what she was about.

"I have been well. I see you arrived with St. Aubyn. How nice, that he should so kindly take you under his wing. But then, he is always helping a lame dog over a stile, as it were—such a *generous, kind* gentleman. At least, *I* have found him so." Her ladyship bestowed a pitying look upon Regina before sweeping away on Lord Wrexham's arm.

Regina drew a ragged breath, then gestured toward her mother. "If you would be so kind, sir, I would rejoin my mother."

Sir William hurried Regina along to her mother, and St. Aubyn glared at him. "Pleasure all mine, dear lady," he declared in parting, looking quite as uncomfortable as he ought.

"They are to play a waltz next. Dance with me," Lord St. Aubyn ordered.

Had she not desired to waltz with him so much, she would have flounced away. The nerve of the man, not only to patronize her but to order her around.

"Spare me your high horse, if you please. What did Sir William say to put you to the blush?"

"Some nonsense about my skill at dancing."

"And then you found yourself next to Lady Monceux. You exchanged polite words?"

"Indeed, my lord." Regina's voice vibrated with her indignation. "She was so gracious as to inform me that you are the kindest of gentlemen, often helping lame dogs over a stile. I am to be congratulated on your *kind* generosity and aid. I trust that was but a fabrication?"

He gave her a disgruntled look. "I have on occasion assisted one in need, and I fund a home for orphans. I do *not* consider you in the same light, you may be sure."

Regina felt awkward. He was kind and thoughtful. For some reason Lady Monceux wished to cause trouble. "I gather she had her reasons for such speech? She implied she had been the recipient of your kindness as well."

He looked truly uncomfortable, and then she recalled a remark she had heard regarding the beautiful widow.

"Perhaps she resents me—or what she perceives as a claim I might have on you?" Regina glared at him. "I warned you that were you not careful someone might think you had offered me a slip on the shoulder! Should I be flattered to be included in such elegant company as Lady Monceux?" Regina was so annoyed at this point that she almost tripped over her words.

"Miss Hawthorne!" He glanced about, obviously wanting to see if anyone might have heard her. Regina was past caring.

"I well know I am beyond the pale. Would you please return me to my mother? I fear I do not feel well, my lord." Regina's scathing look matched her words.

There was nothing Lord St. Aubyn could do but escort Regina to where her mother sat waiting. He bowed over Regina's hand, offered Lady Hawthorne a smile, then left before Regina could think of any other slurs she might heap on him.

Regina perched on the chair that Lord St. Aubyn had vacated before their ill-fated waltz, watching as his lordship disappeared from view, obscured by the many dancers. "Mama, I would like to go home . . . now."

"It is impossible, my dear. If you leave after a waltz with his lordship you will only make the gossip worse. I very much fear you will have to remain until I think it safe to leave." Lady Hawthorne met Regina's horrified gaze with a stern look that her daughter knew well.

Knowing that nothing would sway her mother once she had made up her mind, Regina eased back on her chair to consider ways and means of departure that would not look as though she was slinking away in defeat.

"In the meanwhile," continued her mother, "you will smile and accept partners of whom I approve." She turned her head at the rustle of pink muslin. "Here is Pamela, returned from a visit to the retiring room. Your flounce—it was not difficult to repair?"

"No, Mama. Regina, while I was in there a woman was talking about you. I cannot believe she is a proper lady, for she was very spiteful." Pamela gave her sister a troubled look while settling on a chair at Regina's side.

"You may tell us about it later," Lady Hawthorne declared in an undertone. "I cannot think that unkind words will improve the evening."

Nothing would improve the evening in Regina's opinion. She had begun in such high hopes that matters would get better. Now, not only was her mother annoyed with her, but she herself had insulted Lord St. Aubyn—although goodness knew he deserved it.

Her thoughts reverted to Lord Tarrington's jilting—for that is how she had begun to think of it. Everyone else appeared to believe it. Why had he so abruptly discarded her after so assiduously courting her? For he had certainly been attentive. Then he had simply disappeared, and after that came the announcement in the papers. What had she done wrong? And Miss Talbot done right? Comparisons were odious, but sometimes useful.

Although, Regina reflected, it was not as though her heart was truly engaged. She had liked him very well, but most fortunately had not fallen in love with him. That would have been a disaster. Still, he was handsome and personable, and she had found him charming company. Just, she reminded herself, as she found Lord St. Aubyn charming company. Was she fated to be attracted to the wrong men?

Percy Botham presented himself, bowing politely to her mother, then turning to Regina with a smile she didn't like for some reason.

"The country dance, Miss Hawthorne? Will you be so good as to partner me?" His manner seemed unctuous.

A glance at her mother decided Regina that she had better accept without delay. She smiled. "I should be delighted, sir." Was it possible that one could escape punishment for lies told under duress?

At least he danced well, even if his conversation lacked a certain something. As he returned her to her mother's side, he paused. "I say, you are a smashing girl. Can't think why Torrington preferred Miss Talbot."

"We each have our own inclinations." She smiled, aware that it was more than a little strained, then turned gratefully to seek the gilt chair at her mother's side. When she would have pleaded to depart at once, Sir William thwarted her.

"Dear lady, may I have the delight of partnering your

daughter in the Scotch reel?" His bow was elegant and his manner well bred.

With her mother's gracious nod, there was little Regina could do but agree and accept his hand. It was fortunate that Sir William did very well at a Scotch reel. Such an active dance left little time for any conversation. Even had she had the breath, Regina doubted she would have thought of a thing to say to the man. She was a little put out with Lord St. Aubyn's friends at the moment.

At the conclusion to the reel, she found they were at the far end of the ballroom. Sir William had begun to escort her to her mother, obviously recalling his past failure, when Lord Wrexham stepped into their path.

"Miss Hawthorne, may I request the pleasure of the next dance?" His gaze was fixed on her face.

"See here, Wrexham, ain't at all the thing . . ." Sir William began with a sputter. Whatever else either gentleman might have said would never be known, for at that moment a tall, slender gentleman with dark Byronic looks also joined them.

"Miss Hawthorne, Lucien Jeffries at your service. I was hoping against hope that you would be so kind as to give me the next dance." He held out a beautifully gloved hand and wore an imploring expression on his face. Any girl would have leaped to please such a handsome man. "Sir William will vouch for me, I know."

"Indeed, indeed. Known Jeffries any number of years." Whether or not he was happy to hand her over to the man was something she couldn't guess. She was just relieved to escape the clutches of Lord Wrexham.

Relinquishing her feather-light touch on Sir William's arm, Regina bestowed a delighted look upon Mr. Jeffries. "How lovely. One always enjoys meeting someone new."

Sir William offered a thankful smile, while Lord Wrexham's countenance darkened with fury. Spared his attentions, she sailed off with Mr. Jeffries to take her place in the set then forming.

The first chance she had, she glanced at her new partner and said, "I don't believe I have seen you before, sir."

"Newly returned from Spain, so that's not surprising. My uncle is ill, and had me recalled."

She considered this, and wondered if she should inquire further. When next they met in the pattern of the dance she said, "I trust he is better?"

"Enough." He led her through the next movement with expertise that hadn't been learned on a battlefield. She suspected that he had spent a good deal of his time in Society before going off to Spain. His laconic reply told her nothing other than that his uncle wasn't dead.

At the conclusion of the country dance he correctly returned her to her mother's side. Then, not relinquishing her hand, he spoke to Lady Hawthorne with superb address. After revealing his identity and making known the fact that Sir William vouched for him, he continued, "If I may, I would deem it a great pleasure to take Miss Hawthorne to supper."

Regina peeped up at him to observe that he wore a roguish smile. If that didn't delight her mother, nothing would. Her mother appeared to be acquainted with his family, and that was always helpful. Pamela looked enchanted.

"Do go and enjoy yourselves. Mrs. Beacham always has such interesting fare."

Leaving the admiring Pamela with her mother, Regina walked with her new acquaintance to the dining room, where a vast array of delicacies was offered to tempt them.

Once seated at a dainty table, Regina noted Lord St. Aubyn across the room talking to Lady Monceux. How could he tolerate such an unpleasant creature? Although he didn't seem to be enjoying himself. In fact, he looked more like he was arguing. Pointedly turning away from the sight, Regina concentrated on the elegant and apparently eligible gentleman who had so gallantly rescued her from Lord Wrexham.

"What a nice evening this has been," Regina said, suddenly realizing that it *had* become rather nice, and she owed it to this gentleman. Certainly, she owed little to Lord St. Aubyn. All he had done was to create more trouble for her, for she suspected Lady Monceux was annoyed at him because of his assistance to Regina. Some assistance.

"Would it be possible for you to join me for a drive in the park tomorrow? Or is every gentleman in London lined up at your door, and I should have to fight my way in?" He gazed at her with admiration clear in his eyes.

"What nonsense," Regina said with a chuckle. "I should be pleased to drive out with you on the morrow. I hope the weather proves agreeable. One thing about our weather, you never know what the coming day will bring."

He agreed, then casually led the conversation into a discussion of the Season and its delights.

It was not the sort of conversation that gave a girl the feeling of being esteemed. But on the other hand, there were no double-edged subtleties to plague her either.

Lord St. Aubyn and Lady Monceux passed their table at that moment. Regina looked up at him with what she devoutly hoped was a blank face. They paused.

"Miss Hawthorne. Jeffries, good to see you home again. I trust Miss Hawthorne has brightened your return to Society? She is as talented a dancer as she is a conversationalist."

She bit back a smile when Lady Monceux's eyes flashed with annoyance at his compliment.

Mr. Jeffries rose, his face a polite mask as he faced his old friend and Lady Monceux. He bowed. "I can see I have missed a great deal while gone. I shall have to make up for lost time."

"Jeffries, perhaps you will be so kind as to escort Lady Monceux to her home? I am otherwise engaged and unable to comply with her request."

What Mr. Jeffries thought could not be guessed. He agreed with utmost suavity, taking his friend's place at once. They left immediately, Lady Monceux looking in a temper.

Glad to see Lady Monceux thwarted, and yet annoyed at St. Aubyn for sending off the most considerate gentleman she had met, Regina seethed with frustration. "My lord, you are too, too kind. How good I shall see him tomorrow."

"Well, I thought I was being most considerate." He smiled at her with what appeared to be self-satisfaction. "How would it look were I to take *that* woman home when I brought you? Your mother would not take kindly to such behavior, and I would think myself the worst sort of fool."

"Indeed, it would not have looked well." Regina gave him a severe look and wondered what really went on in his head. She was still annoyed with him; the evening had been difficult, and he had not spared her being gossiped about. Not able to eat a bite of the food on her plate, she rose from the table. "I had best find Mama, else she may worry about me. After all, she may have seen Mr. Jeffries leave with Lady Monceux and think me abandoned."

"I doubt you would ever be abandoned, Miss Hawthorne." St. Aubyn rose from the table as well to walk at her side.

Regina ignored the inflection in his voice. Doubtless she imagined the warmth in it. They returned to the ballroom, where Regina sought her relatives. The ball had lost its appeal for her. She hoped Pamela would agree to leave.

Precisely why she was so angry with Lord St. Aubyn she couldn't have said. There was no doubt that her eyes might have frozen him on the spot if he had chanced to meet her furious gaze. He didn't. They met her mother and Pamela where they had been seated before.

"Mama, are you a trifle tired?" She turned to her sister, trying to gauge her mood. "Pamela, perhaps the hour is growing late for Mama? What do you think?"

Her attempt to encourage thoughtfulness in Pamela

succeeded, for her sister popped up, urging their mother to find her bed. "We do not want you to overdo, dearest Mama."

"Well done," St. Aubyn murmured.

Regina flashed him an annoyed glance, gathered up their scattered belongings, and prepared to depart at once. The walk outside to the carriage was accomplished with light chatter from Lady Hawthorne. Pamela was obviously sorry to leave the ball, but she said not a word.

Regina couldn't wait to get home and away from the aggravating Lord St. Aubyn. When the carriage drew up before the town house, she edged forward, impatient to get out.

"May I hope that you will join me for a drive tomorrow? Or do you go with Jeffries? Perhaps we might take a stroll in the park in the early afternoon?"

"No. Thank you. I shall be otherwise occupied, my lord."

"On second thought, you might well be abandoned, my dear." His voice was wry, as was his expression.

Lady Hawthorne and Pamela had exited the carriage first, so only Regina heard those last words. She bestowed an indignant glare upon St. Aubyn, then accepted the groom's aid in leaving the carriage, with St. Aubyn directly behind her.

Chapter Three

Regina entered the house with more speed than grace, bidding Lord St. Aubyn good evening with enough frost in her voice to ice over the Thames. He seemed about to speak—no doubt to explain his behavior. She gave him a look that revealed her thoughts on that idea, and he left.

"You were a trifle harsh with him, my love," Lady Hawthorne said, with a reproving look at her elder daughter. "I believe he meant well. After all, he could have left us to fend for ourselves after you so rudely slighted him."

"So much for the assistance he claimed to offer. He spent the evening dancing attendance upon Lady Monceux." Regina had placed that at the top of the list of her grievances against his lordship. Actually, there was little else she might complain about. And if pushed, she had to admit that he had not neglected her. An excellent dancer, handsome beyond most men, and sensible in conversation, he possessed few flaws that she could see. But it rankled that he should attend to Lady Monceux. Why had he troubled to take Regina and her mother and Pamela to the Beachams' ball, then ignore Regina when he had claimed he would pay such attentions as would set the gossips in a different direction?

"Not so much as all that, my dear." Lady Hawthorne, though looking tired, led her daughters up the stairs and into the drawing room. Crossing to the fire that still burned in the fireplace, she paused to warm her hands. "It was chilly this evening—and not just in the Beachams' ballroom. Whatever made you treat Lord St. Aubyn so? I was not best pleased when you insisted upon leaving that waltz. I am sure it created gossip."

"Well, is that not what we wished? If they wonder about Lord St. Aubyn, they may forget Lord Torrington." Regina took a turn about the room, then paused. "I quite like Mr. Jeffries. I consented to go for a drive in the park with him on the morrow. I trust that is agreeable with you, Mama?" She bestowed an affectionate look on her mother, then noted how tired she appeared. She went to her side and placed a gentle hand on her arm.

"I know—up to bed." Lady Hawthorne went to the door willingly. "I shall sleep late in the morning. You may, as well. Tomorrow can only offer interesting possibilities, my dear." She turned to Pamela. "You did very well, dearest. I was quite proud of you this evening."

"I liked Mr. Jeffries as well, Mama. I think Regina ought to encourage him." Giving her sister a saucy grin, she hurried out of the room before Regina could think of a reply.

"She ought to do quite well, I believe." Lady Hawthorne leaned on Regina's arm, allowing her to conduct her to her room.

Once in her own blue-and-white room, Regina reflected that her sister had not appeared to suffer from the gossip directed at Regina. If the contretemps with Lord St. Aubyn served to assist in that direction, it was all to the good.

Allowing her maid to undress her, Regina considered that gentleman. Unlike the amiable Mr. Jeffries, St. Aubyn possessed a distinctive air about him. She wondered when he would manage to speak with her. That he would, she was certain. It was what he might say that bothered her. Confrontation with him was fraught with hazards.

Betsy bobbed a curtsy as she stood beside Regina's bed, holding an exquisite bouquet, inquiring pertly where she might place it.

White roses. What did that mean? Pamela claimed that white roses meant silence. Well, did Lord St. Aubyn desire her silence on something? Perhaps they were by way of an apology?

"On the table by the window," Regina said, thinking that while she might like to toss out any offering from St. Aubyn, the roses were innocent and had harmed no one. Why she had the notion that they were tied to her refusal to allow him to speak last evening, she couldn't say. A hunch, perhaps? She'd bet her next quarter's allowance that he would take her to task. Or he might possibly wish to apologize. Now, that was an amusing thought. So . . . why was she not amused? She was terrified!

Selecting the most modest day gown she possessed, a blue kerseymere with white bows appliquéd around the skirt, she quickly dressed. The high, lace-trimmed neck and long sleeves offered discreet covering that was flattering as well. Betsy arranged her hair in a simple twist on the top of her head, allowing soft curls to caress her cheeks. Even on a dim day her hair gleamed with an inner light of its own.

"I ought to do well enough." Regina checked her reflection, nodding with hope that her words were true.

Thanking Betsy for her help, Regina went down to breakfast, peering into the drawing room on her way. The notion that St. Aubyn might be there, prepared to read her a lecture, was silly. Yet she well knew that she had made rude to him last evening, and he merited an apology. Never mind that *he* had abandoned her in favor of Lady Monceux, who was no better than she should be in Regina's opinion.

She would do what she must. Her mother had instilled proper manners in her. Never would she allow someone like St. Aubyn to blot out *all* that she had been taught.

Following a light meal, Regina retired to the drawing room, passing her time with practice on the pianoforte, in particular, a Mozart piece that she was attempting to learn. She listened with satisfaction to a passage that went precisely as it ought. The sound of applause caused her to whirl about and stare at the man in the doorway with apprehension.

"Very pretty." Lord St. Aubyn advanced toward her. Too late she realized she was trapped between the piano and the stool.

She couldn't have moved to save her life.

"Still silent? I thought that perhaps you might have regained the use of your voice by now. Perhaps it is as well, for I have a few words to say to you. It is comforting to know you will not interrupt." He stood, one hand rubbing his jaw as he contemplated her. He was most intimidating.

"My lord," she protested, finding her voice at last, "allow me to bid you welcome and offer an apology for my behavior last evening when you kindly brought us home." It galled her to say the words, but she knew she would know no peace until she did.

"Nicely done, Miss Hawthorne. I trust you practiced that as diligently as you did the Mozart?"

"Odious creature!" She slipped from the bench, confronting him with hands clasped before her. If she didn't hold them she could not be certain what she might do to the man. He not only intimidated, he maddened.

He smiled, his dark brown eyes revealing depths of humor that annoyed her even more.

"It is not amusing, my lord."

"What a haughty piece you are this morning." When she would have objected, he held up a hand sheathed in the finest York tan leather. "Now, allow me to have my say. I also apologize for last evening. I had not intended to desert you in the least. Actually, I feared Lady Monceux might forget she's a lady and be rude to you. I thought it a good idea to protect you."

"That was kind of you," Regina agreed thoughtfully. Why was he not defending Lady Monceux's behavior?

"Lady Monceux and I were friends in the past. In the interest of what once was, and to avoid endangering the plans you and I have made, I could not permit her to damage matters more than they were at the moment. However, I do think the situation served our purpose."

"Indeed, sir?" Regina gestured to the sofa near the fireplace, where, in spite of a pleasant morning sun, a small fire burned to take the damp chill off the room. "I cannot think how that might be."

"Well, do you believe the tabbies are muttering in their tea about you and the departed Lord Torrington today? They will be speculating on what will happen next you meet Lady Monceux, not to mention me. Drive out with me this afternoon." He walked at her side to the sofa.

Regina felt a tinge of apprehension at his nearness. Intimidating? The man was a menace to her nerves. How like him to order her so! Regina smiled sweetly, disposing herself with grace on the sofa, wondering if she ought to summon her maid to lend propriety. Still, she would prefer that no one listen to such a conversation as they were likely to have. Lord St. Aubyn took the wing chair, thankfully a prudent distance from the sofa and her shaken sensibilities.

"Mr. Jeffries kindly invited me to drive with *him*, Lord St. Aubyn. Was that not nice of him? I believe that of all your friends I find him the most pleasing." Regina grew wary at the considering look from his lordship.

"You shall drive out with me, my dear," he said. "Jeffries can take the charming Miss Pamela for a drive. I take it that she is permitted to do such a thing?" One brow winged upward with a hint of his inner amusement.

"Pamela is nineteen, and very well mannered. But I should hope that I am as well. It would be unseemly for me to simply tell Mr. Jeffries I have changed my mind. By the way, speaking of manners, why are you here at *such* an hour?" She ignored his smile, concentrating on proprieties with a glance at the longcase clock against the far wall.

"No changing the subject. Pamela is a pretty little thing, and driving with Jeffries will lend her a nice bit of cachet." He leaned back in the chair, appearing enormously satisfied with his conclusions. "Our drive will set the tabbies to wondering what you are about. Confusion is a marvelous ploy."

"It certainly is! I am as confused as any of those so-called tabbies. Why fobbing Mr. Jeffries off on my sister, then going for a drive with you will serve as a ploy I cannot think." She hoped her expression revealed her annoyance with him. She intended to wither him, but she suspected he was not a man to wither easily.

"Allow me to explain to Jeffries when he arrives. Did he specify a time?" He tilted his head, smiling at her with all his considerable charm.

To her vexation, she promptly replied, offering the time that had been set. Why did St. Aubyn affect her this way? She was not usually a silly girl, so utterly witless.

He immediately rose from the wing chair, bowing over her hand with all the aplomb of a London gentleman. "I shall return in time to meet Jeffries and explain to him. He will understand why we must thwart the gossips."

Overwhelmed by the way he loomed over her, Regina rose from the sofa. It was really little help, however, for he now stood far too close. She could almost feel the texture of his coat; she could detect the scent of his cologne, a spicy fragrance that subtly enhanced his appeal. The man daunted, but this she would not permit. She couldn't retreat, though—the sofa was immediately behind her.

"Please, sir," she said with a wave of her hand, and he took a step away from her. "As to your argument, I wonder if it is quite necessary for another person to know what we have discussed."

"He dislikes gossips as much as I do. Besides, Pamela is a charming girl, not so very much younger than you, and almost as beautiful."

Regina could feel a blush bloom on her face, her skin heating as it spread. "You are without a doubt the most aggravating man in the world."

"I try to please, Miss Hawthorne." His slow grin was

nearly an affront. Those brown eyes could cause havoc in a girl with greater susceptibility.

Wishing that she might do violence to the man who had turned her world upside down, Regina gave him a fulminating glare, then turned to the open doorway. "I gather I shall see you later this afternoon?"

"But of course. I have another request." At her surprised look, he said, "Have your mother obtain vouchers for Almack's. I think that ought to be our next objective."

"You are welcome there, my lord?" She couldn't conceal her disbelief, and knew at once she had overstepped the bounds of what was proper. *Her wretched tongue.*

He reached out to grasp her chin, staring into her eyes. Never had she imagined brown eyes could look so cold. "That was uncalled for, Miss Hawthorne. I am sought after not only for my title, but for the wealth it confers. The patronesses are only too happy to see me." He bit off his words, his voice harsh to her ears.

"Again, I apologize. My deplorable tongue. But you know how critical they are. So many fine people are excluded." All of a sudden she knew that the last person on earth she wished to alienate was Lord St. Aubyn. Precisely why, she would not admit, even to herself.

He dropped his hand at a sound from the hall.

At that moment Pamela appeared at the doorway. "Good morning, Lord St. Aubyn." She glanced about the room, turning a frown upon her sister as though to inquire of a chaperon.

Regina cast a look at his lordship, daring him to tell her sister to prepare for a drive this afternoon. She ought to have known better.

"Miss Pamela, I feel certain that you would be willing to assist your sister in any way you might?"

Oh, he was so suave, so polished. He could charm the paper off the wall, Regina reflected with resentment. He certainly charmed Pamela into agreeing that a drive with Mr. Jeffries would be most agreeable while Regina, seated in St. Aubyn's carriage, gave the quidnuncs something to chew on.

"I think Mr. Jeffries is a very nice gentleman," Pamela said, her voice ringing with sincerity.

Regina compressed her lips before she said something to the effect that he certainly was, which was more than could be said for his friend. What imp possessed her to taunt Lord St. Aubyn she didn't know. She only knew that while she didn't want to alienate him, she devoutly wanted to stab him with words, for want of a better tool.

She might have set her clock by Lord St. Aubyn, so prompt was he. Her mother nodded in greeting as he entered the room. Pamela, garbed in her prettiest blue carriage dress, stood near the window. Regina, dressed in her finest carriage gown of lilac merino with a pretty frill at the neck, stood close to the fireplace.

"A lovely trio, I vow." There was no hint of mockery in his voice or manner. Regina could not fault him, try as she might.

Hard on his heels came Mr. Jeffries. Regina wondered precisely how St. Aubyn intended to make the switch.

"Fancy seeing you here." Mr. Jeffries exhibited a certain amount of wariness that Regina judged was well founded, considering what St. Aubyn planned.

"We have a problem," St. Aubyn began, then gave Jeffries a concise explanation of what had transpired over the past week, leaving out little.

Regina knew she blushed when Mr. Jeffries glanced at her after St. Aubyn revealed the degree of the gossips' damage. It was distressing to have one's mortifications revealed to others. Never mind that she had willingly confided in Lord St. Aubyn. He was different.

"I would be delighted to take Miss Pamela for a drive in the park. I am certain she will be as agreeable a companion as she was a partner in the country dance last evening." He bowed to Pamela, then to Lady Hawthorne.

Lord St. Aubyn turned again to Lady Hawthorne.

"Regina mentioned Almack's? You will see about those vouchers? Today? I am counting on you, my lady. I believe it important for her."

No one commented on his use of her first name, least of all Regina.

Frowning slightly, Lady Hawthorne nodded. "I shall see to it today, you may rest assured. May I hope that the two of you will join us there? Perhaps dinner here first?"

Regina drew a surprised breath. She hadn't anticipated attempting to eat a dinner while in his company. That she thought only of St. Aubyn didn't occur to her until later.

Lord St. Aubyn agreed at once. "I feel sure Jeffries will be only too glad to come, and dinner with such ladies of charm is not to be missed. With two—no three—such enchanting ladies to escort we would be remiss if we did not present ourselves early on. I believe my carriage will hold all of us."

Mr. Jeffries nodded when looked to, and Lady Hawthorne agreed, with something that sounded like relief in her voice. "That is settled, then. We shall see you about half past six of the clock? Lord Hawthorne may join us as well."

"Indeed, ma'am," both gentlemen replied before offering an arm to the young ladies who were to be taken driving.

Pamela gave the appearance of a child about to be taken to Astley's Amphitheater; she sparkled and beamed her delight. Regina wondered if she herself looked nearly as pleased.

The drive in the park behind a match pair of chestnuts was all that she might have wished. "I believe every gossip in Town is present this afternoon. As you said, it ought to serve our purpose well." St. Aubyn frowned, and Regina wondered if she had spoken out of turn.

"I had hoped that you found my company somewhat pleasant, Miss Hawthorne. I am sorry if that is not the case." His face wore the expression of one who has eaten a sour pickle. His chestnuts had responded to the lightest touch of his hands, and now they slowed a trifle.

"Oh, pooh-bah!" Regina snapped with asperity. "You must know that you are top of the trees! I am the most fortunate of creatures to be seen with you." At his low chuckle, she sighed. "What is there about you, my lord, that you cause me to be such an utter idiot?" She turned to give him an exasperated look, only to discover a decided gleam in his dark eyes.

Before she could say another word, he murmured a cautioning and slowed the carriage so to greet the occupants of the oncoming vehicle.

"Lady Jersey and Princess Esterhazy, how lovely to see you again." He tipped his hat, smiled, and captivated them.

Regina thought the very air might melt with his charm.

"Indeed, Lord St. Aubyn." Lady Jersey gave Regina an inquiring look as though she knew her and couldn't quite place her. That was nonsense, of course. Regina had been presented to the ladies some weeks before the Torrington affair, and she had appeared to meet with approval at that time.

"You must have met Miss Regina Hawthorne, Lady Jersey. She is one of the Season's incomparables. You are ever aware of all that goes on in Society." He glanced at Regina. "I must say, I find her company most refreshing."

Regina gave the ladies a smile, longing to throttle him. She murmured appropriate words, then grew silent. He could jolly well handle the patronesses without her help, speaking of her as though she wasn't there.

"I fancy we shall see you at the Assembly rooms come Wednesday evening?" he said with a wickedly enchanting look. Regina wondered if they could resist it.

"You naughty man," Lady Jersey simpered. "You know we are only too pleased to see you . . . all." She signaled to her coachman to proceed, and Regina was left to stew, but not in silence.

"That was impossible! How could you place me in such a humiliating position?" She fiddled with the reticule on her lap, tightening the cords.

"Plain speaking, indeed. In the event that your mother is not able to remind Lady Sefton what is due the Hawthorne name, it will not come amiss to have my endorsement."

"As at the Beachams' ball?" She sniffed her displeasure, turning her shoulder slightly away from him. Lady Sefton, another patroness of Almack's, was known to her mother.

"At least you never disappoint me. As I said, you are refreshing. I never know how you will react to anything."

With that, he continued through the park, returning to the Hawthorne residence just after Jeffries and Pamela. They all entered the drawing room to find Lady Hawthorne in pleased conversation with Lady Sefton. The foursome paused at the doorway, waiting to see what would be said.

"I reminded your mother, dear girls, that you had already been approved for vouchers. I brought the cards with me. I've known your mama for some years, you know. We shall see you all on Wednesday." Lady Sefton rose, smiling at them as she took her leave.

The four moved into the room, with Regina halting by Lord St. Aubyn.

She turned to him to say in softest tones, "So the act in the park was totally unnecessary. What a pity—to waste that smile." She gave him the superior look, narrow-eyed and considering, of a vindicated woman. He ignored her, turning to speak to her mother. Regina thought he was without a doubt the most aggravating male in existence!

After that, tea was brought in and no one had a chance for private conversation. The talk was mostly concerned with the coming attendance at Almack's. Regina sat serene and pleased, although why, she wasn't sure. She darted a glance at his lordship, that powerful, menacing man, who looked as mild as any lamb.

"You appear to have enjoyed your drive, Miss Hawthorne," Lord St. Aubyn said as she escorted him to the stairs.

"True. I wouldn't have missed it for the world. You are a very talented man, you know." What possessed her to say those words in such purring tones she didn't know. Her tongue seemed to take on a life of its own when she was around him.

He shook his head, gazing at her with a confused expression in his eyes. "I hope to please."

"Oh, you do," she whispered. Utterly appalled at what she had not intended to say, she took a hasty step back, only to bump into Mr. Jeffries. Lord St. Aubyn's bark of laughter did not help matters in the least.

The Hawthorne ladies, with Mr. Jeffries and Lord St. Aubyn close behind, entered Almack's Assembly rooms with somewhat cautious steps. Regina felt so tense that had someone touched her she likely would have jumped a foot.

Dinner had been pleasant, with lighthearted chatter and not a word about the coming ordeal. Papa had dined with them but claimed he was required elsewhere.

There were three patronesses attending this evening. Lady Jersey looked down her elegant nose, smiling when she caught sight of Lord St. Aubyn, tolerating the others. Mrs. Drummond-Burrell, on the other hand, froze St. Aubyn and greeted the Hawthorne ladies with tepid enthusiasm—which for her was a great deal. Lady Sefton smiled her welcome, murmuring to Lady Hawthorne that all would be well this evening, she felt certain of it.

She was more confident than Regina, who glanced about her as they made their way to the far side of the room. She did not notice any lessening of hostility. The same spiteful smiles, superior looks, and haughty snubs were still in place. Surely her mother must find the sudden turning away of faces that had once greeted her with smiles a bit difficult to take.

"As soon as the music begins I claim the first dance," Lord St. Aubyn said to Regina in an undertone she found oddly tantalizing.

"You dare? Those women might freeze you with all those cold looks." Regina smiled at him, hiding her hurt.

"Never mind them. Continue to smile. Eventually something will happen to turn the attention from you to another scandal."

"I hadn't realized I had reached the status of a scandal." Regina tried to keep the pain out of her voice but failed.

"Dear girl," he murmured, taking her hand and heading toward the gathering dancers. Behind them Mr. Jeffries walked with Pamela, who was all grace and smiles. Her delight in her escort was not hard to discern.

They were able to form the first set without adding others to their group, and that success set the pattern for the evening. Mr. Jeffries partnered Regina in the next dance, while St. Aubyn took Pamela's hand. After that, only gentlemen who met St. Aubyn's nod of approval were accepted as partners.

Lady Jersey chided St. Aubyn when she chanced to encounter him. "You are more critical than we are, my lord. Shame on you for turning away Lord Wrexham. He presents an acceptable partner for the most selective."

"That is why you partner him, my lady?" he replied with a dark gleam in his eyes.

"Oh, you . . ." She laughed, wandering off to gossip with one of her particular friends.

On the far side of the room Lord Wrexham favored Lord St. Aubyn with a chilling stare. Regina remarked on it.

"I do not like his expression, my lord. I think he is plotting something nasty."

"I have encountered his sort before," Lord St. Aubyn replied, a menacing note in his voice that Regina had not heard before, one that sent a shiver down her spine.

She gave him a thoughtful gaze as he led her out for their second dance. "I do not think I would like to cross you, my lord. I suspect you would make a formidable enemy." Yet she had felt an instinctive trust in his ability to assist her.

"I did say you are a refreshing creature, did I not? Not only that, you are quite astute. I confess I can be as ruthless as the next when it comes to certain matters."

"Such as gossipers?" she guessed.

"Such as gossipers," he confirmed. He swung her into the first pattern of the dance, and she momentarily forgot her troubles in favor of the joy of an excellent partner in a dance she quite enjoyed.

When he returned her to Lady Hawthorne's side, she offered in her well-bred voice, "I believe we are making progress. Several ladies are curious what is afoot. They want to know your intentions, my lord," she concluded with a chuckle. "I am the soul of discretion, saying nothing in many words."

Lord St. Aubyn turned to face Regina. "You are most blessed in parents, Miss Hawthorne. Would that a few other mothers took lessons from yours."

"She is the best," Regina said simply, with a fond smile at her mother.

He and Mr. Jeffries left then to obtain lemonade for the three ladies, who all claimed to be parched.

While they were gone, Lady Jersey returned with Lord Wrexham in tow, both wreathed in smiles. "My dear Lady Hawthorne, allow me to present Lord Wrexham to Miss Hawthorne as an acceptable partner for the next dance."

Trapped in that insidious smile, Lady Hawthorne could only take a deep breath and offer Regina an apologetic look. "Sir." Her expression was not welcoming.

No frosty look from a mother bothered Lord Wrexham. He extended his hand, sweeping Regina off to dance—a waltz. Regina wished she were anywhere but where she was.

What a pity he was so excessively handsome. Had any other gentleman approached her with the same sort of smiles, bows, and excellence of dance, she would have been in alt. Indeed, she would have thought Lord Wrexham a fine gentleman, considered him as a suitor, if he had not approached her with a not-so-subtle suggestion that she join him in a tryst—quite alone—in a delectable little house in St. John's Wood. He had promised myriad delights.

As it was, she longed to punch him in the nose—even if no young lady of her position would dream of doing such a thing.

"You are rather silent, Miss Hawthorne." His voice was low and pleasant, but had no charm.

She strained against his clasp, desiring to keep as much distance between them as possible. "Perhaps I have nothing to say."

"Surely you do not think you will receive an honorable proposal from St. Aubyn?"

Regina gave him a direct look. "Lord St. Aubyn has been all that is proper, sir. I trust him completely." With a faint shock, she realized that this was true. He may be dubbed a rake by Society, but she felt him to be principled.

"And Lady Monceux? Do you think he will give up one so fascinating for your simple charms? Foolish child."

Chapter Four

The drive home was done in rather more silence than Regina could like. Her mother made perceptive comments about the pretty gowns seen and the people with whom she spoke. Pamela chattered happily about the lively music. Neither gentleman said anything other than the most polite comments, and those were extremely guarded.

Once at her front door, Lady Hawthorne invited both men to join them in a glass of sherry, and seemed surprised when they accepted.

Regina was the last to exit the carriage, and she took Lord St. Aubyn's hand with more than a little reluctance. Why was the man looking at her with such disapproval? Surely he must know that she would never have accepted a dance with Lord Wrexham unless there was no possible way of avoiding him.

"I trust this evening has advanced our cause, my lord." Regina held up her head, determined that he would not see how upset she had been.

"You think so?" He escorted her into the house, up the stairs, and with every evidence of pleasure assisted her with removing the wrap she'd worn against the chill of the evening. She shivered as his hand brushed her neck. Even though he wore gloves, he had the strangest effect on her senses. Dropping the wrap on a chair, he went to join Lady Hawthorne.

"It was better than I expected—Almack's," Mr. Jeffries said pensively while he sipped his sherry. "Miss Pamela is a gifted dancer." He bowed politely to her, a slight smile on his face. "Even the lemonade was better than I recalled—although not to compare with this sherry."

Lord St. Aubyn accepted his glass, eyeing the amber liquid with appreciation before taking a sip. "Indeed." He paused for a few moments, then said, "Thanks to Wrexham the tabbies have an entirely new tidbit to speculate about." He gave Regina a look that she felt was distinctly ironic.

"I hope you do not think *I* encouraged him." Had she dared to stamp her foot she would have, but her mother would frown on such childish behavior.

"Perhaps I ought to explain what happened," Lady Hawthorne inserted. "While you were fetching the lemonade we desired, Lady Jersey approached us with Lord Wrexham in tow. She presented him as an acceptable partner to Regina. The poor girl had little choice but to accept. To refuse would have truly set the cat among the pigeons!"

"My lady, you do not know the extent of Wrexham's wickedness." Lord St. Aubyn spoke softly so Pamela would not hear their conversation. He met her knowing gaze over the rim of his glass. "You are aware?" He cast a grateful glance toward Lucien Jeffries, chatting with an animated Pamela about the evening at Almack's.

"Regina often confides in me, my lord. I believe I mentioned before that she apprised me of the shameful offer made by Lord Wrexham the very evening he made it. I counseled her to ignore it, as any well-bred woman would. It was unfortunate that Lady Jersey had to take an interest in the matter. I could think of no way to refuse him without creating a scene. One does *not* like to offend a patroness."

Regina strolled over to the fireplace, staring into the fire while considering what her mother deemed a "matter." Lord St. Aubyn was extremely handsome and personable. Could it be that Lady Jersey had an eye on him for herself? Regina had heard whispers about that lady. Lord Jersey didn't seem to object to her legion of suitors.

It was said that as long as one conducted liaisons with discretion no one minded. St. Aubyn could be just one more conquest. If Lady Jersey nudged Regina into Lord Wrexham's arms, it would leave St. Aubyn free for a dalliance with her. Or was Regina seeing intrigues where none existed? She supposed it would be possible for Wrexham to change his mind, to present a proper offer rather than the scandalous one he had made. What did she know about the workings of the male mind anyway?

Society life in London was of a complex nature. Regina had been more or less jilted by Lord Torrington, which led to an offer of help from Lord St Aubyn. He, in turn, had known a very close relationship with Lady Monceux, who seemed to take strong objection to his being seen with Regina. That she could not possibly know his true reason didn't matter.

Why had St. Aubyn decided to help her? What prompted a gentleman to intervene in a situation that could only be a bother? She longed to ask, but her wretched tongue had plunged her into enough difficulty as it was. Perhaps that was what had driven Lord Torrington away from her side. Apparently not every man desired a wife who was on occasion a bit outspoken.

Yet she had tried so very hard to be prudent when she had been with Lord Torrington. She *had* minded her tongue, she had been as circumspect as possible. Never putting a foot wrong had taxed her nerves, likely made her a trifle stiff. But, she consoled herself, she had been proper, the sort of girl her mother had urged her to be when with a gentleman suitor. Only he hadn't been a suitor, had he? Regina had entertained him, perhaps. He had returned to Katherine Talbot, and that would— within days—result in their marriage.

"What was said when you waltzed with Wrexham?" Lord St. Aubyn inquired, walking over to Regina at the fireplace and standing a trifle too close for her comfort.

"Little. He chided me for my silence and called me a foolish child." That he had stated she would never receive an honorable proposal from Lord St. Aubyn she declined to reveal. After all, that might imply that she hoped for one. That Wrexham had infuriated her she also left unsaid.

"And?"

"I was more concerned with keeping as much distance from him as possible to conduct a sensible conversation, particularly one that required careful consideration."

Lord St. Aubyn looked as her as though he did not believe her. Indeed, he opened his mouth to speak, then snapped it shut. How wise. She was not confident she could withstand prolonged questioning.

Mr. Jeffries had apparently taken note of Lady Hawthorne's air of fatigue. "St. Aubyn, I suggest we allow these ladies to seek their rest. It has been a tiring evening for Lady Hawthorne, I feel certain."

Jules immediately apologized. "Forgive us, my lady. We shall hope to see you all on the morrow."

Before he left the room with Mr. Jeffries, St. Aubyn paused near Regina. "I shall learn all that was said, sooner or later, Miss Hawthorne."

Regina stared after the departing gentlemen with apprehension. She very much feared that St. Aubyn would do precisely that, and she rather thought it might be best to keep a few secrets from him.

The two men clattered down the steps to the ground floor, silent, both deep in thought. Seen on their way by Norton, they left the house quietly, heading for the carriage. The coachman gave a nod at the direction given him and once the gentlemen settled within, he set off.

"Thanks for the ride home, St. Aubyn. It has been an interesting evening," Jeffries said with reflection. "Pamela is more appealing than I had imagined, so the evening was not a total loss. I had rather fancied to escort her elder sister. How sits the wind in that quarter?" The darkness concealed any expression on Jeffries's face.

Jules considered his words. What to say? If Jeffries was considering courting Regina, should he stand in his way? Ought he to caution him about possible problems? "I find Miss Hawthorne interesting, refreshing after the usual silent chit who has nothing to say for herself. I wonder why Torrington tossed her over for Miss Talbot. Not that I ever found Miss Talbot objectionable, but her looks, her demeanor, not to mention her family background can scarcely compare to Regina's."

"Without a doubt. Good grief, have you ever met Mrs. Talbot? The woman is enough to send a man running. I believe Miss Talbot pleasant, nothing more. But her mother—fancy dealing with her in years to come." Jeffries gave a grunt of disgust.

Jules could scarcely disagree with that view. Anyone who met Mrs. Talbot would feel the same. "In contrast, Lady Hawthorne is charming. Regina is fortunate to have so sympathetic a mother. Not all girls do." He paused to think a moment, then added, "Have you met my parents?"

"Liked your father very much. You must miss him a great deal." In a more guarded manner Jeffries continued, "Your mother is all that is proper. I understand she watched over your sister with the greatest care when she was in Town."

Jules thought of his younger sister and dryly agreed, "Yes, Mother is all that is proper and determined to have all around her in like propriety."

He returned to the matter that so puzzled him. What had happened to turn Torrington away from Regina Hawthorne? It baffled him—and demanded a great deal more study. All of which naturally meant that he would be required to spend more time with Regina Hawthorne. Somehow, that did not seem the slightest concern; in fact, he looked forward to seeing her on the morrow. Or, considering the hour, later in the day. He stifled a yawn, dropped Jeffries off at his place, then headed to his own bed with the mien of one who has performed a number of good deeds.

The following morning Regina went down to breakfast to find a pretty bouquet of posies in the entry hall. Thinking they might be for her, possibly from St. Aubyn, she crossed to the exquisite table of fine mahogany inlaid with satinwood. There was a crisp white card tucked into the flowers, and she pulled it out with surprising eagerness. Glancing at her reflection in the gilt-framed looking glass over the table, she could see the flush in her cheeks, and she shook her head in dismay. Pray that she not reveal her interest in him when he was around!

The flowers were not from Lord St. Aubyn. Rather, Lord Wrexham's scrawl appeared on the pasteboard along with the expressed hope that he might have a few words with her later that day!

Why should he wish to speak with her? What could he possibly have to say of interest? Unless . . . Could he rue his sordid offer and wish to make amends? She would not alter her decision regardless. But she would feel a great deal better about herself if he made an honorable offer.

Pamela joined her to enjoy a fine meal of eggs and bacon, toast and tea. They made small talk as they ate. Before Pamela left the table, she paused to study her sister.

"There were flowers in the hall. Did Mr. Jeffries by chance send them to you?"

"No, love. Lord Wrexham sent them to me with the request for a few words later this afternoon."

Pamela slid onto a chair again, her forehead creased in a thoughtful frown. "I wonder what he has to say?"

Not about to tell her innocent sister the distasteful details of Lord Wrexham's previous conversations, Regina merely shrugged. "I cannot imagine. If it is anything interesting, I shall share it with you." She rose from the table to take Pamela's hand, then urged her to the hall.

"Well, I wish a gentleman would send me flowers."

"One will, I know. You are far too pretty to be ignored for long. Just look how the gentlemen thronged after you last evening."

Pamela chuckled. "Well, as to that, quite a few of them asked me about you. They wanted to know all manner of little things. I believe I answered all queries politely without revealing a thing."

"Well, you are indeed growing up! That is a talent every woman must learn. Mama certainly leads the way for us in that area." Both girls chuckled at this bit of wit.

"Perhaps we might go shopping this morning? I should very much like to have a new reticule. I fear I shredded the cords on mine last evening." Pamela touched her sister's arm hesitantly. "Please?"

"Indeed. I suspect mine looks a trifle shabby as well. An evening so fraught with nervous tension is apt to produce frightful results."

Regina chuckled softly before parting from Pamela, but when she viewed the reticule she knew she had mangled while at Almack's, she found the pretty silver-mesh trifle in the same dire condition. Shopping was a must. It would occupy the hours until she had to face Lord Wrexham.

Following a successful shopping expedition and a nearly silent nuncheon, Regina retired to the drawing room, ostensibly to practice that Mozart piece again. She almost felt guilty when her mother praised her for her diligence at her playing. Requesting Betsy to sit by one of the windows with some mending, Regina mentally prepared for what she feared would be an unpleasant interview.

When Norton ushered Lord Wrexham into the drawing room, announcing him with polite deference, Regina was taken aback at the leap of alarm in her heart. Yet, his reputation couldn't be so dreadful, for the butler would have known and indicated his disapproval with a frosty tone. She doubted there was a butler in London who could render a frosty utterance better than Norton.

She rose, recalling as she did how different this was from the recent occasion when Lord St. Aubyn had found her at the pianoforte. She had felt none of this apprehension then, or at least not the same kind.

"Miss Hawthorne, it is very good of you to receive me

after our conversation of last evening." Lord Wrexham made an exquisite bow over her hand, offering a hopeful smile.

"I suppose it is," she replied candidly. "I fear I am a curious soul and would know what you have to say." She studied him, admiring his handsome appearance; his eyes were not set as close together as she had thought. The first time they had met she considered him among the most handsome of gentlemen, but had thought the set of those gray eyes seemed too close. She must have been mistaken.

He looked a trifle disconcerted at her plain speaking but recovered quickly. "I ought not to have said what I did."

She gestured to the sofa, glancing at Betsy to see that she was close enough to keep an eye on them but still not hear everything. "Will you join me, my lord?"

He sat down as though the sofa might collapse beneath him, giving Regina a wary look as he did.

"Thank you for the lovely flowers, sir. I do appreciate them." Regina smile hesitantly, not wishing to seem encouraging, though she knew she must be polite.

He seemed to relax then and leaned forward with an earnest expression on his face. "I have reflected on all I said, and find I do not like myself very well. I ought to have known better than to say *such* things to a young woman of your quality. It was the outside of enough! Will you accept my apology? Forgive me?"

Regina remained silent for a few moments as she recalled the grief his less-than-proper proposal had caused her. Then, reminding herself that one should be prepared to forgive a wrong if an apology is genuinely offered, she nodded. With a solemn expression, she said, "I will admit the proposition you made shocked me to my core, sir. It is not so easy to forget." She had no intention of making matters simple for him. She had shed too many tears for that. He must be made to see how grave his offense was.

"I can only repeat how sorry I am, dear lady."

"Then I must accept your handsome apology, sir. Surely a change of heart must be allowed."

"Are you referring to Torrington?" A calculating expression crossed his face so rapidly she wasn't certain if she actually saw it. Surely she must be mistaken.

Her swift intake of breath was swallowed by chagrin. "Actually, I meant you, Lord Wrexham. Whatever was in the mind of Lord Torrington is beyond my knowledge." While it galled her to admit this, it was nevertheless the truth. "Should you learn what was in Lord Torrington's mind, be so kind as to tell me. I quite long to know." Her laugh was a touch forced.

"I believe I have done it again—offended you when I had not intended to do anything of the sort."

Regina gave him a rueful look. "I fear I often say things I'd not intended. My wretched tongue!"

He smiled with great charm and lightly patted her hand where it rested on the sofa. "Then you can understand my dilemma. Would you drive out with me this afternoon?"

Regina wondered what St. Aubyn would make of such an event. He would not approve, she was certain of that. Yet if she refused Lord Wrexham he would believe she was not sincere in her acceptance of his apology.

"Oh, excuse me," Pamela cried, pausing at the doorway with a very arrested expression on her face. Gentlemen of such charm and attraction did not appear in the Hawthorne drawing room every day.

"I believe you have not met my younger sister, Pamela." Regina tried to conceal her reluctance as best she could. It was easy to see that Pamela was impressed with Lord Wrexham. It was to be hoped that he considered her far too young to be of interest to him.

He rose at once and crossed the room to bow low over her hand. "Miss Pamela, I am delighted to make your acquaintance at long last."

He was a charming devil, Regina had to concede that. No matter she had forgiven him, she had thought him the villain for too long to put it out of her mind yet.

Pamela blushed, and shyly went to stand near Regina.
Uncomfortable with the two of them eyeing one another
over her head, Regina rose as well and edged toward
the door.

With a hasty glance at the longcase clock, Lord Wrexham turned to Regina. "I have enjoyed my chat with
you, Miss Hawthorne. I am most grateful to receive
your forgiveness."

She gave him a cautioning look, which he appeared to
interpret correctly as a warning to say nothing more. He
paused near the door to turn a questioning face to Regina. "May I call for you about five of the clock?"

Something within her urged caution. "Would tomorrow be acceptable? I must talk with my mother first."

He assumed a wry expression and nodded. "So be it.
I shall look forward to our drive with anticipation." He
bade both of them good-bye, then disappeared down
the stairs.

"Well, at least today you have Betsy in here to lend
propriety. I cannot imagine what Lord St. Aubyn thought
when you received him alone." Pamela didn't meet her
sister's gaze, but idly plunked a few of the ivory keys on
the pianoforte.

"That is neither here nor there. I had best report to
Mama that Lord Wrexham called," Regina said, hoping
to escape before Pamela could ask uncomfortable
questions.

"Regina, why was Lord Wrexham apologizing? Did he
say something last evening that was uncalled for?"

Turning slowly to face her sister, now seated on the
little stool before the pianoforte, Regina sought the right
words. "He felt he had said something to vex me, dear.
Of course I accepted his request for forgiveness." She
hurried out of the room, hoping that what she had said
satisfied Pamela's curiosity. Her sister knew little or
nothing of what had transpired—and a good thing too.
The girl would never be able to conceal her feelings,
particularly if she thought her dear older sister had been
ill-treated.

When Regina told her mother about Lord Wrexham's call, she received a troubled look in return.

"I confess I do not know what to think of him," Lady Hawthorne mused. "He is from a fine family and the highest *ton*. He certainly is a handsome man. You must do as you think best, dear."

Regina nodded her appreciation that her mother believed her to be sensible enough to deal with the matter. "I will go down to keep Pamela company, Mama. There may be other callers, you know."

Her return to the drawing room coincided with Lord St. Aubyn's arrival. She stood at the top of the stairs, waiting for him to join her, then they entered the room together.

"Well, this is a day for guests," Pamela said gaily. "Lord Wrexham left not long ago. Only fancy, he came to apologize to Regina." She immediately realized she had spoken out of turn and turned scarlet. "Oh, dear."

With relief, Regina watched Pamela flee the room. "She seems to have inherited the wretched Hawthorne tongue." Then she awaited St. Aubyn's comments.

"Wrexham was here to apologize to you? For what, may I ask?" St. Aubyn led Regina to the sofa and seated her, with a glance at where Betsy still plied her needle. Then he joined her, sitting a bit too close.

She edged away from him, and he followed her. "He apologized for everything, if you must know."

"Noble of him, after causing you so much grief." St. Aubyn leaned against the sofa, placing his arm across the back, almost, but not quite, touching Regina's shoulder.

"In fairness to him, he did not know that." She shifted again. How odd that she felt such breathlessness and sensations that had been absent when Lord Wrexham was here. Perhaps she was acquiring the palpitations that so many women complained about. Her heart was assuredly beating faster than usual, and her mouth felt dry. Even though St. Aubyn's hand did not touch her shoulder, she could almost feel it, sense it. He was very disturbing, far too much so for her peace of mind.

"I thought we might go for a drive this afternoon."

"Would you like a drink? Sherry? Tea, perhaps?" Regina knew her voice sounded too high. She swallowed with care, taking a deep breath, trying to calm her nerves.

"Yes, I would enjoy some of that fine sherry we had last evening. And I *would* like your company for a drive."

"I will be delighted to drive out with you, my lord." Regina escaped to pour a glass of sherry, then returned to hand it to him. When she sat again, she made certain that she was a greater distance from him.

Norton surprised her at that moment by bringing in a tea tray, with Pamela immediately behind him, her color restored to normal.

"I thought the least we might do was offer Lord St. Aubyn some refreshment." Pamela busied herself with teacups and tiny plates that she filled with delicacies. Ignoring the glass of sherry that Lord St. Aubyn held, she made to offer him what she had prepared.

"You may give that to me, dear. Lord St. Aubyn will likely wait a few moments. He will probably want to finish his sherry." Regina met her sister's distressed gaze with sympathy. "Why do you not have some, and I can offer his lordship tea—if he desires any?" She turned to face St. Aubyn, immediately noting the amusement in his eyes. He was a good man; he kindly did not tease Pamela. She counted that to his credit.

He handed his empty sherry glass to Pamela. "As long as you are at the tea tray, I will have some now. It was most thoughtful of you to order it for us. Your sister will likely need fortification for our drive."

"Oh, is she driving out with you? She is going with Lord Wrexham tomorrow. I must say, Regina does keep busy." She gave Lord St. Aubyn an innocent smile, then took a bite from a toasted tea cake.

"Was I to know about this?" St. Aubyn inquired in a dangerously silken tone.

"I intended to inform you, although I am not quite

certain why you need to know." Regina hoped her voice didn't sound as shaken to him as it did to her.

They finished the tea in silence broken only by an occasional comment from Pamela. When enough crumbs graced the china and the tea reached an acceptable level in the teapot, St. Aubyn turned to face her.

"I suggest you fetch your bonnet and reticule. We can leave for our drive immediately. We have a few things to discuss."

He didn't have to glance at Pamela for Regina to know precisely what he meant. The dear girl couldn't know she was tattling out of turn. "Of course. Pamela, come help me to pick out a bonnet, will you?" Regina was going to take no chances on more spilled confidences.

Hurrying out of the room with St. Aubyn's rich chuckle in her ears, she made short work of plopping on her head the first bonnet Pamela handed her. She grabbed up a convenient reticule and gloves and returned to the drawing room to find his lordship standing before a window. He turned at the sound of her footsteps.

"Amazing. I made sure you would be another ten minutes at the very least. And a ravishing picture you offer, my dear. Let us go at once, I can scarce wait to display you to one and all."

"I shall lose my sweetness if you keep this up," Regina cautioned as he escorted her down the stairs to Norton, who guarded the front door.

Within minutes she was ensconced in the high-perch phaeton and they were on their way to the park. She waited with some trepidation for what he would say.

"Now, kindly explain what transpired to permit a drive with Wrexham tomorrow afternoon."

"Well . . ." Regina gave him a hesitant look. St. Aubyn was impossible; you could rarely tell what he was thinking. "Lord Wrexham sent flowers, along with a note requesting I see him when he came to call. He was most apologetic. I confess I did not immediately grant forgiveness. There were too many tears for that to happen," she said thoughtfully, recalling the many dampened pillows.

"Eventually, I did accept his seemingly heartfelt apology."

"Seemingly?" He jumped on the word, sharp and quick.

"Just so. I cannot see into his heart. I would like to believe he is sincere. One can never know, though." She sighed, gazing across the green of the park. This was not quite the way she would like to spend a drive with Lord St. Aubyn.

He said nothing more for a time, appearing to digest her news. "The day after tomorrow is the wedding. You will go with me. I want you to look your most ravishing—which ought not be too difficult for you to accomplish. We will arrive at the last moment, when all are seated. I would take seats somewhere in the center, I believe."

Regina swallowed uncomfortably, thinking of the stir their entrance would produce. "You feel we must do this?"

"You were only too ready a few days ago. Cold feet?"

"Certainly not! I am not sure what to wear, however. I doubt I can assess what would appear ravishing to you."

"Describe your favorite dresses, the ones likely to fall into that category."

To her amazement he listened carefully to her brief descriptions. When she concluded, he mulled over the lot for a few minutes, then said, "Wear the blue jaconet with the lace trim. And perhaps a white hat. Do you have such an item? One with a fetching brim, maybe a touch of feathers."

"I shall oblige, sir." The wedding had assumed all the charm of a hanging.

Chapter Five

She did not own a white hat. And that was not the least of her troubles. Her best blue afternoon gown was scarcely suitable for attending a wedding. Ravishing?

"You could add some trim to that gown, you know," Pamela suggested. She was curled up against the pillows on Regina's bed, only too happy to offer ideas if she wasn't required to do anything.

"What is it, dear?" Lady Hawthorne paused in the doorway, her head tilted in inquiry.

"Lord St. Aubyn said I ought to wear something blue—'ravishing' was the word he used. And he thought a white hat would be nice. I do not *have* a white hat." She gave her mother a stubborn look, holding up her favorite blue afternoon gown before her while studying its effect in her looking glass.

"I think Pamela is right. Have Betsy sew a bit of lace at the neckline. It is a trifle plain as it is now. And you can simply purchase a white hat. I cannot see where the obstacles are. But then, I suspect you truly do not wish to attend this wedding, do you?" She gave Regina a look of sympathy.

"You must know I do not!" Regina draped the gown across a chair. "I can just see it all. I shall walk into the church on the arm of one of the prime rakes in London to attend the wedding of the man I once thought to marry. Heads will turn, people will stare, and everything will be worse than ever. Can you not hear what the gossips will say? 'The poor dear, come to see her rival wed to the one she thought to marry.' "

"Oh, I doubt it will be as frightful as all that," her mother said thoughtfully. "I cannot believe Lord St. Aubyn would knowingly subject you to such a cruel situation. I suggest you go to the milliner—take Pamela with you—and find an utterly captivating white hat. I think a touch of blue would be nice—perhaps a feather or something."

Regina reluctantly smiled at her mother's suggestion. That vague bit about a feather was designed to turn Regina's mind to shopping and away from the ordeal she faced.

"Oh, do let's go," Pamela pleaded.

"Find a new bonnet for Pamela as well. She deserves something for her cooperation. I shall stay home to rest." Lady Hawthorne contrived to look fragile and unable to do more than hold a teacup.

"Of course, Mama." Regina glanced at the delicate little gold clock on the mantel, noting the time. "Come, Pamela. Put on that green pelisse and meet me in the hall in twenty minutes. We will have a wonderful time."

Once Pamela had left the room, Regina turned to face her mother, a rueful look in her eyes. "I dread the morrow. I have never been one to seek attention, particularly this sort." She slipped on her brown pelisse.

"That is why it is important you should be dressed with the greatest care. Lord St. Aubyn has the right of it, my love. You must look utterly ravishing. People *must* wonder what was wrong with Lord Torrington that he could bear to leave your side, much less turn to the Talbot girl. Have no worry. I feel all will turn out as we wish."

"It is not merely for me, Mama. I have feared that my, er, notoriety would somehow taint Pamela. I would do almost anything to keep that from happening. I do not fear spinsterhood, but I would sincerely regret if Pamela were denied a splendid match because of this rubbish."

"Scarcely rubbish, my dear. We may feel it is utter stupidity, but there are many who look on gossip as a spark of truth. You know . . . where there is smoke, there is fire."

"I cannot see that smoke has a thing to do with this." She gave her mother a sudden grin and a kiss on the cheek. Then grabbing her reticule and a tiny golden-brown hat with a dashing brim and a stiff plume of feathers, she picked up a pair of gloves and walked out of her room. The hat quickly dealt with, she pulled on the gloves while pausing at the top of the stairs. "I shall find the most gorgeous, meltingly beautiful hat the milliner has in her shop. Beware! It is likely to cost a small fortune."

"For a good cause, I feel certain." If there was a hint of anxiety on her ladyship's face, it was not seen by her departing daughter.

Regina joined Pamela in the entryway, with Betsy discreetly lurking just behind her. Norton opened the door, only to discover Lord St. Aubyn in the act of raising his hand to knock.

"Lord St. Aubyn! What a pity! We were on the verge of departing."

Regina stared at the handsome gentleman standing before her, wondering why on earth she should go to the trouble of finding a new hat. He would capture all eyes when they entered that church on the morrow. There could not be a man in Town who could hold a candle to his elegance. And that the elegance seemed so natural, so unaffected, made the effect all the more devastating.

"Good morning." He smiled. His eyes lit with humor, and delightful crinkles appeared at the corners of them. If she was not mistaken, there was a dimple lurking in his left cheek. It simply was not fair for a man to be so utterly fascinating. Every woman in the church would fall under his spell. How could they help it?

"Good morning. Is there something you wished to see me—or Mama—about?"

"You are about to go shopping?" At her nod, he continued. "I shall go with you." At her narrowed look, he added, "Not that I have any doubts about your talents when it comes to selecting a hat. I merely wish to admire it."

Any objection she might have had was foiled with that last remark. What could she say without sounding pettish? "Very well. Pamela comes with me, as does Betsy." She was not about to leave Pamela behind, and Betsy would lend a nice touch of respectability, as well as carry the hatboxes.

"Propriety is such a fine thing, is it not?" He bestowed a lazy grin on her, nodded at Norton, then offered his arm to her. "The day slips by; we had best be on our way." Quite as though she was the one to delay their departure! Oh, the odious creature.

"Well, I was *on* my way out when you appeared." She gave him an offended look, marching along at his side and entering the landau with the utmost dignity. Only when she was seated did she wonder where he obtained all his carriages. To date she had seen his curricle, the high-perch phaeton, and now this landau. For an unmarried gentleman, he possessed quite a number of vehicles. Doubtless he had a traveling carriage in his mews as well. When he had declared he had wealth to support his title, he had not been exaggerating. While he might have inherited the landau and the traveling carriage, the phaeton and curricle were the sort owned by a gentleman on the town. She knew there were many men in Town who merely rented a vehicle when they wished one. Carriages were not inexpensive, nor was all that went with them.

St. Aubyn settled next to her, with Pamela and Betsy seated on the far side. He made a few innocuous comments, but Regina scarcely heard them. She was far too conscious of the man at her side. Well, it was to be expected, she supposed. He had never been known to take up an unmarried girl, one making her come-out to Society. It was hardly surprising that she ought to feel a wee bit out of the ordinary.

The landau came to a halt before a millinery shop that Regina had not patronized before. It was an elegant little place, neatly painted and quite appealing. Regina gave St. Aubyn a quizzical look.

"I have it on the best authority that this milliner has the finest selection of hats and bonnets in London. Come—do not quibble. I will be the soul of discretion."

Regina gave him a mystified look, accepting his assistance from the carriage, then watched with approval as the footman handed Pamela and Betsy down with equal courtesy. St. Aubyn set a standard that could be emulated by all.

As might have been expected, Lord St. Aubyn had been right. Never before had Regina seen such hats.

Pamela immediately fell in love with a dear confection of Pomona green satin with a turned-up brim, low on each side, lined with white satin to frame her face in a pleasing manner. Since it went nicely with her pelisse of the same green, Regina could see that it was the thing to buy.

Her own hat of golden-brown satin that matched her pelisse was set aside so she might try on a variety of hats and bonnets. She wandered about the shop, scrutinizing the wares on display. The soft gray of the walls offered a superb backdrop for the various colors.

She saw St. Aubyn murmur something to the woman who ran the shop, and within moments she had fetched a hat that was the precise thing for the blue dress. Held out for Regina's inspection was what the milliner called a Spanish hat. The white satin hat had a blue rim and was ornamented with delicate silk cornflowers of the same blue.

"It is perfect," breathed Regina as the deferential woman placed it on her head. The contrast of the white and blue with the russet of her hair was very nice indeed. Within a short time, the purchases were made; Regina had ample funds with her in spite of the rather dear prices.

When St. Aubyn escorted the women to the landau, Regina found a chance to comment, "I vow, you must have had experience in shopping for bonnets. You knew precisely where to go for the finest."

"I am accounted to have a good knowledge of the City, Miss Hawthorne." He had that closed expression on his face again, one that told her to cease her probing.

She persisted. "For whom do you collect such knowledge, sir?"

"If you must know, it is not as you may think. I have on occasion purchased a bonnet for my younger sister. She lives in the country, declining Society, yet still enjoys a piece of modish headgear."

Sensing that she had again stepped beyond bounds, Regina stilled her wayward tongue. She had thought that perhaps he bought hats for Lady Monceux. Of course, if he had, he'd not likely tell her, anyway.

Why was it she couldn't keep a sensible tongue in her head when she was with Lord St. Aubyn? Why, when she had ridden out with Lord Torrington, she had been on her best behavior. Nothing but the most proper observations left her lips, and she had certainly never contradicted him. That was how she had been taught to act. A young lady should never voice opinions or disagree with her escort. Indeed, she should always defer to the gentleman. With Lord St. Aubyn, all sensible conversation left her head, and she was not above contradicting him.

When they were promptly set down at the Hawthorne residence, Regina regretted the brevity of their trip. She would have liked to saunter along Bond Street to peer into windows, possibly select some trifle, certainly a treat for her mother. Now she was home. He lingered.

"Please, sir, do come in."

The lightning glance he gave her was followed by his nod of agreement. After a word with his coachman, he entered the house with them.

Regina sent him a questioning look. "Would you care for a glass of sherry, or perhaps tea?" She gathered that he had something on his mind; it was obvious he wanted to talk. She wondered what he would say.

"Good, good," he said absently as he handed his hat

and gloves to Norton, then ushered Regina up the stairs, trailed by Pamela and Betsy.

Pamela went to show her mother the new bonnet. Betsy settled in the chair on the far side of the room once again, picking up the mending that seemed to have found a permanent place there now.

Regina poured him a glass of sherry, then handed it to him with care. He looked ill at ease, staring into the glass of amber liquid as though it offered an answer.

At last he spoke. "I confess I have an ulterior motive for helping restore you to your proper position in Society. It did not begin that way; it only occurred to me just now. I want you to know that."

Quite surprised, Regina sank down on the convenient sofa and stared at him with perplexed eyes.

"I had not planned to say anything to you, but when you asked about my shopping for bonnets it came to me that you might help me. At first I had thought of nothing more than a kind of settling of scores with those gossips. Now I believe you can come to a sort of rescue, if you will."

Intrigued, Regina motioned him to join her on the sofa. She hoped Pamela would remain upstairs a trifle longer, for she suspected St. Aubyn wouldn't say a word about his plan were Pamela present.

"The sister I mentioned is living quite isolated in the country. We have an estate not too far out of London where she makes her home. I believe she must be close to you in age. She was Pamela's age when she left Society for seclusion."

"Seclusion?" Regain could see that it was not an easy matter for St. Aubyn to talk about his sister. Why did he use such a strange word as "seclusion" for her withdrawal from London? A sound at the door drew her attention.

"Mama said the bonnet is exactly what she would have wished," Pamela said, happily unaware that she was unwelcome.

"That's nice, dear." Regina sighed with vexation. She

would never order Pamela to leave; she was too old to be told to go to her room. But, oh, how she wished she might.

"We shall continue this discussion at a later time," Lord St. Aubyn murmured, setting his empty glass on the closest table. "I will call for you tomorrow morning half an hour before the ceremony."

"I will be ready and waiting for you, my lord," Regina said, feeling sympathy for him for the first time. Whatever it was he wished her to do for his sister, never mind the reason, she would attempt to do her best. She told herself it was the least she might do to help someone who was attempting to help her.

"Good-bye, my lord." Pamela stared at his retreating figure with curiosity. "He didn't even say good-bye. I say, did I interrupt something?"

"Nothing that cannot be continued at a later time, my dear. So, Mama was pleased with the new bonnet?"

She withstood the searching look from her sister with fortitude. Lord St. Aubyn might continue that curious and interesting conversation later on, and he might not. But she hoped very much to know the whole of it.

The discussion of the merits of the new hat and bonnet kept them occupied until it was time for Regina to dress for her carriage ride with Lord Wrexham.

She had not expected to drive out with him ever again—not after his improper suggestion. Perhaps he had truly suffered a change of heart? She hoped so.

Wearing a carriage dress of pea-green faille that had a pretty double frill of cream lace at the neck, Regina felt ready to endure the occasion. In any event, she decided, as she put on the neat chip straw bonnet with a rolled brim and a cluster of silk flowers to one side, she would be able to see his face. While the bonnet did not conceal her expression, neither would it prevent her from seeing his. And she very much wanted to watch his face.

The drive was a distinct letdown. Nothing to which she might take exception was said. He was propriety itself.

She found herself looking for fault, scolding herself for being disappointed when she could find none.

"It appears the weather will be quite nice for the wedding tomorrow," he offered.

"Indeed. I think there is nothing more agreeable than good weather for a wedding. So nasty if the gowns are ruined by rain." Could any conversation be more insipid? She was determined to be proper if it killed her, however, and the weather made such an unobjectionable topic.

He returned her to the Hawthorne residence with great courtesy. It was silly to feel uneasy. She dismissed her qualms with resolute determination and smiled at Lord Wrexham, hoping she looked pleasant.

He smiled in return, bowing over her hand with exactitude in parting. He did not hold her hand too long, nor did he gaze at her with the speculative note in his eyes that once had been there.

She reported to her mother that all had gone well.

"Dear, I am so relieved. Now all that has to be faced is the wedding tomorrow."

They exchanged a bleak look of the sort not usually connected with weddings.

Fortunately, the day proved to be bright and sunny. Even if she didn't particularly care for Katherine Talbot, Regina was glad she had a lovely wedding day. Happy is the bride the sun shines on, her old nanny used to say.

Following her bath, Regina dressed in her undergarments and Betsy brushed her hair until it gleamed bright and healthy. The wedding was at eleven of the clock and Regina, garbed in the simple yet exquisite gown of smoky blue, was prepared well in time. She fingered the delicate lace that Betsy had added to the neck of the gown. It was the perfect finishing touch.

"Your hat, dear." Lady Hawthorne picked up the new hat and set it atop Regina's neatly coiffed head. "It is exactly right."

"Mother, you are certain I am doing the right thing? I

am so tired of gossip and speculation. Why cannot people simply allow me to live in peace?" Regina clasped her mother's hand, seeking comfort.

"I know, dear. It is difficult to understand. Just realize that you have the support of an excellent gentleman, not to mention your family."

"Some call him a rake." Regina exchanged a troubled look with her mother.

"I believe your father was considered extremely dashing when he was a young man—and see how sedate he is now. I could not wish for a better husband and father, even if he seldom goes with me to parties. It is said that there is no better husband than a reformed rake, my dear."

"Mother! I do not plan on marrying the man!"

If her mother had private thoughts on this interesting subject, she didn't reveal what they might be.

"Draw on your gloves and pick up your reticule. It is such a nice touch that it matches the dress. How fine a day it is proving to be!"

"I feel as though I am going to a funeral."

"I know, dear, I know," her mother said, soothing her girl as in the past. "You will be home again before you know it."

Regina was ready and waiting for Lord St. Aubyn as she had promised, pacing back and forth in the small library off the entry hall. When she heard the door-knocker she tensed. Silly, but she worried as much about what Lord St. Aubyn would think of her garb as that gathering at the church. She stiffened her spine, determined that he would not know how terrified she was.

"Hello, Regina." His voice was low, polite. She ignored his improper use of her given name. After all, he was a rake, and she supposed rakes had different rules.

"Good day to you, my lord." She stood, waiting, breath suspended, while he inspected her costume. Was it what he had hoped her to wear? Why it mattered so much escaped her. Never had she allowed the possible opinion of her escort to weigh so keenly with her.

"Well, my lord, I believe she did quite well," Lady Hawthorne said from behind him.

"Indeed she did, my lady. She far and away exceeded my hopes. Not even the bride can outshine her, I vow."

"I shouldn't wish to diminish what should be a happy day for Katherine Talbot," Regina objected.

"Commendable, indeed. Come. It will be difficult to get near the church. I have the landau so I won't have to worry about the carriage, and we shall arrive in style."

With leaden feet Regina walked to the conveyance, entered it, and settled on the velvet-covered seats. She gave one final smile to her mother before she concentrated on what was to come. Surely it could not be as bad as she feared.

They set off.

The streets were unusually busy with gigs, curricles, hackneys, and drays going every which way. When they at last drew up before the church, Regina felt as though her nerves were frayed to the snapping point.

"What a pity I cannot have a case of the vapors, my lord. I should welcome one at this moment."

His smile was warm and comforting. "Brace yourself. There will not be a single woman in there who can compare to your beauty. I can see the thoughts now—'How could Lord Torrington turn away from Miss Hawthorne?' Come, allow me to take your arm."

Regina doubted that she possessed the beauty he claimed, but she thought he was kind to offer her comfort with his words.

Feeling as though she was walking in a nightmare, she placed her hand on his arm, only to have him draw her close, an intimate closeness as though they were extremely friendly. Her skirt swished against him as they walked up the few steps to the porch, then went inside, allowing the door to shut behind them with a thud.

The light was dim and the interior vast. Regina could see a large number of people seated near the front of the church. The sun beaming through the high windows revealed dust motes lazily floating above the assembled guests.

They slowly made their way down the aisle to a section near the center. Mr. Jeffries sat there, with two vacant places next to him. He turned his head, a look of welcome on his handsome face.

"Go on," St. Aubyn murmured to Regina in a voice no one could possibly have overheard.

Never had she been so aware of people watching her. Whispers abounded. Were the stares unkind or merely curious? She glanced at Lord St. Aubyn to see what his reaction might be.

He smiled. It was a warm, encompassing smile that completely took away her fears. She turned her head to see Mr. Jeffries, on her other side, offering a most approving nod. She settled down and relaxed just a hair.

The bridesmaid, Persys Timothy, a cousin of the bride, her head crowned with rosebuds and her dress of the palest pink, came down the aisle first, followed by Lady Jocelyn Robards, the groom's sister, dressed in like fashion.

Regina fancied that Miss Timothy would seek a new home. Who wouldn't wish to get away from the dreadful Mrs. Talbot? And Lady Jocelyn would scarcely wish to live with the newlywed couple, particularly after she'd had the ordering of that home for a number of years. How awkward that would prove to be for the bride. It was a time of change for the entire party.

The ladies calling on the Hawthorne residence had been only too eager to contemplate the future of those involved. All discussion had been conducted with unkind glances at the silent Regina, who had borne their sharp words and glances with fortitude. The situation had been discussed over endless cups of tea and biscuits, with no conclusions reached. But she was made aware of their gleeful pity.

At first avoiding a look at Lord Torrington, Regina took note of the bride. "She's lovely," she whispered to St. Aubyn. And she was. The white satin gown draped her slim form in perfect folds, flared out by the satin rouleau at the hem. It had puffed sleeves and a low neck edged in fragile-looking lace, and sheer lace formed an overskirt that fell from the brief bodice. White roses crowned the delicate lace veil that cascaded down her back to touch her elbows, and her arms were concealed by long white gloves. The gown must have cost a fortune. Mrs. Talbot would, of course, have insisted on the finest when her daughter married a marquis.

Then Regina turned her attention to the groom. With thudding heart and moist palms, she slowly directed her gaze to where he stood waiting for his bride. Her heart sank to her toes. He looked at Katherine with such love in his eyes that it nearly blinded one to see it. A woman would be thrilled to see love like that in the eyes of the man she married. Heaven knew, Regina would feel that way—if the occasion ever occurred.

So that was it. He truly loved Katherine! Perhaps they had had some misunderstanding that caused a rift during his courtship. Such things happened. While apart, he had decided to escort Regina, not realizing what Society was thinking or expecting of him. Or, for that matter, what she was led to believe and expect.

Her anger at him crumbled in the light of his love. She certainly hadn't been able to compete. Who could?

Jules studied, as unobtrusively as he might, the face of the beautiful woman at his side while she contemplated the wedding party. He knew just when she turned her attention to the groom. Her cheeks paled and she clasped her hands tightly in her lap. A look of wonderment crossed her face, and he turned to see what had caused it.

It seemed that the wedding was a true love match, if Torrington's expression was anything to go by. The man wore a rare smile, more than fond, at the sight of his lovely bride. Jules wondered how this might influence his own campaign to restore Regina to her proper place in Society without the supposed jilting hanging over her.

He glanced about him uneasily. Jeffries had promised to assist. Sir William could be counted on. As to Wrexham, try as he might, Jules did not trust the man. If he had been so stupid as to offer Regina a slip on the shoulder once, might he not do so again? True, the chap was on best behavior at the moment. But . . .

As to Percy Botham, if he didn't strangle the fellow first, he would likely persuade him to mind his chatter, confining it to unobjectionable matters.

The bishop droned on, the fateful words were recited, then the couple disappeared into the vestry to sign the register. The deed was done.

The difficult part of restoring Regina was under way.

She was composed now. No clutching of the hands or pale cheeks could be seen. He smiled at her, offering support. She caught his gaze with her remarkable blue eyes, almost smoky—like her gown.

"It is almost over, my dear girl," he found himself saying by way of consolation.

Her answering look proved that she had undergone an ordeal, one that she was only too glad was over.

Then the bridal party returned to march triumphantly down the aisle. As they disappeared from view, the people attending slowly rose and began to drift out of the sanctuary.

"Well, that is that," Miss Hawthorne declared in a soft voice. She lifted her chin, challenging any who dared to comment or say an unkind word. She was quite magnificent. She rose to her feet, accepted the arm Jules offered, then began the tedious process of departure.

"What did you think of the wedding?" Jeffries asked.

"Lovely. Utterly lovely. That gown was a masterpiece. Everything was . . . lovely." Her smile was brave and most admirable. Jules doubled his resolve to help her. And with any luck at all, she would help him with his sister, Lady Amelia.

Chapter Six

Mrs. Dudley stepped in front of Regina so that she was compelled either to stop or to walk around her. She suspected it was best to stop and allow the woman to speak. With a glance at Lord St. Aubyn that held more than a little appeal in it, she gave the lady an inquiring look.

"Good morning, Mrs. Dudley. It was a lovely wedding, was it not?" Regina held on to her composure with difficulty, hoping Mrs. Dudley didn't see her tremble.

"I am that surprised, Miss Hawthorne." Mrs. Dudley darted a look at Lord St. Aubyn, then returned her piercing gaze to Regina. "I confess I had not expected to see *you* here, of all people."

"I see no reason why," Regina replied with a calm she didn't feel. "I suppose I knew both bride and groom as well as most of the guests present did. Would you not agree, Lord St. Aubyn?"

"Indeed, Miss Hawthorne; probably better than many. Come, I imagine the carriage is waiting. I've invited Jeffries to join us. I trust that is agreeable?"

"I do enjoy his company. He is such a delightful gentleman." Regina half turned to seek the tall figure of their friend. He was not far away, and he smiled as their gazes met. Regina returned that smile.

Mrs. Dudley's eyes widened at this tidbit, which she no doubt intended to add to her store of gossip. Regina reflected that weddings and funerals provided such a wealth of news—almost as much as balls and parties.

Lord St. Aubyn led Regina away from the gossipy Mrs.

Dudley, ignoring any other who would seek a word with "Rejected Regina."

She placed a not-quite-steady hand on his arm as they left the church. Mr. Jeffries walked immediately behind them like a rear guard. "Thank goodness! 'Tis done. Perhaps the magpies can find something else of curiosity now. I believe I have served quite enough, thank you."

At that moment she caught sight of Lady Monceux, who appeared to be making her way in their direction. Yes, she was. Not only that—she succeeded in reaching them before they could manage to arrive at the carriage, which was trapped in the crush. It appeared they were to be joined.

"Lord St. Aubyn and poor Miss Hawthorne! And Mr. Jeffries as well! Was that not a precious wedding? Although I myself would prefer a quiet affair with just the closest of friends and family. What sort of wedding would you like, Miss Hawthorne—if you have a wedding, that is." She tittered a dainty laugh, batting her lashes deliciously at both St. Aubyn and Mr. Jeffries.

Regina considered that since Mr. Jeffries was heir apparent to the elderly and never married Viscount Quellan that Lady Monceux didn't wish to neglect a possible parti.

"In the event that I marry, I should wish it to be an intimate affair. Quiet and cozy, without the Society gossips and the ill feeling one finds on occasion. But perhaps I shall end up a spinster. One never knows, does one? Although, as you are a widow, you are quite safe from that state, are you not?" Everyone knew that Lord Monceux had not lived long after marrying a woman greatly his junior. A few wits claimed she drove him to his grave.

Mr. Jeffries took a step closer to Regina, and she felt quite protected with St. Aubyn standing at her other side. She took her hand from his arm to toy with her reticule. Lady Monceux had not missed that gesture or where Regina's hand had rested. Her eyes narrowed and she looked thoughtful. She pouted and sidled up to Lord St. Aubyn.

"I wonder if I might beg a ride with you, my lord. It will be impossible to find a hackney in all this squeeze." She contrived to sound delicate, definitely a woman to be cosseted. And she well knew that with his excellent manners there was no way Lord St. Aubyn would deny her.

"Naturally we shall assist you, Lady Monceux."

Regina gave him a sideways glance and noted with satisfaction that he looked annoyed for a few moments. At this point there was a break in the traffic, and his coachman maneuvered the landau to where they waited.

Mr. Jeffries assisted Lady Monceux into the carriage. Lord St. Aubyn helped Regina. As the vehicle proceeded, Lord St. Aubyn sat, arms folded, beside Regina, while Mr. Jeffries, looking uncomfortable, sat beside Lady Monceux.

"How pleasant this is," Lady Monceux said. She settled on the seat with a flounce and placed a hand on Mr. Jeffries's arm, but sent a dazzling smile at St. Aubyn, across from her. "Far nicer than some old hackney. I dislike taking my carriage out when I know there is to be a mass of people. So tiresome to wait."

"How fortunate you are that there are those who will take pity on you," Regina said sweetly.

Lady Monceux cast her a puzzled look, as though not certain if Regina was teasing or serious.

To Regina's enormous satisfaction, they took Lady Monceux to her town house first. An angry expression briefly crossed her face, but when she turned to St. Aubyn she was all smiles and charm and fluttering lashes.

With her sugary thanks echoing in their ears, the carriage continued on to the Hawthorne residence. Regina was surprised that St. Aubyn didn't take Mr. Jeffries to his home first. Then she decided that there was to be no mention of St. Aubyn's sister at present. Or would he say anything in front of Mr. Jeffries? Well, she would soon find out.

Both gentlemen left the carriage to enter the house with Regina. She was glad of their company, for little could be said about the wedding if guests were present, particularly gentlemen.

The gave Norton their hats and gloves, indicating to Regina that they expected to stay for a while. She walked slowly up the stairs to the drawing room, wondering why Mr. Jeffries had joined them. Lord St. Aubyn, she suspected, wished to speak of his sister. But Mr. Jeffries?

Pamela rushed to greet them, flying down the stairs from her bedroom, followed more sedately by Lady Hawthorne, who wore a look of anxious inquiry.

"How was the wedding?" Pamela cried. "I should have liked to attend. What was her gown like? Gorgeous? And her brides-maids? How many brides-men did they have? Do tell us everything." Pamela just barely restrained herself from dancing about the room.

"Two each of attendants," Regina replied with a laugh. "And I shall give you all the details of gowns and so forth later. The gentlemen were there, and I'd not wish to bore them. But do know that everything was of the finest."

Lady Hawthorne touched Pamela lightly on the arm. "Please arrange for tea, dear." The girl went off with good grace, obviously intent on a speedy return.

Giving her mother a grateful look, Regina suggested that the gentlemen be seated. Mr. Jeffries selected the sofa where Regina perched. Lord St. Aubyn chose to stand by the fireplace. There was a pause before he spoke.

"I am glad you are here, my lady. There is something I would ask of your daughter, and I would that you know of it as well." He gave her a rather sober look.

"Is that so? Explain, if you please." Lady Hawthorne chose a chair opposite the sofa where Mr. Jeffries and Regina sat. Once ensconced on the dainty armchair, she folded her hands in her lap, waiting.

"I have a sister now living just outside of London. She has been there for several years, ever since the man she expected to marry turned to another. They had been on the verge of an engagement, with the announcement anticipated at any day. Suddenly a notice was in the papers of his coming marriage to another. There was a rumor that he was placed in a compromising position, but I have no sure knowledge of that. My sister was desolate and found the gossip unbearable." He ignored Regina's gasp.

Regina closed her eyes, then gave St. Aubyn a look of sympathy. Small wonder he had wanted to help her. He knew full well how devastating such an event would be for a young woman. It explained his sympathy and his desire to help.

"Instead of remaining in Town to defy the gossip"— he bowed to Regina with an expression of approval— "she fled to the country and has been there ever since, refusing to see anyone, much less return to London."

Regina imagined how difficult it must be for St. Aubyn to discuss this with people who were practically strangers, although he seemed to have known Mr. Jeffries for a long time. She failed to know what she might do to help, however. If this sister refused to see anyone, what could be done? A glance at Mr. Jeffries revealed that he was equally mystified. She returned her gaze to Lord St. Aubyn.

He continued, gazing at Regina while he spoke. "I would like to have Miss Hawthorne and Lucien come with me to visit her. It need not be a long visit, perhaps no more than a few days. My mother lives there as well, so there would be no thought of any impropriety."

Regina turned her head to meet the concerned look in her mother's eyes. At her nod, Regina declared, "I should be most willing to visit your sister, my lord."

"I met her years ago and would like to renew my friendship with her," Mr. Jeffries said. "This happened while I was gone. I'm sorry to learn of it. She is such a delicate creature. What a nasty jolt for Amelia."

"As I have reason to know." Regina rose from the

sofa to face St. Aubyn. "Decide when it would be best to visit and let us know. I will be ready when you need me."

Pamela glided into the room, followed closely by Norton with a newly opened bottle of wine and a maid with a tray of tea, tiny cakes, and the necessary china. Norton offered the gentlemen a glass of canary.

Thankful to have something with which to occupy her hands, Regina accepted her steaming cup of tea. She sipped the fragrant bohea from a cup as thin as eggshells while peeping at her mother. That lady sat on the delicate chair, seeming deep in thought.

It was a pleasant room in spite of its vast size. The pale gold walls so nicely offset the rich blue of the sofa and chairs that ranged along the walls and dotted the room here and there. A fleeting glance at the mahogany longcase clock reminded Regina that the wedding had not occupied a great deal of the morning. She wondered what the gentlemen planned to do for the remainder of the day, but didn't ask them. That might imply she wished to be with them. Not that she didn't—it just would be improper to broach the subject. Lord St. Aubyn would likely give her that icy look down his aristocratic nose. Mr. Jeffries would smile benignly.

Norton placed the tray bearing the wine on the sofa table, then left, seeing that the maid departed before him.

"I hoped that Miss Hawthorne and Miss Pamela could take the air with us in the landau this afternoon." There was a hint of a query in St. Aubyn's voice that her mother immediately answered.

"I think that would be lovely." She smiled at the gentlemen, a sympathetic expression that brought instant smiles in return. "Regina? Pamela? Would that not be pleasant?"

"We would be delighted," Regina replied after a glance exchanged with her sister.

"Until then, ladies." Mr. Jeffries rose to join his friend, setting his glass on the tray by the wine.

Regina admired their bows, elegant and so proper.

"Lovely manners," Lady Hawthorne said with a sigh.

When the front door had closed behind them, Pamela plopped onto the sofa beside Regina. "I should like to know why I am invited. I usually am not allowed to go along, and after all—I am nineteen."

Regina met her mother's gaze. "Well, dear, I believe we tend to forget how old you are."

"Indeed, Pamela, a little less bouncing and flouncing around the room and more decorum would not come amiss." Lady Hawthorne gave her daughter a minatory look. "Perhaps, just perhaps, you might be allowed more outings, more dinners and balls. One needs good manners, you know."

"In which case I ought to have a new dress or two. Regina's dresses do not fit me well." She looked down at her bosom and sighed. "I am too flat, unlike my dear sister, who has a fine figure and an enviable bosom."

Regina choked on a mouthful of tea, requiring a thump on the back from Pamela. "Please remember not to say things like that when we are around others, my dear."

"What do you think I am? An utter nodcock? I wonder if Lord St. Aubyn's brother will be coming to London soon."

"I was unaware he had a brother," Regina said slowly. There was so much she didn't know and longed to find out about the enigmatic Lord St. Aubyn.

"He is closer to my age—Thomas Montegrew. He has a sister named Amelia, too." Pamela gave Regina a virtuous look. "I asked, so that is how I learned."

Shaking her head, Regina didn't reveal that she knew about Amelia. "Pamela, you will be the undoing of us yet."

"At least I am not gossiped about." Then realizing how cruel that sounded, Pamela slid over to give her sister a hug. "I am a wretch. You are right. My tongue will get me into trouble one of these days."

"I suspect that it runs in the family," Regina murmured quietly.

"Is Cornelius coming home for the summer, Mama?" Pamela turned to her mother for a reply.

"I believe so, dear. He leaves Eton to prepare for Oxford. Dear boy, I wish *he* were as studious as his father was at school. Your father was an excellent scholar." She gave Regina a smile, while her eyes twinkled with remembered conversation.

A leisurely nuncheon was followed by a protracted discussion on what ought to be worn for their drive.

Pamela demanded to know when she could go to the mantua-maker. "If I am invited anywhere interesting it would be dreadful to appear in some old rag."

That resulted in an involved discussion of colors, fabrics, and styles, not to mention a suitable time. Pamela wanted to go at once and was restrained only by a promise of selecting her new gowns on the morrow.

With a few words about the time to meet, Jules left Lucien Jeffries at his place, then headed out of town to the residence of his mother and sister. He could easily make the distance and return in time to take Regina Hawthorne for a drive. He just hoped his mother would be amenable to guests. He knew what his sister's opinion would be, and he didn't intend to let her know of his invitation. The element of surprise ought to work in his favor.

Henrietta, Countess of St. Aubyn was a proper lady who ruled her home with an iron hand. If she loved her children, none of them was aware of it, for she seemed determined to remain aloof from all contact. She ordered the house kept in perfection, even overseeing the redecoration of the dower house. At every opportunity she admonished her eldest son, reminding him of his need to marry.

Indeed, Jules had a greater fondness for his nanny than for his mother. He had, however, found his father to be an agreeable person. It was a pity he had died at such a relatively young age. Jules would rather have had his parent than the title. As well, his father might have had a softening effect on his wife. Lord knew, no one else did.

When he turned in between the stone pillars that marked the boundary of the property and the avenue to the house, Jules knew a quickening of pride. He loved his home, even if he did have to cope with his mother there. He inspected the condition of all he saw as they approached the house, a relatively new building designed by Sir John Soane when the old home—a Tudor structure riddled with dry rot—had suffered a serious fire. Instead of repairing, he had built on higher ground, a more desirable location in his estimation, with a splendid view of the home park.

The door opened and he saw Wilmot hurry out of the house and down to the bottom of the steps. With a pleased nod, the old retainer accepted his master's greeting, replying calmly when Jules asked about the family.

"Her ladyship is in the small sitting room. Lady Amelia is in her own rooms, my lord. Mr. Thomas is expected any day, from what her ladyship said. We have his room prepared. It will be nice to have him around again."

Beyond a tightening of his mouth, Jules said nothing. His own rooms were always in readiness, for the staff never knew when he might pop down for a visit. He suspected his servants were as eager for Amelia to return to London as he was. Perhaps even more so, for they well knew how Lady St. Aubyn treated her only daughter.

Instead of finding his sister to engage her in the light banter that he enjoyed, Jules sought out his mother.

He paused at the door to the sitting room his mother favored, noting that not a piece of the heavy oak furnishings had been moved since he was last here. The cherry velvet hangings at the windows gave a cheerful aspect to the room—especially welcome, given his mother's cold disposition. She looked up to see him, seeming not the least surprised.

"Well, and what brings you to home? Come to tell me you are to be wed, perhaps?" She bestowed an arch look on him, with a smile that was as cunning as her interest.

"No. But I intend to do a bit of looking about. I do have something to discuss. I am bringing several people for a short visit—friends of mine."

"You know how your sister would feel about that. Why I must be cursed with such a dull girl I shall never know." She put her needlework on a table, then gave Jules her full attention. "Why? And who?"

"Miss Regina Hawthorne was in expectation of wedding Lord Torrington. Everyone else was of the same opinion, but he had other ideas." He concluded his explanation with what he had accomplished. "Miss Hawthorne was persuaded to hold up her head, attend the wedding, and in general act as though she was not the least affected by his desertion."

"Your doing?" his mother inquired, startling Jules with her perceptiveness.

"Yes, well, I did encourage her to attend Almack's, balls, and the like. And along with Lucien I escorted her to the wedding." He strolled to the fireplace, noting that even on a fine day his mother insisted upon a fire.

"Lucien Jeffries has returned to Town? I thought him off in France or somewhere." She leaned against the back of her chair, studying Jules with narrowed eyes.

"His uncle, Viscount Quellan, is not in the best of health, and he requested Lucien to return. He has perked up some, but Lucien is mindful of the necessity to be near."

"That's right, Lucien is his heir. And you would bring him along with Miss Hawthorne? When?" Lady St. Aubyn rose from her chair to walk stiffly to the window. She turned to gaze at her son, no smile on her face.

"Whenever you think it convenient. Miss Hawthorne has assured me that she is willing to come whenever needed. Her mother approves, by the way." Jules fiddled with a book on the sofa table, wondering if what he sought to do was really wise. What if his sister refused to join them?

"Ha! Susan Hawthorne likely thinks to promote an alliance with you." Lady St. Aubyn turned again to stare out of the window, looking her normal haughty self. "What made you champion Miss Hawthorne? If Torrington finished with her, why should any other man take an interest?"

"You must know why I took, indeed still take, her part. Because of Amelia. And as to why Torrington broke the connection, I have no idea. Perhaps he came to see he loved Miss Talbot."

"Love! Bah! That is a lot of nonsense—the sort of twaddle in which Susan Hawthorne might indulge, considering she chose to marry a mere baron rather than an earl."

Jules stepped closer. "Did Father have an interest in Lady Hawthorne before she married?" It would explain his mother's dislike of the charming Lady Hawthorne.

"I did not say that. I merely scorned her choice of husbands." The stiff back became even more rigid.

Suspecting that he'd not learn anything more, Jules turned the subject. "So—you would not object to my guests?" She could make the visit uncomfortable even if the house was now his.

She shrugged. "This is *your* house. Why you had to tear down the home of your ancestors is more than I can see. Just because of a slight fire." She sniffed.

"You forget the dry rot," Jules retorted ironically. "As soon as Regina is free we will be down here."

"You call her Regina? Such rag-manners were not allowed in my day." This remark was accompanied by another sniff, and Lady St. Aubyn gave her son a wintry look.

"I refer to her as Miss Hawthorne most times."

"But you think of her as Regina? Curious."

Annoyed with himself as well as with his mother, Jules turned on his heel and walked to the door. "We ought to be here within the week. Order the rooms readied— but not a word to Amelia, mind you. When is Thomas due?"

"Any day now."

"Perhaps if I brought Miss Pamela Hawthorne along she could keep Thomas amused—charming girl."

"Three rooms? They will be ready."

Jules paused, bid his mother a curt farewell, then marched back to the front door.

"Leaving, sir?" Wilmot hurried to open the door for his employer. "We should have welcomed your stay."

"I am bringing guests within the week. I thought it prudent to warn my mother. Don't want Amelia to know about it, however. See that rooms are prepared for three."

Jules knew that Wilmot would relay the news to the housekeeper, and that good woman would have all in readiness, complete with flowers in the rooms.

The coachman had him back in London in good time for the afternoon drive. He picked up Lucien, then went along to the Hawthorne residence.

"Trust all was well with your mother? Your sister as well?" Lucien gave Jules a curious look.

"Mother is her usual self. I didn't see Amelia. She has her rooms and seldom leaves them. I shall have to think of some stratagem to persuade her to join us."

"An old friend to visit is not sufficient?"

"You sound offended; don't be. I doubt she would care no matter who came to see her. I fancy she is so used to being alone that she scarce thinks of the reason anymore. It has become a habit." Jules chewed his lip for a moment.

"Habits can be broken."

"'If you say so. Perhaps Re . . . Miss Hawthorne can think of something. She seems to be a resourceful person." Jules paused a few minutes, then continued. "Thomas is coming home. I thought perhaps I would invite Miss Pamela to join us, make the numbers even."

"And your mother approved?"

"She is certain that Thomas is not the slightest inclined in the petticoat line. Little does she know. However, I suspect Miss Pamela will provide no more than a diversion. He is too young to settle down at his age."

"And you are thinking about it?" Lucian gazed at Jules with patent amusement. "That will be the day."

Jules rubbed his chin, distracted by thoughts of his sister and how Regina Hawthorne might persuade her to return to her former life. "Well, we all have to go sometime," he at last admitted absently.

Lucien just laughed. Jules was happy to see they had drawn up before the Hawthorne residence. Springing out of the carriage, he ran lightly up the few steps to the entrance, then went in when Norton opened the door. Lucien followed on his heels.

They were greeted by the sight of the Hawthorne young ladies coming down the stairs, garbed in attractive carriage dresses.

Regina drew on a glove, smiling with anticipated pleasure at the treat of a drive with such distinguished gentlemen. "Welcome. You see, we are on time."

"That is because I believe it is rude to keep people waiting," Pamela inserted.

"You will have to train my younger brother, in that event. He seems to have not the slightest concept of time."

"Except when it comes to racehorses, or so I understand," Pamela said with a grin.

"Word does get around, I see." Lord St. Aubyn offered his arm to Regina.

She accepted his escort, noting Mr. Jeffries doing the pretty for Pamela. That little wretch had better learn to control her tongue or she would be in hot water. Fancy her telling Thomas Montegrew to pay attention to the clock!

"Your brother is leaving Eton? Will he be at your home when we are there?" Regina wondered what he was like.

"Yes. I thought perhaps Miss Pamela might come with us. She could amuse Thomas while we attempt to entertain my sister. Amelia has always been protective of Thomas. If she thinks there is some young lady tossing her cap at him, she may decide to inspect her. At least she might leave her rooms."

"I expect she has every comfort possible there?"

"Of course. I would never permit her to suffer in the slightest." He looked offended at the mere thought.

"I wonder if life has been made *too* comfortable for her. It might be no bad thing for her to be sufficiently annoyed to come down and complain to you." Regina gave him a conspiratorial grin.

He returned her smile as he settled beside her in the landau. "I knew I did the right thing when I sought your help."

Regina was aware that Mr. Jeffries watched them, but he gave no indication of approval or censure at her joking. It had not been an easy matter, but she was coming to put the episode of the wedding behind her. She hoped others would as well!

The first person they saw when they entered the park was Lady Monceux. In her fine black carriage accented in bright yellow, she sat with Lord Wrexham at her side. She gave Regina a smug smile, while Lord Wrexham looked chagrined.

"It would seem that both Lady Monceux and Lord Wrexham have found consolation, my lord," Regina murmured.

"Why should they?" Pamela demanded.

"Hush, dear," Regina said, without considering that there were gentlemen present. She could feel her face heating with a blush. "That is, they are friends, that is all."

"That is a strange answer, if you ask me," Pamela muttered.

"I believe Miss Pamela will get along nicely with my brother." Lord St. Aubyn turned to meet Regina's gaze, a gleam of amusement in his eyes. "I spoke with my mother," he added after a time. "She would welcome you whenever it is possible for you to come."

Regina considered the engagements in the coming week, then replied, "Perhaps Tuesday, next?"

"Tuesday it shall be, in that event."

What would that visit bring? Regina clasped her hands in sudden trepidation.

Chapter Seven

"I hope it is the right thing to do, Mama." Regina gave her mother a troubled look before turning to inspect the clothes she had selected as suitable for a stay of up to several days. It would have helped if Lord St. Aubyn had been more specific as to the duration of their visit.

"If anyone can understand what that poor girl has gone through, it is you, my dear. Remember, not every woman has the same amount of fortitude. You are blessed with common sense, but I trust you also have sensibilities to feel what this girl has suffered." Lady Hawthorne gave her eldest a concerned and sympathetic look.

"She is scarcely a girl, Mama. She is older than I am, and I am twenty-one." Regina held up a Norwich shawl, wondering if it might be needed.

"I know." If Lady Hawthorne added mentally, "and still unwed," Regina saw no sign of it. "It may be that Lord St. Aubyn is not certain how his sister will react to his guests. If she stubbornly refuses to see you, there is little that can be done. You may as well return home. It cannot be denied that being jilted is a stigma hard to overcome. Should she consent to meet with you, however, the visit can be prolonged. And if, by some happy chance, she finds you agreeable, perhaps you may be able to do some good. Surely it is worth a try?"

"Of course, Mama. I will try my very best to help her, if I have the chance. I only hope that Pamela will mind her tongue while we are there. From what you have said,

Lady St. Aubyn is not particularly friendly. What a pity Lady Amelia doesn't have a mother like you."

"Thank you, dear. What are we going to do about Pamela's clothes? She has been such a hoyden these past years that I felt little inclined to spend money on a gown that would be quickly ruined."

"Let's see what we can devise. She's a dear, and I think the day will come when some gentleman will see her worth." How long that might take was another matter.

The process of turning Pamela into a nicely dressed young lady took less time than anticipated. The mantua-maker promised to complete two gowns for her quickly. One dress was a gown that had been ordered, then the order canceled before completion; it was a simple matter to fit it to Pamela. That the shade of blue muslin was particularly pleasing was a bonus.

Sundays were always quiet days, and this particular one was no exception. There was church, followed by a pleasant meal at which their father treated the girls to a brief lecture on proper behavior, aimed—it was to be thought—at Pamela.

"Papa, I promise to do my best." If her mien was a trifle indignant, it was not too surprising. Pamela always insisted she meant well, people simply misunderstood her.

Lord Hawthorne studied Pamela from under shaggy brows and nodded. "I expect you will."

When the two girls at last escaped to the confines of the strip of garden behind the house, Pamela sighed. "I wonder if this visit is worth the trouble. Mama fusses so, as does Papa. Surely I am not required to assist you with helping Lady Amelia."

Regina patted her arm in consolation. "I suspect Lord St. Aubyn invited you to make equal numbers, since his younger brother is coming home from Oxford. If he is as hay-go-mad as I suspect, you won't have to worry about propriety as much as if he was a scholar or a dandy. Just take care not to annoy Lady St. Aubyn."

"I shall avoid her at all costs, you may be sure." Pamela made a frightful face, causing both young women to chuckle. Regina sobered at once, wishing she could avoid her as well.

By Tuesday the girls had all in readiness.

Lady Hawthorne took a look at the equipage that drew up before the house and declared, "Excellent, my dears. You will travel in the finest style." She kissed each girl, bid them be good, and then stood aside as Lord St. Aubyn entered with Mr. Jeffries behind him.

There was to be no time wasted in conversation. With an apology to Lady Hawthorne for their haste, Lord St. Aubyn and Mr. Jeffries ushered the girls to the traveling coach. They entered the carriage only too happily. At least, Pamela did.

Regina had reservations regarding her ability to communicate with Lady Amelia. Even if she allowed it, what could Regina say? It was such a sensitive subject, so personal. Regina felt as though she might be trespassing.

The two young women sat together facing forward, while the gentlemen sat facing the rear of the coach. Pamela had the unfortunate tendency to become ill when traveling, particularly when facing the rear. Regina thought it proper to sit with her, so as to offer comfort if need be. She doubted if gentlemen were inclined to tending a queasy female.

Pamela peered out the window, unwilling to miss a thing, which fortunately kept her mind off her stomach. Regina resigned herself to ignoring her sister's slightly indecorous comportment. She had more on her mind than Pamela's minor infractions.

Regina was agreeably surprised to see how modern the St. Aubyn country house proved to be. It possessed a pleasing aspect, with sparkling white stucco and exquisite details in the finest of taste. Her mother had mentioned the disastrous fire that had necessitated construction of the new house.

"I gather you selected the design, sir?" she said to

Lord St. Aubyn after he had helped her from the carriage. "It is quite lovely." She admired the front door
and fanlight.

"Sir John Soane was responsible for most of it. Clever
chap, you know. Thought of any number of elegant little
touches. My mother still prefers the old house, however."

Since Regina had little experience with architects or
building at all, she merely nodded and went up the steps,
far more worried about meeting Lady St. Aubyn than
about studying the design of the house. If the lady preferred the older house to this, she must be very hard
to please!

They entered a hall of impressive proportions, their
footsteps echoing on the black-and-white marble tiles as
they advanced to be met by the housekeeper.

Regina knew her mother would have made a point of
meeting someone who had come to help her daughter.
Apparently Lady St. Aubyn felt differently.

"Mrs. Wilmot will show you to your rooms. The maids
will assist you. Let them know if there is anything you
need," St. Aubyn offered. "When you are settled, come
down. The drawing room is on the first floor—the doors
will be open."

The adjoining bedrooms were very pretty, and Pamela
pronounced her bed first-rate. Perhaps Lord St. Aubyn
had more to do with the decoration than his mother did.

Pamela hung back. "Must we go down?"

"I never thought you a coward, dear. Perhaps it won't
be too trying." Regina wondered if she was reassuring
herself rather than her sister. Would Lady St. Aubyn be
there to welcome them to the house? It wasn't precisely
hers, but of course she would live there until her elder
son married. She fancied he would have to do that before
long. Even with a brother, he would likely want an heir.
That thought displeased Regina for some reason.

"Well, I've never been accused of cowardice!" Pamela
marched off in a huff.

Regina trailed after her, wondering in which direction
Lady Amelia's rooms might be. The house was larger

than her first impression. There must be any number of bedrooms on this second floor. The scent of spring flowers perfumed the air, along with the pleasing aroma of beeswax. Had she not been so nervous, Regina would have quite enjoyed it.

Pamela paused before the doors to the drawing room, waiting for Regina to join her. Apparently she felt some of the same apprehension.

"Come in, come in." Lord St. Aubyn crossed the length of the large room to join them. Regina took note of a rather imposing woman standing some distance behind him. Even Mr. Jeffries kept his distance from her.

Lady St. Aubyn was tall, stout, correctly garbed, but had the coldest expression on her face Regina could imagine. She felt as welcome as a slug in a lettuce patch.

How nice it would have been if her mother could have seen Pamela curtsy to the countess. It just proved that even the most unlikely girl could do well if challenged.

"Good day, ma'am." Regina stepped forward to make her curtsy, thanking heaven she didn't trip on her skirt or wobble. Girls did at times, making for an embarrassing occasion.

"Delighted to meet you, Miss Hawthorne," the countess said in an austere manner. "I hope that Amelia will agree to see you. I confess I have lost all patience with the girl. She does not take after anyone in *my* family."

It was to be sincerely hoped that none of the children took after her ladyship's family. Regina bowed her head, hoping she might find the right words.

Seeming aware of the effect his mother had on people, Lord St. Aubyn suggested that they inspect the gardens. Regina hoped he might set forth his plans for her to meet his sister at the same time. Obviously, his mother had little interest, other than to wish that her daughter be gone.

Once free of the house, the four strolled around the shrubbery until they were a short distance away. There was a relaxation of all present and their mood lightened.

Lord St. Aubyn drew Regina aside to point out a

unique bloom. "I requested that the housekeeper not cater to my sister. There will be no more meals brought to her. The maids will no longer scurry to do her slightest bidding, nor will they fetch books for her from the library. If she wants something to read, she will have to leave her rooms. If she should become hungry, food will be found in the dining room. You see—I listened to you, Miss Hawthorne. I suspect my sister will be getting angry about now."

"Does she know we are here?" Regina queried.

"No idea that anyone other than Mother is in the house. Servants, of course—but they will be oddly occupied with other tasks." He looked self-satisfied.

"Should we be in the library or the dining room?" Regina smiled at the notion of hiding in the library—wherever that might be—to confront a very annoyed Lady Amelia. "What does she like to read?"

"I don't know. She orders what she wants from Hatchard's. I stopped that, put an end to orders from anywhere." His look was benign; he sounded amused. "I believe Lucien had a good notion when he said her withdrawal had become a habit."

"Oh, dear," Regina said, making a face. "She truly won't be best pleased with you, in that event."

"Shall we brave the library first?" He held out his hand to her, and Regina found the oddest comfort in his touch. Comfort . . . and something else she couldn't name, other than to say it was a delicious feeling. Excitement? Tingling? It was almost like touching one of those extraordinary electric machines that her little brother thought so marvelous. Perhaps it was merely the novel idea of doing something so different, yet important.

"Yes. If I was deprived of all new books, I fancy I would go hunting for something else." Regina looked back to see Mr. Jeffries and Pamela headed to where an archery butt was set up.

"Your sister is not the conventional young miss, is she?" Lord St. Aubyn murmured as they returned to the central hall of the house.

"Perhaps not, but she is a dear." Regina found herself whispering, not just because the house was a grand place; she had seen many that were impressive. She feared her voice might carry and alert Lady Amelia that a stranger was within. "Where go we do now?"

He led her to a room that truly did impress her. In the present vogue, the library was a vast room with bookcases ranging along the walls. Busts of long-dead poets and writers peered down from atop. A massive desk was flanked by a pair of globes, and surrounded by any number of comfortable-looking chairs, an elegant set of library steps in the latest design, fine Argand lamps, and hundreds of books. Regina inspected a few of the titles, particularly the books on birds and flowers.

"Well, if she couldn't find something here, she would be hard to please." But then, Lady St. Aubyn didn't like the house. Perhaps being difficult to please ran in the family? Did that perhaps include Lord St. Aubyn?

"I believe I shall leave you alone, if you do not mind. She won't want to see me. Should Amelia come in here, it would give you an opportunity to talk with her. I trust you to know how to approach the subject."

It seemed to Regina that he had more confidence in her than she did. Trust to luck, perhaps?

It was odd how bereft she felt when he left. The room might have hundreds and hundreds of books, but it seemed frightfully empty without him. She pulled a book from a shelf to flip through the pages, then restored it, only to do the same with another.

Perhaps Lady Amelia would simply read an old book over? There was no guarantee that she would come storming down to the library. Regina wondered if this wasn't a harebrained scheme. An hour passed while she examined several books on flowers, all gorgeously illustrated with excellent descriptions. Pity she was no gardener.

A maid came with a tray of tea and tiny biscuits, plus a note from Lord St. Aubyn apologizing for leaving her on her own. Perhaps wait just a bit longer, then she was to join them for lunch.

Regina took a restoring sip of tea, then folded the note after admiring the strong, decisive slant of his writing. Well, she could think of far worse things than perusing beautiful books in the comfort of this library.

A soft sound alerted her. She spun around to see a pretty young woman slightly older than she was.

"What are you doing here? Who are you?" She tilted a haughty nose and folded her arms.

"Regina Hawthorne," Regina replied simply, hanging on to the book *Wild Flowers of Britain* as though her life depended on it. She would not permit Lady Amelia to see how nervous she was. "Do you mind that I am here?"

Lady Amelia sputtered, "I desire privacy." She took a few steps into the room to confront Regina with a hostile face not too unlike her brother's when he was angry. She wore a plain sprigged muslin in green and white with a simple ruff at the neck. Lady Amelia might be in the country, but she was rigged out in the best of last year's fashion. Probably her brother's purchase, considering how caring he was of her.

"Why? If I may say so, you are very lovely. Those dark brown eyes are extremely pretty, and your hair color is quite in vogue this year. You have a pleasing voice. Although you ought not frown—wrinkles are impossible to avoid, you know." Regina spoke in her most kindly manner, attempting not to anger Lady Amelia any more than she already had. Her temper became her, bringing a pretty rose to her cheeks and a sparkle to her brown eyes.

"I have never heard anything so outrageous. Were you not too old, I would say you are one of Thomas's friends." She gave Regina a searching examination.

"I have not had the pleasure of meeting Thomas. I do know the circumstances that keep you here."

Lady Amelia's eyes blazed with anger. "How dare you! You know nothing of the matter. How could you?"

"Because I have suffered the same indignity. Do you think you are the only woman who has had her lover turn to another?" Regina placed the large volume on a table, then crossed her arms before her. "I do not know if you read the papers, but if you do, you'd have seen the notice of the marriage of Katherine Talbot to the Marquis of Torrington. I had fully expected to see *my* name listed there."

There was no reply, although Regina though she detected a softening of her expression. "It is not easy for me to talk about it. I confess I did not love him as perhaps I should, but I had been led to have expectations. I thought he would ask me to marry him." Regina gave a rueful moue, then looked down before continuing. "Needless to say, he did not. Your brother Jules insisted I must attend the wedding. I thought him an unfeeling monster, but I did go." She peeped at Lady Amelia to note her reaction.

"Stupidity! How like Jules to be so uncaring. He cannot know what I have suffered—or you, for that matter." Her anger appeared to be moderating.

"He had the right of it, however. At the wedding I came to terms with the marriage, the reality that Lord Torrington truly loved Miss Talbot. I cannot say that it was easy, for it wasn't. I was very aware of hostile glances, gossips hunting for something to chew over during afternoon calls. I received a few snubs, more than a few prying questions. But I shall survive all that, and put it behind me. Without pretentious behavior on my part there will be nothing as fuel for the gossips."

"Are you saying *I* am pretentious? That I have no raison d'être for my withdrawal from a cruel society? How dare you?" She advanced a few more steps toward Regina, looking as though she might like to box Regina's ears.

Regina gestured to an arrangement of two upholstered chairs. "Let us sit. I am weary of this standing and confronting one another. We have too much in common to be at odds."

Slowly, with a wary and suspicious look on her face, Lady Amelia took one of the chairs. Regina thankfully sank onto the other, her legs having become more and more undependable.

"You wish to remain here, secluded, for always?" Regina suspected this might be a sore point, but she had to approach the problem of Lady Amelia's future. "What if your elder brother should marry? He ought to, you know. He should have an heir, even if there is Thomas."

"I would remain here." But Lady Amelia sounded less sure, almost wavering.

"It might be difficult for you, with another woman, one perhaps unsympathetic to your ordeal. When children come you would not have the quiet, nor might she be inclined to pamper you as your mother and brother have."

"He ordered no more meals in my room! I wrote for books and received a letter to the effect that they could no longer send me what I want. As I said, he is a monster."

"A very indulgent monster," Regina said softly. "How long has it been? When did you withdraw from Society?"

"Two years and one month," Lady Amelia whispered. "Oh, the humiliation, the hurt. Unless you have known it, you cannot imagine."

"I suppose if I told you that others eventually forget and that your friends want only your happiness you would not listen."

Lady Amelia jumped to her feet, clapping her hands over her ears. "I will not listen to you! You have no sensibilities."

Regina rose as well, shaking her head in sympathy. Had Lord St. Aubyn not stepped in and urged her to face the facts, she might have sunk into a similar decline. "I shall leave you for the nonce." She stepped toward the door that Lady Amelia had shut when she entered, then paused. "Oh, Lucien Jeffries begged to be remembered to you."

Lady Amelia lowered her hands, giving Regina a puzzled look. "Lucien is not here, is he? I thought he was in France or somewhere."

"Indeed, he is here, along with my younger sister and your elder brother." Regina studied Lady Amelia's reaction. She made no reply, but Regina took heart at the confusion on her face.

"My sister is a romp, but I believe that somewhere in this world is a husband for her, the right sort of man. I shouldn't wonder but the same would hold true for you."

With that, Regina turned, left the room, and wandered about the halls, hunting for Lord St. Aubyn.

He found her, as it was.

"Lady Amelia came into the library and discovered me there." Regina noted the worried frown and placed a reassuring hand on his arm. "It went better than I had expected."

"Walk with me in the garden. I would know all that was said." They left the house, seeking the herbaceous border.

Regina related the words that had been exchanged, taking note that when she mentioned that Lord St. Aubyn was likely to bring a wife to this house, he nodded ever so slightly. She felt a distinct chill.

"You intend to marry, then?" It was none of her affair, but some inner desire to know prompted the query.

"Without a doubt."

Regina could not explain why this answer depressed her. Surely she had no fondness for the man. He was quite determined to have his way, whatever anyone else might wish—never mind that he had been right. Not only that, she had such a strange reaction to him. She couldn't explain that, either, other than to acknowledge that he was a remarkably handsome man. Doubtless he charmed women without conscious thought. And, she admitted, he had charmed her as well.

"I mentioned that Mr. Jeffries is here. She had an odd reaction to that bit of news. However, she expressed no desire to see him."

"I think you made progress. We shall stay the night,

and I hope you will try again. We have allowed her sensibilities to override common sense. This state of affairs has gone on long enough." He looked so fiercely determined that Regina had no doubt that eventually he would win, and Lady Amelia would find herself in London. But to what effect? Would she consent to mixing in Society?

"You look doubtful. I assure you that I fully intend to restore my sister to her proper place in Society."

"I will do all I can to help. I merely wonder if we do the right thing."

"Rubbish. It is not natural for a woman to hide away as she has done. Had she mourned his death, it would have been but a year." He paused to gaze down at Regina, his dark eyes seeming to probe hers.

"She said it was two years and a month since he tossed her over for another woman. Did he wed the woman?"

"Oh, indeed he did. I believe it was considered a good match. She had a fine dowry and was deemed pretty by some, but she was not as lovely as Amelia. I have seen nothing of them since the marriage. They do not come to Town."

"That is to the good. If we persuade Lady Amelia to return to the city, he will not be around to haunt her." Regina took a deep breath, then continued, "I am glad I attended the wedding. It would not have been a good thing for me to marry Lord Torrington. It would have been a disaster. I did not love him, and he loves Katherine."

Lord St. Aubyn took her hand, tucked it in the crook of his arm, and then continued to saunter along the path. The scents of spring flowers hung in the air, perfuming every step. He made no remark on her confession. She hoped she hadn't given him an aversion to her. It might be best to change the topic.

"Does Lady Amelia ever come out to the garden? I could not bear to remain inside on such a heavenly day with all this beauty outside my door." Regina looked up, found her gaze trapped with his. All thoughts of flowers and scenery vanished, replaced by a warmth of feeling she'd not known before. They came to a halt, utterly engrossed in each other, only to have the extraordinary mood shattered by a shout from the house.

Lord St. Aubyn turned, muttered something rude, and then apologized. "Thomas is home."

Shaking herself free of the strange feeling that had overcome her, Regina smiled. "I should like to meet your little brother."

"Not so little, I fear. He bids fare to top me if he keeps growing." They walked back toward the house.

Thomas strode along the path to meet them. "I say, this is famous. Did I hear right? Amelia actually spoke with a stranger?" He cast a curious look at Regina, then bowed, evidently recalling his manners. "If 'tis true, we are most indebted to you, ma'am."

"Miss Hawthorne, this is my rag-mannered brother, Thomas, down from Eton. Regina has a sister here with her as well. Miss Pamela should be somewhere about. Lucien Jeffries also came down with us this morning."

Thomas gave his brother an arrested look. "Old Lucien here? How interesting."

"Join us for luncheon. Cook ought to have something to tempt your appetite. As I recall, it never took much persuasion for you to make a good meal."

St. Aubyn took his brother's arm without releasing his comforting hold on Regina. She wondered why. It would be best not to attempt to read anything into his words or actions. As to that remarkable episode just now, she couldn't begin to decide what she had felt, let alone what had gone on in Lord St. Aubyn's mind.

They sauntered up the steps to the veranda that stretched across the rear of the house, only to meet Lucien and Pamela.

Introductions, exclamations, and a wary sizing up on the part of Pamela and Thomas followed. It appeared to Regina that the two younger people took to each other with guarded interest. She doubted if anything might

come of it: both were too young to think of marriage—
at least Thomas was.

They all came to a halt in the vastness of the entryway.
Standing near the door leading to the breakfast room
was Lady Amelia.

Thomas immediately marched over to place a sound
kiss on his sister's cheek. "Good to see you, Amelia."

She didn't reply, but Regina noted that she did search
Lucien Jeffries's face.

"You have met Regina Hawthorne. This is her sister,
Pamela." St. Aubyn gestured, drawing his sister forward.

"And we met ages ago, did we not, Amelia?' Mr. Jeffries stepped forward to offer his hand. It was hesitantly
accepted, although Lady Amelia did little but murmur a
greeting to him and the others.

Regina thought she seemed changed from her earlier
mood.

Lady Amelia turned to her elder brother. "I decided
that if I was not to starve, I would have to join you. It
was not well done of you, Jules." After her gentle rebuke
she latched on to Thomas. "Lead me in to lunch."

Once her back was turned, Lord St. Aubyn gave Regina a jubilant smile. In an undertone so his sister could
not hear he said, "She can hate me all she pleases. I
shall win this battle."

Regina gave him a cautioning look. "I'd not be too
certain of that, my lord. She seems a rather determined
woman in spite of her apparent docility. It will not be as
simple as you would like, I believe. Beware."

"I am rarely mistaken. I shall be the victor."

"I trust you will not regret it."

Chapter Eight

It was a pity that Lady St. Aubyn joined them for luncheon. Her severe countenance cast a pall over the few attempts at conversation, and she dominated what little was said, offering her acerbic opinions on a variety of matters, particularly her daughter.

She sat at the head of the table, with her elder son at the foot. Lady Amelia perched silently next to him, with her brother Thomas at her other side. Pamela was placed next to Mr. Jeffries. Regina sat between him and Lord St. Aubyn, where she might observe Lady Amelia directly across from her. Even the impulsive Pamela found the neighboring Lady St. Aubyn intimidating and said little, other than a few quiet comments to Mr. Jeffries. Lord St. Aubyn had little to say, to Regina's regret.

Indeed, only Thomas seemed interested in the food placed on the table. He ate well, contributing amusing comments from time to time, and seemed not to notice the strained atmosphere.

It appeared that Lady St. Aubyn would make up for the lot of them. She spoke of the previous Sunday's sermon while casting contemptuous looks at Lady Amelia. "As the rector said in his text, 'Her enemies looked at her and laughed at her destruction.' It is found in the book of Lamentations, but it might have been written about Amelia. They shall continue to laugh at you unless you stiffen your spine and return to London. It is utter foolishness to hide in your rooms. I will say this for Jules—he managed to get you out of your rooms. Would

that he took you with him to London!'' The coldness in
her eyes ought to have frozen Lady Amelia on the spot.

Regina felt pity for the girl. What a shame that she
couldn't have had a sympathetic mother. It convinced
Regina that it was necessary to whisk Lady Amelia from
her present home to London, and with any luck at all
into the arms of a presentable gentleman. Almack's
would be a starting place. The matrimonial bazaar—as
some called it—was where any man or woman would
seek a spouse. Certainly, the cream of Society would be
found at Almack's Assembly rooms.

She exchanged a speaking look with Lord St. Aubyn,
wishing she might discuss the problem with him now that
she had talked—even if briefly—with Lady Amelia.
Surely they ought to be able to think of some means of
persuading the pretty Lady Amelia to attempt a stay in
the City. If she married, she would be free of her mother,
and that ought to be sufficient motivation to nudge her
out of her rooms!

The pudding came, but only Thomas made inroads on
his portion. Regina could see the wisdom in not eating
meals with Lady St. Aubyn; she quite took one's appetite away.

At last the meal drew to a close. Lady St. Aubyn
placed her silver on her plate and proceeded to stare
expectantly at her elder son.

Jules leaned back in his chair, then surveyed the table.
''I thought perhaps you all might like to enjoy the lake
for a bit. There are boats if you wish to row. Or you
could sit in the shade of the willows. Amelia, I would
particularly deem it a pleasure to have you join us.''

Thomas swallowed the last bite from a plate that had
been piled high with pudding, then turned to the pretty
woman at his side. ''Dash it all, Amelia, too nice a day
to remain cooped up in the house.''

''Bring a book along if you must, but I think you might
enjoy relaxing by the lake. 'Tis a peaceful place.'' St.
Aubyn glanced at her, hope briefly crossing his face. His

voice had been casual, as though he didn't care in the least whether she came or not.

Lady Amelia cast her gaze about the occupants of the room and raised her brows as though to comment on the number of people who would also be there. "Really?"

His mouth firmed as though he bit back a retort.

Regina thought it a pity if Lady Amelia refused to join them. In her way, that young woman was just as difficult as Lady St Aubyn was. Both women were as stubborn as might be. It seemed to Regina, though she had not been around her long, that Lady Amelia had grown to accept her seclusion; indeed, she appeared to relish her solitude, or as Mr. Jeffries said, it had become a habit with her. Of course, with the new restrictions in place, she might find it trying in short order.

"I would enjoy another chat, Lady Amelia." Regina hoped that by adding her mite she might help her host.

"It seems as though I have no alternative," Amelia replied at last, giving her eldest brother an annoyed look.

If she was merely annoyed at this point, it seemed as though she might be reachable. Regina considered what had been accomplished since their arrival and took heart.

Surely Lady Amelia ought to be curious to know more about what had happened to Regina. Hadn't her mother always said there is comfort in sharing troubles? Sometimes it seemed to help merely to talk about the incident. It lessened the sense of humiliation, brought matters into a proper sense of proportion. It seemed to Regina that Lady Amelia had allowed her jilting to overshadow her entire life. Not that it hadn't assumed enormous importance for Regina. But one eventually had to continue with life or risk being petrified in time.

She hadn't thought anyone observed her lack of hunger, but as they left the table St. Aubyn murmured dryly, "We shall make up for this by having tea served on the terrace later. I feel certain Mother will not desire to eat out-of-doors. I believe she considers it quite barbaric."

Regina had to smile at that. It fit her image of Lady

St. Aubyn very well. Stickler for propriety, indeed! Even Lady Hawthorne enjoyed an alfresco meal on occasion.

Pamela tucked her arm into the crook of Regina's, matching her steps. "I think I shall persuade Thomas to row me out on the lake. I wonder if there is a parasol I might borrow?"

Lord St. Aubyn evidently overheard her happy words, for he entered their conversation. "There are a number of parasols around—left by guests, for the most part. I'll ask that several be brought so you might choose one you like." He went immediately to speak to a footman.

When he returned, Regina met his gaze. "An outing on the lake sounds delightful, my lord. I hope Lady Amelia joins us."

"Lucien is in the process of guiding her out to the terrace at this very moment." He glanced toward the tall doors that led to the attractive terrace at the back of the house. "She asked him what he had been doing. Knowing Lucien, it could take some time for him to relate all. He has led a busy life until now. Pity his uncle has taken so ill. I know it is hard for Lucien to linger about with little to keep him occupied."

He flashed a sudden grin at her, and Regina had the queerest sensation of being wrapped in warmth.

"Thomas, can you row a boat?" Pamela demanded as that young gentleman sauntered in their direction.

"Dear . . ." Regina murmured in protest of her sister's forwardness.

Thomas looked affronted that anyone would call him to account for such a basic skill. "Of course I can. Come, I shall prove to you how clever I am with oars."

The housekeeper appeared with a collection of parasols, from which Pamela chose one.

Watching Thomas stroll off with Pamela on his arm— a parasol twirling gaily over her shoulder—Regina decided her little sister was not so dreadful after all. She had achieved what she wished, and Thomas seemed in a cheerful mood, judging by his face.

The housekeeper placed the collection of parasols on

a table, then departed. Lady St. Aubyn retired to her room for an afternoon nap. Regina was shortly left alone in the entry with Lord St. Aubyn.

She looked about her. "You have a charming home. I cannot think how your mother could prefer the inconvenience of a very old house to the appeal of this one." Then she realized she had done it again—spoken her thoughts. "I beg your pardon, that was rude to speak so of your mother. You do have the strangest effect on me. I am not usually so outspoken. But I confess I find it impossible to understand her feelings. This must be one of the loveliest homes I've ever seen."

"Thank you. It is always nice to hear kind words. I trust your stay here will prove equally agreeable for you."

Again she felt the warmth of his smile wrap around her. How odd that it could have such an intense effect. She had to admit it was a delightful feeling.

"Come, let us make our way to where the boats are. I would talk with you." He took her arm after offering her a simple white parasol with fringe trim.

Accepting the pretty trifle, Regina wondered how best to approach the matter of his sister's dilemma. She ignored the pleasant sensation of having her arm tucked so close to his side. Really, she had to get a better hold on her emotions. "Well, I wanted to talk with you, too. What shall we plan next? Your sister did not want to listen to what I had to say, but I think I did make her a trifle curious. She claimed I have no sensibilities. If she but knew! It is a pity she is so stubborn. Is that a trait that runs in your family?" Regina gave him a mischievous look. "I would guess that it does, for you seem to have a share as well."

They left the house and crossed the terrace to take the steps down to the pathway leading to the lake. Regina was kept close to his side in spite of her teasing.

"Stubbornness is not always bad." He gave her what could only be termed a cool look, sending her heart into flutters of apprehension. "Determination to see a thing through to the end might be called stubbornness, yet I think it an admirable trait." His face now wore that closed expression again, and Regina sighed. It wasn't that she wished to attract him, she reminded herself. It seemed, though, that for a time they were destined to work together for mutual aims, and it would be nice to be on pleasant terms.

It was a pretty vista. The lake was closer than she had thought. When they had wandered in the garden previously, she hadn't paid the slightest attention to what was beyond. He had a way of totally absorbing her interest that was a bit disconcerting when she thought about it.

Trees rimmed the irregular shore, willows draping their feathery greenery into the water here and there while limes and maples arched their limbs high above. A cluster of graceful larch waved their branches in the delicate breeze. While there were clouds above, none looked to bring rain. The lake invited one to enjoy its appeal.

Resolved to convey her thoughts about Lady Amelia, Regina began. "I believe she must be jolted out of her belief that she is the only one who has ever endured such a happening. She did not like hearing what I said. Perhaps I should be equally determined—if you wish—to make her see what a waste it is for her to bury herself in the country merely because some man chose to marry another woman. Who knows, Lady Amelia might have had a narrow escape. That man she hoped to wed might have turned out to be the monster she claims you are. And I do not believe that for a moment. I do not think you would ever harm anyone for whom you care." Regina bestowed an earnest gaze on the man at her side, hoping he would offer a comment on her thoughts.

They had reached the lake now. Ignoring the others, St. Aubyn ushered her into a small rowboat, dropped the oars into the locks, and then joined her. Within minutes they were well out on the lake, far from the others, yet within sight.

"I do not think our words will carry far. The breeze ought to send them the opposite direction."

"What are your thoughts on the subject, my lord? You know your sister far better than I do." Regina was not about to allow him to drift off to other matters as the boat glided along with the current.

"First of all, you are right in that I would never intentionally hurt one for whom I had regard. And I agree with you as to persuading Amelia that the chap she thought to marry was a bounder—or at least that he was not worthy of her. I certainly had a suspicion or two about him. But I've heard nothing of him since his marriage—and that occurred off in the country, somewhere in Sussex, I believe."

"So, she has not seen him since he left London? That is good, I fancy. And if we can persuade her to return to the City she is not likely to encounter him—correct?" Regina shifted on the wooden seat, slowly twirling the parasol.

"I should hope so. Nothing is ever definite in this life, I have found." He stared off across the lake, frowning, then continued his aimless rowing.

"Well, that is certainly true. Yet we cannot give up, can we? As I said, I am glad you urged me to attend that wedding ceremony, sir. It opened my eyes, although I confess I would rather have avoided the entire event."

He sighed. "I don't suppose I can persuade you to call me Jules?"

She shook her head, giving him a reproving look. "It would never do. What if I so forgot myself as to address you as Jules in front of others? Although I do think it a very nice name." Rather than meet the knowing look that was sure to be in his eyes, she turned her gaze to the far side of the lake. "I see your sister is walking with Mr. Jeffries. That is progress. I thought perhaps she might loll in the shade of the willow with a book, as you suggested."

"If I suggested she take a walk, she would have been certain to read a book. When I suggested the reverse, she perversely took a walk. I am sure you know your own sister that well? You have a brother, do you not?"

She nodded, smiling a little at the thought of the scamp. "Cornelius. He is a sad trial to my father, far too often being sent home from Eton. I will be glad when he begins Oxford next year. He is growing too old for the sort of pranks in which he indulges."

"You will likely have to wait until after he departs those hallowed halls for that, if Thomas is anything to go by." He dipped the oars into the water and commenced rowing strongly away from Pamela and Thomas's boat, where an argument was obviously in progress.

"At least Thomas is not one to allow Pamela to say outrageous things without opposition. She is a dear, but . . ." Regina shrugged, then returned her thoughts to Lady Amelia.

Jules studied his companion without seeming to do so. What a lovely creature she was. It was a trifle difficult to concentrate on his sister's problems when the charming Miss Hawthorne sat across from him. He had been very aware of her at luncheon—so near, yet so far. The meal had been an ordeal—trial by Mother, he thought wryly. If Regina Hawthorne hadn't been put off by his insistence that she attend that miserable wedding, she must find his family intolerable. Any woman he married would have to be a saint to put up with his mother. Not that he contemplated marrying Regina Hawthorne—or anyone else, for that matter. Thomas could well continue as heir apparent.

But Regina was truly a beautiful woman. Her freshness was appealing, especially when compared to the somewhat jaded charms of Beatrice. Lady Monceux was a rapacious woman, always wanting more—of material things as well as him. However, he had done with her, and he hoped she understood that their affair was over.

On the other hand, Henry Fleming, the cad who had lured Amelia into thinking they would be wed, had not seemed to be that interested in her dowry. He had never inquired about it so far as Jules knew, and Jules was the one who had all the details. So why had he dropped her like a hot coal to marry the other woman?

He glanced across the lake again and saw his dear sister obviously having a difference of opinion with Lucien. She shook her finger at him, then charged off in the opposite direction, toward the house. Jules frowned. That wasn't supposed to happen. Hastily, he turned the boat toward the little dock and rowed with far more energy than heretofore.

"Is something wrong?"

"Yes, Miss Hawthorne, something must be wrong, for Amelia is rushing back to the house. Unless I miss my guess, she has quarreled with Lucien. I had better find out why." He knew his mother would take no interest in the spat. She would have been far happier to have Amelia married, or at least in London. Anywhere so that she might know peace.

Once at shore, he assisted Miss Hawthorne out of the boat, then left her side to catch up with Amelia.

"I gather you had a difference of opinion with Lucien. I trust you were not rude to a guest of mine."

She halted, staring at Jules with pursed lips and eyes full of anger. That her bosom was heaving was but another clue. She was furious.

"That . . . that man! He dares to criticize me, tell me that I am a coward."

"It is his opinion, I daresay he is entitled to it. Why does he think you a coward?" he queried. Jules led her to a group of chairs placed on the terrace so as to view the lake. He urged her to sit, then took a nearby chair to face her. She studied her hands, then tilted her face at a defiant angle.

"He says I hide down here. I am not hiding. I simply view Society as utterly beastly." She sniffed, nose in the air as though she thought Jules would argue. "But then, Lucien was never one to be concerned about a woman's sensibilities. He is an unfeeling monster."

"Lucien is no monster, Amelia. He is a fine gentleman, as good as they come. As to Society, they are inclined to be frightful," Jules admitted. "At least some of them. Ask Regina Hawthorne. Her experience with Society scandalmongers isn't so different from yours. You must understand that you are not the first woman who has been set aside for someone else, nor will you be the last." Jules waited for the explosion. Surprisingly, it didn't happen. Amelia merely stared at him, then went into the house. In a way her silent departure was worse than a storm.

Tea, when at last served on the terrace, was subdued. Cook sent out a tray that had not only a huge pot of bohea but also plates of buttered scones and dainty ginger biscuits. It was not unusual for guests to be famished after sharing a luncheon with his mother. Certainly, Regina looked pleased.

"I had hoped to chat with Lady Amelia," Regina confided to Jules after she had poured tea for all present.

"She will miss her tea. Perhaps she will return." Jules wasn't too hopeful that she would, though. Stubborn as any could be, that was Amelia.

"Perhaps. Otherwise I shall attempt to speak with her later—unless she is determined not to listen to what I have to say. As the Scriptures say, there are none so blind as those who will not see—and that applies as well to hearing, I imagine."

It did seem that Amelia had decided not to listen to Regina. Tea finished, the guests scattered to their rooms to dress for dinner. Jules sat for a time over his cooling cup of tea, reflecting on the day. All was not lost, he concluded. At least Regina had provoked Amelia to some degree, and Lucien had added his mite. But they had much left to do. Jules cared for his only sister, and as head of the family he must try to help her.

Regina changed into a simple dress suitable for an evening in the country. It was a lavender muslin trimmed with yards of fine lace. Pamela wore her pink muslin that had little silk rosebuds clustered here and there. With her cheeks rosy from her afternoon in the fresh air, she looked particularly pretty.

They descended the broad stairs to the ground floor, where the dining room was located, to hunt for the others.

"I wonder if Lady Amelia will join us?" Pamela whispered.

"She was most unhappy with Mr. Jeffries earlier. Poor man, he looked so blue deviled." She exchanged a significant look with her sister.

At the bottom of the stairs they paused, looking about. "We are here," Lord St. Aubyn said from the tall door that led to the terrace. "Come join us."

Lady Amelia was not present. Lucien Jeffries wore a long face. Thomas seemed unmoved by whatever had been said. He had found some cheese and was nipping off chunks with a small knife.

Conversation was awkward. No one wished to mention the disagreement that had taken place. When the gong sounded for dinner, they silently filed into the elegant dining room. The rosewood table gleamed with silver and crystal, fine china, and exquisite linen. Beeswax tapers lent a golden glow to the room, the soft light kind to Lady St. Aubyn when she took her place.

There was a vacant place at dinner; Amelia had refused to join them. Instead of requesting dinner in her room, she had cleverly gone down to the kitchen, helped herself to what she wished, then retired to her rooms.

The evening went downhill following dinner—an indifferent meal presented by a cook of small talent. Evidently Lady St. Aubyn was not particular about her meals. Regina judged that Lord St. Aubyn had little to say regarding what went on in this house. At least at present.

At Lord St. Aubyn's request, she played the pianoforte after dinner. There was music for her, a Mozart sonata. It was a favorite of hers, not memorized but much practiced. She wound her way through the crisp ripples of the allegro, then shifted into the reflective nature of the andante, rather relishing its dreamy mood. The sprightly rondo and concluding allegro reprise brought her to the end. Since the others were still occupied, she turned a page to commence the next sonata, not so well known to her but suited to her mood—tranquil and soothing. At least the adagio was, though the allegretto was suitable for dancing. Mozart did have some quite light-hearted moments!

The gentlemen indulged in a few halfhearted games of cards while Pamela wandered about, restless and likely wishing she was home. There was an air of something in the offing, a note of suspense lingering in the room. Regina felt it acutely from where she sat, taking comfort in the Mozart she played.

At last Regina rose from the pianoforte, gathered her sister, and made her excuses. "We shall see you in the morning, sirs."

Lord St. Aubyn walked to the bottom of the stairs with them. "The music was lovely. Never have I enjoyed hearing Mozart as much as this evening. You play uncommonly well."

"The corners appeared well thumbed. Someone else in this house likes to play that music as well." She waited to see if he would say who else enjoyed the pianoforte.

"Both my sister and I had a teacher. I suspect she performs better than I do. She has neglected her music for some time—unless she plays when no one else is here." He seemed to consider this possibility, but said nothing more.

Deciding that the conversation had ended, Regina bade him a civil good night. She accepted her night candle from a footman, then joined Pamela to climb the stairs to their respective rooms.

Alas, morning proved to be little better in regards to their hopes. Lady Amelia again did not join them.

Following a light meal, both in quantity and in mood, for Lady St. Aubyn also did not join them, Regina set out to explore the garden and continue her plotting. For that was how she now considered it. What a pity she did not write plays. But then, she suspected that people rarely behaved as a playwright would have them act. Still, the notion gave her an idea.

"Why do you look so pleased with yourself?" Lord St. Aubyn—she dared not even think of him as Jules, wish though she might—asked as he joined her.

"Did I—look pleased, that is? I was thinking that I am busy plotting and wishing I might persuade people to act as I wish, much like parts in a play."

He chuckled. "What an interesting notion. And what parts would you have us play?" He placed her hand on his arm, then sauntered along the path toward the lake.

"I would have Lucien Jeffries charm Lady Amelia into returning to the City. He does seem to admire her. Perhaps he is not interested in marriage, but I believe he would stand her a good friend. And none of us can have too many genuine friends."

"Is that how you think of me?" He looked down at her, a quizzical light in is dark eyes.

"Why, yes, I do think of you . . . as a friend." It occurred to Regina that she would welcome him as more than a friend, but she pushed that thought firmly away. Had she not had enough trouble of late? "Only a friend would care enough to help such a case as I have been."

"I assure you that I have found it not the least onerous. You are an apt pupil and I have enjoyed the teaching so far. There is still a bit of ground to cover, you know. It would be best if you were to engage yourself to another gentleman. That would definitely put an end to speculation."

"There is no one yet to whom I might turn," Regina replied. Then, changing the subject somewhat, she said, "What a pity we cannot persuade Lady Amelia that she would not have the slightest bit of trouble in London." Regina considered the matter a little, then continued, "Is she concerned about you? That is, if she thought you were about to align yourself with one whom she deemed unacceptable, would she come to rescue you?"

"She ever liked to order me about whilst we were growing up. I doubt she has changed in that regard. What do you have in mind?"

"Hint to her rather plainly that you are about to contract an alliance with someone she knows, someone she does not particularly like. Then take yourself off to London. She just might decide to follow you. Especially if she really disliked this woman."

"She detests Lady Monceux. Perhaps it might work."

Chapter Nine

"Perhaps Mother has the right of it," Lord St. Aubyn mused aloud.

Lady Amelia, who had surprisingly joined them for tea, gave her brother an alarmed look. "Mother?" she said faintly. "Whenever did you agree with anything Mother had to say?"

"She believes it is time I took a wife." He bestowed a bland look on his sister that could have meant anything.

Lady Amelia darted a glance at Regina, looked concerned, then murmured, "And who might that be? Have you chosen anyone to whom you will pay your addresses?"

Regina wished she might feel more amused, but the prospect of Lord St. Aubyn marrying to please that dragon of a mother could not be a happy thought, if indeed he intended to do just that.

"I know a number of women in London who are quite acceptable."

"Not Lady Monceux, I trust?" Lady Amelia's voice was a trifle sharp. She clasped her hands tightly before her and seemed to be on the verge of jumping to her feet.

Regina thought it unfair of Lord St. Aubyn to tease his sister so. But perhaps it was not merely teasing. He did need an heir, and so a wife.

Lady Amelia leaned toward him, ignoring her cooling tea. "Surely there ought to be someone better?"

"I am no longer a boy you can browbeat into doing your wishes, Amelia. If I choose to marry Lady Monceux—or anyone else—it is none of your affair."

He hadn't actually said he intended to wed the lady, Regina noted. But then, he hadn't denied it either. She began to see the extent of his cleverness, and it was a bit chilling. It certainly ended Lady Amelia's comments regarding a wife, particularly Lady Monceux.

Lucien Jeffries rose to stroll along the terrace. Since the weather was exceptionally fine, they'd enjoyed a bit of tea while viewing the lake and its surrounds. He suddenly turned to face Lady Amelia.

"If you had not been so secluded here you would have a better idea as to what goes on in the City. I can recall when you liked to be au courant with the very latest. Now, dear girl, you are becoming frumpish; your clothes are sadly out of date. Moreover, you do not have the slightest notion of who is who in Society. Perhaps it is as well that you are become a recluse, since you have no care for yourself or anyone else."

"That is vastly unfair, Mr. Jeffries." Lady Amelia jumped to her feet, set her cup down on the small table, then made to return to the house.

"Running away, Amelia?" Lucien taunted.

She gave him a dagger glance, then with a sniff marched into the house, head held high and fists clenched at her sides.

"Oh, very good, Lucien." Lord St. Aubyn clapped a couple of times in praise. "If the one item doesn't shake her, the other should."

"You urged me to provoke her, and she is so easy to annoy." Lucien Jeffries grinned at his good friend. "It is a good thing we are cronies from a long way back. I'd not do this for merely anyone. Amelia is a nice lady. She deserves better than to be holed up in this house, charming as it might be—even with your mother in residence."

"Without a doubt Amelia is easily riled, just as she can irritate me beyond belief. As to Mother, I believe it is more than time that I see the renovation of the dower house completed. Perhaps I can persuade her to oversee the project. She does so enjoy ordering people about."

"Friends often have differences, I believe," Regina

said, with a pointed look toward Pamela, who was teasing Thomas Montegrew. But the thought occurred to her that the dower house would be needed only in the event that Lord St. Aubyn married and wished to have his wife escape the malevolent tongue so often wielded by his mother. What woman would relish sharing a house with her?

Lord St. Aubyn merely chuckled in a most aggravating manner and said nothing more to give a clue as to why he would want the dower house in good condition. He assisted Regina out of her chair with a courtly air and escorted her into the house, pausing at the bottom of the stairs while he thought for a few moments. Regina waited patiently to discover what was on his mind.

"We have planted the seeds. She will have to make up her mind what to do—and she will likely accomplish that far better when the house is empty of guests." He had retained hold of her hand, and now absently caressed it. Did he have the faintest idea what his touch did to her senses?

"Possibly." She suddenly wished she knew what he was really thinking, what lurked behind those dark and unfathomable eyes. With great prudence she withdrew her hand from his clasp.

"We are a distraction now," he continued. "But—she has had a taste of company, seen your modish garments, and listened to polite conversation again. We can but hope. I think it is time for us to return to London. You will not wish to absent yourself for too long. Others may think you have fled in disgrace or some such nonsense. Yes, it is best we go." He stared at Regina as though he anticipated some manner of rebuke or argument.

"As you wish, my lord. How soon shall we depart?" She attempted to present a calm face.

"As soon as you can be ready."

Had she not been watching him, she would have missed the gleam that flared in his eyes so quickly. He dared to tease her?

"I shall not waste a moment, my lord." She flashed him a look from eyes as wintry as the Arctic sky.

Instant departure, indeed! Annoyed that he placed the burden of their departure on her shoulders, she whisked up the stairs to her room, then decided to take her time in packing the few things she had brought with her. Once done, she did the same for Pamela. A tug on the bellpull brought a maid, who promptly took their cases to the front door and handed them to the footman. Regina followed at a leisurely pace.

"When you decide to go, you do not waste time, do you?" Regina commented as she left the house, only to find him there before her. It was amazing that his case was being stowed in the boot as hers was brought from the house. But then, there were doubtless servants hovering to do his bidding. She hadn't seen all that many maids around.

"Time is of the essence, is it not?" he remarked. Then in a rather loud voice he continued speaking. "You do not wish to miss the next assembly at Almack's, do you? I daresay Miss Pamela wants to order a new gown. Such a charming young lady, and so well suited to the latest fashions, as are you, dear girl. I quite admired that blue sarcenet you wore this past Wednesday. Dear Lady Monceux is always up to the minute with fashions."

Regina frowned. He was not only speaking loudly, he was uttering a lot of rubbish. He had never called her "dear girl" in that odious tone before. And he certainly had not given any indication he thought Pamela suited to the latest fashions—unless he had thought and not spoken. Her own blue sarcenet was hardly worth the praise he now heaped on it. She gave him a confused look, wondering why he had mentioned Lady Monceux to her. She scarce knew the woman, and what little she did know was more than enough.

He, in turn, gazed pointedly at the upper window that stood ajar. Regina followed his direction. As far as she could calculate, it was likely the window of one of Lady

Amelia's rooms. Regina immediately guessed what was afoot. It would not come amiss to add her bit.

"Indeed, sir. Almack's is not something any lady would choose to miss. I trust you go as well? And what about the Hetherings' ball? It is bound to be a crush, for everyone who is anyone will be there." She was certain that her clear tones reached that upper window quite easily.

"Of course. How many engagements are formed at balls? That is where a good many marriages are contracted, as you well know." He gave Regina a narrow look, and added in a soft voice, "*You* still have a way to go, my dear girl. I doubt the gossips have yet forgotten all that has happened, not in a few days. Stiffen your spine, and we shall see you through the difficult days, for I daresay there are a few yet to come."

For no reason in particular, the words from Lady Monceux returned. Did Lord St. Aubyn really consider Regina a lame dog, someone who needed help over a stile? That she should be deemed an irksome responsibility by anyone was not to be endured. Regina gave St. Aubyn an incensed look, which he fortunately did not see, and hoped fervently that her sister would not be long. She could not wait to return to London. Of a sudden, she longed to be as far as possible from this infuriating man.

Pamela and Thomas hurried from the house. Without delay the two young women entered the traveling coach, closely followed by the men. Thomas elected to ride along beside the carriage, claiming he had no wish to be squashed inside.

Of Lady St. Aubyn there had been no sign. Regina would send her a proper letter of appreciation once she arrived home.

She had been her imposing self at luncheon. It had been as dreadful as the meal yesterday, perhaps worse, for she picked on Lady Amelia without ceasing. Why ever did Amelia wish to remain closeted here? Or was it a matter of a place to live in London? Perhaps Lady St. Aubyn would go with her. Surely they would be able to reside with Lord St. Aubyn. Regina's mother had said the St. Aubyn London house was marvelous, one of the finest in the city. Pity that the family wasn't the sort to which one might warm. Never mind that his elegant lordship deigned to assist her. He merely endured the association, she was sure. She hadn't missed the odd looks he sent her way from time to time.

Regina pitied the woman who would marry Lord St. Aubyn, if indeed he intended to wed. And if he actually contemplated Lady Monceux, heaven help him! And what would Lady St. Aubyn think of Lady Monceux? Not a great deal, Regina reckoned. She made a face at the very thought of such a marriage.

"You are quite all right, Miss Hawthorne?" Lord St. Aubyn inquired. He exchanged a glance with Lucien Jeffries. "I trust all is well?"

"I shall be glad to return home. I hope that our visit will assist your sister in deciding to return to London. It is a pity that she took her jilting so deeply." Regina strove to remain as cool as she could. It would never do to let him see that he had the power to rattle her. But then, if he felt as though he was assisting a lame dog over a stile, perhaps she ought to set him free of obligation. She added, "Should your sister decide to join you in London, you will wish to turn your efforts to restoring her to her proper place in Society. I feel quite able to handle whatever comes my way now."

"You do?" He didn't look convinced.

"Have you seen the tabbies at their worst, Miss Hawthorne?" Mr. Jeffries crossed his arms before him, studying her with a disconcerting expression.

Pamela shifted on the cushioned seat, then with a glance at her sister said, "Well, I do not see how they could be worse than we have seen. I, for one, would prefer not to have Regina in tears again over that wretched man."

Mortified that her sister should reveal such a personal detail, Regina hurried to speak. "I do not care a scrap for that 'wretched man,' believe me. I confess I do mind the snubs and the hurtful little gibes." She wished she might have added a remark about Lady Monceux's nasty comments, but on the wild chance that Lord St. Aubyn actually might marry the woman, she felt it best to remain silent.

The remainder of the drive to London offered little in the way of conversation and certainly no excitement—no dashing highwayman appeared and nothing else of note happened either. Regina considered what faced her in the coming days, wondering if Lord St. Aubyn really intended to escort her to Almack's. Unlikely—particularly if his sister came haring after them.

At the Hawthorne residence they parted with civil remarks. Once inside, the door shut, Lady Hawthorne inquired about the brief visit and was content with Regina's comments on the beautiful house, how dreadful Lady St. Aubyn was, and how sorry she felt for Lady Amelia.

"Well, dear, things have a way of sorting themselves out, I am sure. Perhaps now Lady Amelia will consider what she is missing and alter her opinion."

"He allowed her to think he might ask Lady Monceux to marry him. More than likely she will want Lord St. Aubyn to see what a mistake such an alliance would be. From what she said, I had the feeling she did not approve of that woman. It is possible she will wish to thwart any connection in that regard." Regina exchanged a speaking look with her mother, content that the dear lady understood precisely what was left unsaid.

"I cannot say I could disagree with her. Now, what do you plan to wear to Almack's come Wednesday? Does Lord St. Aubyn intend to escort us again?" Lady Hawthorne gave Regina a casual glance as they sauntered up the stairs to her room.

"He might. I suspect it depends on whether or not his sister rises to the bait he set for her."

With that, Lady Hawthorne had to be satisfied for the time being.

As to Regina, she decided that the best thing to do was order a new gown. It wouldn't be ready for Wednesday, but she would be stunning for those attending the Hetherings' party.

Jules settled back in his dining chair, listening to the ramblings of his brother with a tolerant ear.

"Think Amelia will actually take the bait you gave her?" Thomas ceased his chatting and now studied his elder brother with a forthright gaze.

"Who knows? Do you intend to join me at Almack's this Wednesday? Miss Pamela would welcome your company, I fancy. Or do you two intend to quarrel forever?"

"Not quarreling. Amiable disagreement." Thomas accepted the change of subject with apparent goodwill.

"Heaven protect me from amiable disagreement in that event." Jules didn't know what he wanted, but surely a wife who would be an agreeable companion would be desirable. His thoughts strayed to the easily incensed Miss Hawthorne. In many respects she was a delightful bit of baggage, rising to his teasing with such dependability. He couldn't fathom what had turned Torrington to the other woman, the one he married. She couldn't hold a candle to Regina Hawthorne. Perhaps he considered Regina too forthcoming. She was not slow to state her opinion of matters, that was certain.

"Were you serious about finding a wife?" Thomas seemed uncomfortable, yet determined to know.

"I suppose the day has come when I must." He had no intention of inviting Beatrice to share his name. It was safer to say nothing of his plans—in the event he actually acquired any. Thomas was not given to tittle-tattle, but it didn't hurt to be careful.

"Mind you find someone you can enjoy, and not just tolerate."

"True," Jules agreed, thinking of his late father. He suspected that his mother had harangued the poor man to his grave. Jules suspected that old Lord Monceux had found Beatrice to be just such a wife as well. Poor man.

"I believe I'll go to Almack's with you. A ticket ought not be too difficult to obtain."

"Not for you. At present you are my heir, and the patronesses are rather fond of heirs, I believe. Besides, you are an amiable lad and dance tolerably well, I understand."

At this high praise, Thomas looked faintly embarrassed. "Shall I go with you to pick up the Hawthorne party?"

"I believe Lucien intends to join us."

"Does he have a regard for Miss Pamela or Miss Hawthorne?" Thomas wore a carefully indifferent expression, the sort that one who is interested but doesn't want you to know it might wear.

Jules gave his brother a thoughtful look. "Neither, I fancy."

Come Wednesday evening, the Hawthorne ladies were ready and waiting, for none of them were of the belief that gentlemen ought to be kept dawdling merely so the ladies could make an impression with a dramatic entrance.

Regina was confident that she looked her best in a gown of fine white lutestring trimmed with tiny clusters of pink roses tucked in the flounce at the hem and at the front of the bodice. White gloves, a long shawl, and a reticule of delicate pink completed her ensemble. Pamela also wore white, but in a soft muslin with innumerable tucks on the lower skirt, embellished by knots of rich green and a matching green reticule. Regina longed to drape her scarf more artistically around her shoulders, but that might upset her fragile calm.

The ride to Almack's was remarkably short, and the occupants of the carriage had little to say, other than exchanging mere commonplaces. Within a brief time they had entered the portals, presented their tickets, and marched up the stairs.

Lord Wrexham was the first person Regina spotted when they had gone through the formalities. She turned her back on him, pretending she'd not noticed his presence. Perhaps he had apologized, but she was still uncertain as to his motives. She wanted to believe the best about people, but she was also wary of almost everyone.

"Dearest, there are some excellent chairs on the far side. I believe they are just what we want," Lady Hawthorne murmured.

Thankful that she had such a discreet mother, Regina promptly followed her, tugging Pamela along.

Mrs. Dudley stepped forward to inquire about the health of the various Hawthorne family members. Her eyes darted from Lady Hawthorne to Regina, ignoring Pamela.

"You look well, Miss Hawthorne. I must say, your color is remarkably fine, all things considered. I've not seen you these past days."

"Miss Hawthorne and Miss Pamela traveled to my estate to meet Lady St. Aubyn and my sister, Amelia. It was a brief stay, but country air does much to restore roses to a pretty lady's cheeks." Stepping forth to insert himself into the exchange, Lord St. Aubyn looked quite superior.

Mrs. Dudley looked about to pop with curiosity. "Do tell," she begged.

"You know how country visits are. I must say, we all enjoyed Miss Hawthorne's talented performance on the pianoforte. Are you at all musical, Mrs. Dudley?"

Since that woman's abiding interest was gossip, all she could do at his query was goggle at him.

He smiled and led Regina off to the seats Lady Hawthorne had her eye on.

"Masterful, indeed, sir," Regina snapped.

"I rather thought so."

"You *are* aware that she is a premier gossip?" Regina walked stiffly at his side, incensed at his behavior and the revelation that she and Pamela had gone to visit his home. There was nothing improper about their visit, but the gossips would attempt to read all manner of things into it. That particularly vexed her in view of what he had intimated regarding Lady Monceux.

"That is why I informed her of your visit. How quickly

the word will travel. It is well known what a stickler for propriety my mother is. If she received you, it should give some of these other ladies something to mull over."

"I cannot like it," Regina protested. "Your mother did not invite us; she was scarcely present while we were there." And when she was, she became the dragon, she thought to herself.

"You do not have to like it. Do recall that I am in charge of this rescue undertaking." His eyes were cold, and he wore that look of hauteur again. He was every inch the earl, cloaked in his rank and his wealth.

"So I understand. But do know this—I have a vital role to play in your little drama. Be so kind as to consult with me from time to time." She flashed him a look of warning before turning away.

Jules watched Regina Hawthorne leave his side. She drifted along as though borne by a delicate wind, not revealing by so much as an eyelash how angry she undoubtedly was. Why was it that he so enjoyed teasing her? He had never before done such a thing, not since he was a boy, at any rate. And he was no boy now. He observed Wrexham leading her into the first dance, a stately minuet.

There was bound to be a waltz later on, and Jules intended it should be his. She was an excellent dancer; he enjoyed holding her in his arms—and not merely to tease her by holding her a trifle too close.

In the interim he saw Lucien and Thomas vie to dance with Pamela Hawthorne. He sauntered over to join Lady Hawthorne.

"Miss Pamela is all the rage this evening. I expect a discreet battle to erupt at any moment."

"You are kind. I believe my girls will come out of this scandal with reputation and manners unharmed. I appreciate all you do. Cornelius is too young to be of assistance." She smiled wryly.

"I would have the next waltz with Miss Hawthorne," Jules suddenly declared. "She has permission?"

"Indeed. Lady Sefton was so kind as to grant it last

time we were here." She scanned the floor, found her daughter with Lord Wrexham, and frowned.

"You have a concern regarding her present partner?"

"Possibly. Pamela thinks him quite handsome."

"Miss Pamela is disposed to think kindly of any gentleman who dances well, I suspect." Jules noted she didn't say what Regina thought of the chap.

Jules claimed Regina for the next waltz with her mother's fond nod to speed them on their way to the dance floor. To hold her closely was a temptation too great to ignore. He enjoyed the flare of anger in her eyes; it brought that smoky hue to the fore.

"Lord St. Aubyn, may I remind you to keep a proper distance?" Frost hung on her words.

"But this is proper . . . for us. Did you enjoy your dance with Wrexham?"

"*He* was all that was proper." She raised a delicate brow, her eyes having a naughty gleam in them.

"Odd, I had the impression that he was persona non grata with you." Jules studied her face, watching the thoughts flit across it. At first he had not been able to read her mind, but it seemed that with time he had learned to know what she was thinking—at least, much of the time.

"I confess that I do not completely trust him, but he has attempted to make amends for his blunder. And what can be accomplished during a minuet?" She directed an innocent gaze up into his eyes.

Jules smiled. "Allow me to demonstrate sometime."

"I do not know if I trust that smile, my lord. If you must know, it was a rather wicked one."

"Dear girl, I trust you are not as forthcoming when with other gentlemen?" He gave her a look of mock concern.

"Well"—she tilted her head to one side, as he spun them around in a slow, beguiling turn—"no. For some peculiar reason I find myself saying the most outrageous things to you. I wonder why?"

Jules suspected that he wore a rather smug expression,

had anyone cared to examine it. Thankful that the waltz
kept them eternally revolving, he sought to learn more.

"I imagine you have learned to trust me, Miss
Hawthorne

"Trust you? That is a bit like trusting that a tiger will
not devour you if you simply look the other way. Not
that I have been around a tiger, but it seems to me from
what I have read about them that they are not to be
trusted in the least."

"I am wounded," Jules said with a chuckle. "As I have
said before, you are most refreshing."

"I cannot help but wonder . . ."

She stopped abruptly, and he speculated as to what she
had intended to say. Did she still mull over Torrington's
rejection, wonder why he turned away from her to another woman? Goodness knew, Jules had turned the matter over in his mind any number of times and not found
an answer.

The music ended, to his surprise. Fortunately, he was
in sufficient command of himself that he managed a
graceful conclusion, then strolled around the perimeter
of the room toward where her mother sat, known gossips
to either side of her.

"Why do we not seek a bit of refreshment?"

She glanced toward her mother and nodded. "Commendable idea, my lord. Even tepid lemonade is better
than nosy questions."

"I see Wrexham is ushering your sister to dance."

She frowned, and he acknowledged that her concern
was legitimate.

"I would not encourage her in that direction, my lord.
Is there anything I can do?"

"You *trust* me to give you the right answer? I am
touched." He arched a brow, offering her a grin.

"Do not mock me, sirrah! Cornelius is too young, and
my father is never around when I want him. Besides, you
understand the situation as no one else does."

Jules sobered at once. He must not allow his fondness
for teasing her to overrule the need to guide, however

subtly. "I should not be surprised if he seeks your concern." At Regina's questioning look, he added, "Perhaps he thinks you will substitute yourself for Miss Pamela."

"I would if it proved necessary."

"Let us devoutly hope it may never come to that."

Obviously recalling the proposition Lord Wrexham had made her, she blushed and turned her gaze to the floor.

"You attend the Hetherings' ball?"

"I said I would. Pamela does as well. My mother is a good friend of Mrs. Hethering."

"The invitations are fewer than before?"

"Yes." Turning to meet his gaze, she continued, "So many hostesses are like sheep, following the leaders. If I am snubbed by one, others are likely to follow."

"Perhaps I shall request that my esteemed parent join me after all."

He didn't answer the question in her eyes, and she was too proper to ask why he suddenly wanted his dragon of a mother to join him in London when he had done his best to exclude her from his life.

They left early, for Lady Hawthorne was tired of the endless queries, all phrased so delicately. Parrying them was definitely fatiguing.

Regina paid no heed to her sister, who sat as though she held a great secret.

Sensing that the ladies were indeed tired, the gentlemen departed once the Hawthorne residence had been safely reached. Pamela dashed up to her room, leaving Regina to mull over the events with their mother. They weighed the evening while walking up the stairs to their rooms.

Come morning, all slept late except for Pamela. That young lady tiptoed down to the ground floor and slid out to meet a distinguished gentleman sitting in his curricle.

"Lord Wrexham. It is a lovely day, is it not?"

Chapter Ten

"Where is Pamela?" Regina inquired of Norton, pausing by the breakfast room door. Her sister, usually found eagerly sampling the morning offerings, was not in evidence. "She is not in her room, either."

"I cannot say, miss." The butler looked offended that he should be questioned regarding a young lady who was known to be impulsive.

Putting her capricious sister out of her mind, Regina turned her attention to a sketchy meal. She had slept far too late, and she wanted to go to the mantua-maker as soon as she might. That new gown for the Hetherings' ball must be ordered as quickly as possible. Fortunately, she knew just the effect she wanted.

"Have you seen Pamela, dear?" Lady Hawthorne inquired as she entered the cheerful breakfast room. Her dress of cherry-striped muslin became her, lending color to her delicate face.

"No." Regina could think of nothing to add to that brief reply, and so only gave her mother a concerned look. "You look all-in, Mama. Perhaps you should have a quiet day? I can take Pamela and a maid with me to choose my gown."

"That might be advisable. I declare I cannot recall when it has taken me so long to recover from an illness."

"Trying to do too much." Regina felt guilty that she had allowed her mother to go with them the evening before. Surely there might have been another means?

"Good morning, all," Pamela caroled from the doorway. She looked fresh, all rosy-cheeked and sparkling eyes.

"I searched for you a bit ago. Where were you?" Regina approved the pretty dress worn by her sister, although it did make her look older. It was hard to remember that Pamela was no longer the little girl that she had protected while growing up.

"Must I tell you of my every move?" Pamela snapped. "I was in the park—and I did not go by myself, either. I know how you feel about going off alone."

"Pamela, you will apologize to your sister." Lady Hawthorne gave her younger daughter a reproving look. "I believe I shall leave you two. I think a quiet day will suit me well." Her ladyship drifted out of the room, leaving behind a scent of lavender and two daughters at odds with one another.

"I am counting on you to go shopping with me this morning." Regina studied Pamela cautiously. Was she being overly concerned? Her sister was so young in many ways, never mind she had reached the great age of nineteen. It was quite possible still to be naïve, and Pamela was definitely that.

"Fine. I will go whenever you please. I think I'll order a new gown for the Hetherings' ball as well. You are not the only one who wants a husband, you know." She gave Regina a defiant look, tilting her nose in the air.

"I have high hopes for you, my dear. With all this gossip, it is unlikely that I shall contract a marriage, in spite of Lord St. Aubyn's insistence. There is no reason that you should not find an eligible gentleman who will cherish you as you deserve."

"I'm a wretch, Regina." Pamela assumed a forlorn expression. "I know you want the best for me, and honestly, I will try to catch the eye of some eligible. But *not* Thomas Montegrew! He is the most annoying, aggravating person in the world! He makes me so angry, always telling me what I can and cannot do. He is worse than you." At the astonished stare from her sister, she plumped herself on a chair and shook her head. "I did it again. I'm sorry."

"All I can say is that you are certainly not yourself this morning. Come, I have lost interest in food. Let's go to the mantua-maker. We shall both of us order a new gown and astound all with our magnificence."

Pamela laughed, as intended.

Deciding that she had been imagining things, Regina took her sister's arm and they repaired to their rooms. Within less time than one would have believed, they were off, with Betsy along to lend propriety and a footman to carry packages.

In her stylish shop Madame Clotilde, her improbably red hair peeking out from beneath a gorgeous turban, greeted her longtime customers with a genuine smile. When the need was explained, she left them a moment, then returned with a folder of drawings. From this she brought forth the perfect sketch for Regina.

"Gold tissue, with this pattern of leaves appliquéd in gold satin. You will capture all eyes, Miss Hawthorne." She pulled out another sketch to show Pamela. "And for you, a gown of white muslin, but of incredible simplicity that will stun all."

Pamela stared at the exquisitely simple gown, tied beneath the bosom with a blue cord and having a pleated back, giving the skirt a charming fullness. What made it different was a clever design done in white embroidery with tiny blue flowers here and there. "Perfect!"

Succumbing to a pretty lace ruff for the neck of a favorite day dress that needed something, Regina paid for it, then the young women sallied forth to find the proper slippers and dainty hats to do justice to the new gowns that were promised to be ready for the ball.

"Oh, is that not Lord Wrexham?" Pamela nudged her sister, discreetly peeping in his direction.

"Yes, it is." Regina hadn't meant her voice to be quite so chilly. She still didn't wish to explain to Pamela what Wrexham had done. Even if he had apologized, the words had been spoken, the proposition made, and that

was difficult to wipe from her memory. She knew she
ought to be more forgiving; however, it was not easy
to do.

"Well, I do not think you need to be so condescending
to him. He seems quite eligible to me." Pamela was in
a huff again, giving Regina scowling looks and refusing
to take her hand when they crossed the street. "Stop
treating me like an infant." Pamela made a childish pout
that entirely refuted her claim to adult conduct.

"Come, let's see what we might find in this shoe shop."
Regina ignored her sister's peevishness, assigning it to
being young and impatient, not to mention desirous of
attracting a court of admirers. The slippers were found,
as were evening hats to complement their gowns. Pamela's was a demi-turban of very fine muslin tied with a
tiny blue bow, while Regina chose a dainty confection of
twisted gold satin and pearls.

They returned to the house in harmony with one another, and nothing more was said about Lord Wrexham.

The days flew by, with Pamela taking early-morning
walks in the park, denying any wish for her sister's company. Regina was a bit hurt that she was unwanted, but
it was delightful to see how Pamela's cheeks bloomed
and her eyes sparkled when she returned.

Lady Amelia wrote Regina guarded letters, full of
questions and hesitant curiosity. Regina replied, taking
her time to compose letters full of encouragement. But
it was not an easy task, for Regina still suffered the little
snubs and gibes when out and about. The invitations to
balls and parties were fewer. She tried not to let her
mother see how this affected her, for it did that dear
lady no good at all to realize the extent of the gossip's
damage.

When Lord St. Aubyn and his brother, Thomas, appeared a few days later, Regina had to admit she was
greatly relieved. She had begun to think he had abandoned her.

Pamela seemed oddly ill at ease when she faced
Thomas Montegrew. Lips compressed, eyes flashing, she

sat as far from him as she could and turned aside when he joined her.

Taking no notice of her sister, Regina gathered the letters from Amelia to share with Lord St. Aubyn. "I thought you would be pleased to know that Amelia seems to be much closer to joining you in the City. She appears to consider such a move."

"Actually, that is why I am here. I had a brief letter from her this morning with the news to expect her tomorrow. I believe the first thing she wishes to do is to visit the mantua-maker and you, not necessarily in that order." He smiled, and Regina returned it in full measure. It was a warm, encompassing smile that made her quite ignore the low-voiced conversation between Pamela and Thomas.

Regina listened to Lord St. Aubyn talk about his plans for Amelia and his mother, absently noticing that the air between Pamela and Thomas had become decidedly frosty. Resolving to learn more later, she paid attention to the details that St. Aubyn offered. It sounded pleasant, and she told him so.

"I owe you a great deal. Had you not spoken with Amelia, she most likely would still be buried in the country, refusing to see anyone."

"Well, it is good to know that a ruse can be helpful. Sometimes that is not the case." She glanced at Thomas and Pamela, distressed to see them at daggers drawn. "Is something wrong, Mr. Montegrew?"

"Ask your sister. And ask her what she is doing sneaking off to go driving in the morning with Lord Wrexham." Thomas ignored Pamela's indignant gasp. "It is for your own good that I warn you. Do not see him again. To be driving out with Wrexham is above all things objectionable for a young miss like you—unless you wish to be thought fast."

"And I should like to know who has made you an arbiter of manners, Thomas Montegrew." Pamela glared at him, no longer trying to keep her voice down.

"Evidently *I* have more common sense than one young

lady I know." He crossed his arms, giving her a superior look. "I shall say no more than this—if you do not cease, you will most definitely come to grief."

"Pamela! You didn't! You haven't! You have?" Regina was horrified beyond measure to think her sister had not only concealed something like this from her, but had gone with Lord Wrexham above all others!

"I do not see why it is a crime," Pamela said righteously. "He is everywhere accepted. You once thought him quite fine. Merely because he didn't ask you to marry him is no reason that *I* should reject his kind offers to drive in the park. He has been all that is gentlemanly."

"Oh, love. I beg you cease." Regina gave Lord St. Aubyn an anguished look. He knew what she had endured. How could she reveal to Pamela the improper proposition that Lord Wrexham had offered her? It was a very painful matter, and she had wanted to keep from sullying Pamela's ears with such a tale.

But now the situation had changed. For one thing, Wrexham had apologized. She had hoped he was sincere, but the seed of doubt grew. What could be in Wrexham's mind that he sought Pamela's company? She was not the least bit like the other young women he preferred. Did he truly want a wife? Regina rubbed her forehead in concern.

"I daresay Pamela will agree that the distress she is causing you, not to mention our rejection of Wrexham as a suitable escort, will change her mind." Lord St. Aubyn spoke in a pleasant manner—not as though he wanted to shake Pamela until her bones rattled, which he likely did. Regina knew she wouldn't mind giving the foolish girl a shaking or two.

"No, I must speak." Regina stiffened her spine. "Lord Wrexham offered me a great insult, a highly improper advance." Regina closed her eyes a moment before continuing. "While he has apologized, I find it difficult to overlook what he said. Please do not associate with him."

"Well, he asked for a dance at the Hethering ball tomorrow evening, and I promised him one." Pamela was a touch defiant, but Regina could see she was upset by the reactions of Regina and Lord St. Aubyn. Had Thomas been the only one to complain, it would have been different.

"I cannot insist, but I beg you deny him," Regina said.

"I found him very courteous." Pamela gave Thomas a mutinous glare. "I shall dance with whomever I please."

This bit of willful conduct would be dealt with later. Regina wanted nothing more than to end the matter for the moment. "Will your sister attend, Lord St. Aubyn?" Regina sought to turn attention from Pamela's wayward behavior, and what better means than Lady Amelia?

"I doubt she will have a decent gown to wear, but we shall see. Needless to say, I will look for you."

So he would not escort her. That was understandable, with his sister arriving. But Regina felt saddened at the loss of his support.

"We will be pleased to see Lady Amelia if she is able to come."

"Perhaps Madame Clotilde would have something she might wear," Pamela said, her voice and manner subdued. "Women sometimes order gowns and then must cancel them for one reason or another."

"I know." Lord St. Aubyn gave Pamela such a look that she must have felt encroaching. Regina knew she would.

The two men rose, made their bows, and shortly left the house.

Pamela rose from her chair, prepared to escape before her sister could interrogate her regarding Lord Wrexham.

"Just a moment—I would talk with you," Regina began, rising to go to her sister's side.

"I refuse to listen to another word. *I* do not think him so dreadful. Just because he insulted you after you were jilted does not mean I cannot have a bit of fun. He's so handsome." Pamela's sulk was much like her childhood reaction when scolded.

"I wonder what Mother will say to that?" Regina was

not one to tell tales, but this was shocking. What to do? With a troubled heart she watched her sister march off to her room.

Regina hated to think what it would have been like had Mrs. Hethering not been a friend of her mother's. The lady was polite, but she looked as though she wished she were not under an obligation to have the Hawthornes at her ball.

It seemed that matters grew worse, not better. It was noted that Lord St. Aubyn was not at Regina's side, and Mrs. Dudley, that wealthy and nasty gossip, couldn't wait to accost her. She planted herself before Regina, going so far as to clasp her arm so that Regina couldn't escape.

"I see Lord St. Aubyn is not at your side this evening, Miss Hawthorne." Her protruding pale blue eyes avidly searched Regina's expression for any clues.

Regina smiled in spite of longing to dump a vase of flowers over the gossiping head of her questioner. "Since I am not his lordship's keeper, what he does is not my concern."

"Well! Plain speaking, indeed." Mrs. Dudley was clearly offended, and dropped Regina's arm in a huff.

"As you say, ma'am." Regina curtsied and hurried on her way to a far corner and her mother.

"That dreadful woman! If only she weren't so rich. Not a soul would have her on a guest list otherwise."

"Look, there are Lady Amelia, her mother, and Lord St. Aubyn," Pamela whispered behind a discreetly raised fan.

Regina spun slowly around to see Lady Amelia wearing a simple and exquisite gown of pale blue trimmed with fine lace. Lady St. Aubyn wore black, and beside her Lord St. Aubyn was a contrast in pale gray and plum.

Lady Amelia soon spied Regina. She said something to her brother, then immediately came toward the Hawthornes. "See, I am come to the City. I shall depend on your encouragement," Amelia cried with a gaiety that seemed forced.

"I am not sure I can be all that much help," Regina began, only to be cut short by his lordship.

"Nonsense! Who better to know friend from foe?" He turned to greet Lucien Jeffries and Thomas, who had walked up to join the group.

Thomas bowed to the ladies, then sought Pamela. "You promised me a dance. I would talk with you."

With a minatory look from her mother, Pamela agreed and sauntered off with the one man who seemed to care what she did.

"Lady Amelia, I am pleased to see you in Town," Lucien Jeffries said, with the first genuine smile Regina had seen this evening. She didn't count the polite grimace from Lord St. Aubyn. He looked as though his dinner hadn't agreed with him. On the other hand, it might have resulted from listening to his mother. That lady could give anyone indigestion.

"Dance with me, Regina," Lord St. Aubyn said. "I would know how things are with you."

Regina nodded, accepting his hand to be led to the dance floor. The candlelight lent a soft glow to the room, for Mrs. Hethering had spared no expense in having so great a number of beeswax tapers. Regina glanced up to admire her partner. The plum coat so well became St. Aubyn. But then, he had such fine taste that everything he wore was just right. She could see that Thomas emulated his brother in dress, if a trifle more colorfully. He wore a blue velvet coat that complemented Pamela's white gown to perfection.

"Now then, how have these last days been? There was little chance to speak, with Thomas and Miss Pamela arguing."

"They do brangle. As to my days, they have varied. I was quizzed about you when I arrived. Mrs. Dudley persisted, and I fear I was a trifle rude to her, for which I shall never be forgiven, I know."

"A pity women like Mrs. Dudley must be tolerated."

"All that lovely money cannot be overlooked, particularly when she has connections to some of the best families. I have sometimes wondered if she uses a touch of coercion or subtle threats to retain her position." Then Regina realized what she had uttered and gave him a mortified look. "I do beg your pardon. My wretched tongue. At times I say things I have no intention in the least of uttering!"

"You are delightful, my dear girl. As I have said before, most refreshing." A smile lit his eyes.

Was his smile a touch patronizing? She recalled the words about helping a lame dog over a stile and wondered if he still felt that way. How unfortunate that at that moment she spotted Lady Monceux across the room laughing up at Lord Wrexham. The lady did not attend Almack's, for the patronesses did not approve her in the least. But she was everywhere else received. Tonight she dazzled the eye with green gauze spangled with gold glitter. Even the drapery over her arms was spangled gauze. Regina was thankful when the turn of the dance took her gaze elsewhere.

"I trust your sister has not forgotten the dances. She seems to be enjoying Mr. Jeffries's company." Regina thought it prudent to ignore St. Aubyn's comments on her character— refreshing or otherwise.

"She does, in spite of their bickering. I swear that at times they remind me of Thomas and Miss Pamela."

She nodded, smiling as she supposed she ought, trying to ignore the delicious feeling of being close to him and having her hand clasped securely in his—even if for only a brief time.

At the conclusion of the dance, Regina was claimed by Mr. Jeffries, who spent what time they were able to speak extolling the charms of Lady Amelia. She bore it with a fortitude she didn't know she possessed.

It was when the dance concluded that she spotted her sister on the far side of the ballroom with Lord Wrexham. She eyed the pair with misgivings. There was something remarkably odd about his interest, yet she could scarce bring it up again. Any more words, and Pamela would totally cease to speak with her! And she didn't know how to find out what his motives might be unless she sought him out. Then how to discover them?

She excused Mr. Jeffries, wishing him to Lady Amelia's side, when she discovered Lady Monceux sidling up to her.

"Lady Monceux, how nice to see you again." It was anything but; however, one must preserve one's manners.

"Ah, the little lame dog. You look enchanting this evening, just the thing for a girl in her second Season and, shall we say, anxious about her chances for a good marriage?"

"Forthright speech, my lady," Regina exclaimed softly. The last thing she wished to do was draw attention to their conversation, however much she might like to retort in kind.

"Bah! You would never take advice from me, so I shall not attempt to offer any. But do note how Lucien Jeffries hangs about Lady Amelia. And also pay attention to your champion, St. Aubyn, when he next dances with me. Look elsewhere, dear girl. Perhaps Lord Wrexham might do? Or does your sister seek to whisk him from under your nose?" She gave a pointed look in their direction, where Pamela bloomed under the practiced charm dispensed by Wrexham.

"I devoutly hope not. Lord Wrexham may be all that is fashionable, but he does not please my tastes. I'd not wish him for my sister." Regina closed her eyes. She had done it again—spoken without due consideration for the person at her side. Would she repeat those foolish words to Wrexham? Nothing would surprise her. Regina wondered if she simply ought to retire to a nunnery or something. Perhaps Lady Amelia had the right idea after all.

Lady Monceux smirked, bid her a sweet farewell, then drifted off to chat with another lady.

After that, Regina lost count of her partners. It seemed that Lord St. Aubyn had fulfilled his offer to have his friends dance with her. Every one, to a man, made some comment about St. Aubyn. She also noted, however, that the men seemed agreeably surprised in her dancing ability as well as her conversation. Not that she said much. Thinking back on two of her chats this evening, Regina decided it best to be silent when possible.

"Regina," Lord St. Aubyn said when the latest of her partners had returned her to her mother's chair.

"What is it, my lord?" She revolved to gaze up into his face.

"We have a problem."

At the worried expression that now settled on his face Regina glanced at her mother, received a nod of permission, then suggested, "Perhaps you might wish a cup of punch?"

"Punch, it is. I would rather be away from others."

She knew better than to think he wished to flirt with her. After all, if she was no better than a lame dog, she ought not expect such attentions! "What has happened?"

"Henry Fleming is back in London . . . without a wife."

"And he is . . .?"

"Forgive me, you wouldn't know. He is the man who jilted Amelia two years ago."

Regina was quite thankful that she was not the questionable Mr. Fleming. Judging by Lord St. Aubyn's expression, the gentleman would not fare well.

"Without his wife? I do not understand. He simply did not bring her with him?"

"Apparently she died a year ago—in childbirth, it is said. Now that he is out of mourning, it appears he is on the hunt for another wife. I have no idea what Amelia might do if she sees him, or meets him!"

"God forbid." Regina turned to seek out the figure in the pretty blue gown. Lady Amelia had been a success this evening, and not merely with the curious. A good many distinguished gentlemen had paid her court. Mr. Jeffries had hovered close whenever possible. "She has been having a marvelous time this evening by the looks of it."

"I wonder if Fleming thinks to establish contact with Amelia?" St. Aubyn sounded more than worried. He had a fierceness in his voice that chilled.

"Would he have the effrontery to do that? Surely he must know that any attentions from him would be highly objectionable. How would he dare?"

"Oh, he jolly well could and might."

"May I help?" She owed St. Aubyn, and perhaps this might repay some of her debt.

"No! I'd not put you in that position."

"Whom else could you trust? I insist." She wondered what she was letting herself in for.

Lord St. Aubyn looked reluctant, his brow puckered. "I shall have one of my friends suggest he might wish to ask you to dance. Perhaps you might mouse about as to his plans."

"He is here?" She was aghast at the thought of what might happen were Amelia to see Mr. Fleming on her first foray into Society.

"He just arrived and is near the door."

Regina needed no prompting to turn slowly and examine the gentleman who had obviously just entered the room. He stood chatting with his hostess with the ease of a man of distinction. His garb appeared to be the latest, his hair was styled in a modish Brutus cut. That handsome profile was enough to send flutters to a girl's heart. Regina could well understand his appeal—she thought him a dashing gallant.

"Well?" There was a wealth of meaning in that one word. "It is likely more than you anticipated. He will not be an easy conquest. However, I suspect you will have no trouble charming him." He said those last words with a dry note in his voice, and Regina wondered at that.

"What do I do?" Poor Amelia must be protected— and what, after all, did Regina actually have to lose? It would seem that while St. Aubyn's friends were perfectly willing to dance with her, none were interested beyond that.

"Try to keep him away from where Amelia is, if possible," he instructed. Then he stroked his chin and mused aloud. "I would give much to know his plans."

She was dubious as to how this might be accomplished

and said so. She set her barely tasted glass of punch on a table, then turned away from the sight of Mr. Fleming charming his hostess. "I do not know how to sound him out."

"I can understand your hesitation. Perhaps if I have it made known that you possess a fine dowry, have excellent ancestors, and have beauty that is not only skin-deep he will consider you his prey for the evening."

"What can I say after such a delightful commendation?"

"Your eyes are smoking with rage."

"Is it to be wondered at? You . . . you make me so utterly furious. I cannot think how it is that you are the darling of Society. I should like to crown you!"

He studied her with a curious expression on his handsome face.

She had done it again, spoken without guarding her tongue. If she survived this Season, she would definitely go into hiding—if not before then.

"How stimulating you are. Most women keep those thoughts to themselves."

Utterly mortified at this point, Regina compressed her lips, longing to hit the infuriating man. "Well? Perhaps *I* am not the one to lure the information from Mr. Fleming after all?"

"If he is half the man I think him to be, he will be fascinated by you."

She looked everywhere but at Lord St. Aubyn. He did not have to so continually mock her. "You tease. But, if you are serious, proceed."

She missed the slow smile that lit his face. "Come with me. I know just the man to do the job."

Chapter Eleven

Lucien Jeffries looked puzzled when Lord St. Aubyn and Regina walked up to him, as though he wondered why they sought him at this point of the evening. After all, Lady Amelia was dancing very nicely with Sir William. That gentleman was far too kind to make the slightest reference to the cause for her absence from Society.

"Have you observed the late arrival, Lucien?" St. Aubyn inquired with an arch of a brow.

"Too busy keeping an eye on your sister. Egad, you would think she had never left Town." He appeared frustrated.

"Henry Fleming just entered the ballroom. I would like you to introduce Miss Hawthorne to him."

"To Fleming? I mean to say, old man," Lucien sputtered.

Lord St. Aubyn gave him a cautioning look, and Lucien bowed.

"So be it. On your head, Jules."

"I'll persuade Amelia to leave as soon as possible. Just give me ten minutes or so."

If Lord St. Aubyn had any doubts about sending Regina into the lion's den, he concealed them well.

Regina walked beside her escort in utter silence. She couldn't think of a thing to say. What a pity she couldn't ask Mr. Jeffries how a young lady went about fascinating a knave. It would be improper, but did that matter anymore?

But then, she had said more outrageous things to Lord

St. Aubyn recently then she had ever dreamt she might say to anyone, ever. It was a pity she found him so intriguing and attractive. It was not merely his reputation as a rake that fascinated her. What drew her interest was the other facets of his character, the ones that she suspected Society rarely, if ever, was permitted to see. She doubted if her young brother would be so caring of a sister, concerned to the point that he would allow another woman to risk her reputation to help—for that is what her involvement amounted to, was it not? But then, had she not decided that she'd might as well consider herself a spinster? It was for Pamela that she braved the gossips and plunged into Society.

Lord St. Aubyn thought she might be restored to her proper place in Society. Maybe. But why—if he sought to help her—did he seem to do his best to thwart her progress? She glanced about her, wondering if anyone could guess the war that waged within her. Surely, being seen with Mr. Fleming could not improve her standing. Yet she wanted to help Lady Amelia. That she also wished to please Lord St. Aubyn she banished from her mind.

The walk across the ballroom was brief. Regina's thoughts whirled through her head, confusing and conflicting.

She glimpsed her sister standing up to dance with Lord Wrexham. If she hadn't promised to lure—and wasn't that a silly word—Mr. Fleming, she would have somehow prevented that from taking place. Fascinate the man, Lord St. Aubyn had said. Stupidity! Why had he not turned to Lady Monceux to lure the man away from Lady Amelia? She certainly had the charm and experience.

Mr. Jeffries drew her to a halt close to where Mrs. Hethering chatted with the newcomer. Lucien paused as though something had just occurred to him, then turned and looked at Mr. Fleming as though he'd just seen him for the first time this evening.

"Fleming, can it be you? I thought you at your estate

in the country. It has been a long time." Lucien sounded polite, almost friendly, certainly not like someone who would rather have Fleming's guts for garters, as Cornelius was wont to remark. At times little brothers came up with the most appropriate sayings, even if they were not at all proper.

"Good to see you, Jeffries." He appeared genuinely pleased to see Mr. Jeffries, but at once turned his gaze to Regina. "I do not believe I have met the lovely lady. Would you do the honors?" Mr. Fleming bowed elegantly to Regina.

She thought his gaze quite speculative. Did he inspect her golden gown as to cost? Or perhaps calculate her vulnerability to his charms?

She'd had time to take note of his excellent bearing, good-looking features, and eyes that seemed to sparkle at her, making her feel unique. Oh, he would be devilish with a young girl in her first Season. She could see why St. Aubyn insisted that his sister must not see him. The mere sight of Mr. Fleming would crush her newfound courage. It would be best if Lord St. Aubyn could prepare her, let her know the man was in town.

With obvious reluctance, Lucien Jeffries introduced Regina to Henry Fleming. It was almost amusing, for his unwillingness made it appear as though he didn't wish Mr. Fleming to meet her for reasons of his own, as though he wanted her for himself. Hilarious, she thought grimly.

"Miss Hawthorne, a pleasure, I assure you. Is your father not Baron Hawthorne?" At her nod of agreement, he smiled—very predatory, that smile. "He is famous for his wit and his astute management of his property."

She'd wager he thought more of the management angle, for her father was scarcely known for a sense of humor. She murmured something appropriate, sounding as much like a shy miss as possible.

"Perhaps you would be so kind as to grant me a dance? Jeffries, might I beg you share this treasure you have found?"

"Mr. Jeffries was about to escort me to find something to drink." The slight pressure from Mr. Jeffries's hand reminded Regina, had she needed such, that she had a role to play.

Mrs. Hethering stepped into the conversation at this point, suggesting that dear Mr. Fleming become acquainted while escorting Miss Hawthorne to where the wine punch was to be found. She was certain that Mr. Jeffries would be so obliging as to relinquish his claim to Miss Hawthorne's company.

"*Your* famous wine punch? I have thought of it often while in the country, ma'am." Mr. Fleming bowed, lingering over the matron's hand a moment longer than necessary.

"Well," she said in a fluttery manner, "it is considered excellent, if I do say so." She waved them off, then turned to Mr. Jeffries. "How lovely to see him again. Such a pity his wife died."

Regina wondered if Mr. Fleming thought it a great pity. There was no evidence that he mourned, if his sky-blue velvet coat was anything to go by—not to mention his roving eye. She could not say it was pleasant to be the focus of it. But then, she knew more about him than he suspected.

"You have been in the country for some time, Mr. Fleming?" She smiled at him, the way Lord St. Aubyn had assured her was bewitching.

"Indeed. I've spent the past year in mourning. My wife and child died over a year ago, you see."

"You poor man," Regina gushed, hating herself as she did so. She never gushed. Mr. Fleming seemed enchanted, however. She took a step closer to him, fluttering her ashes. "You need consolation. I am sure that Society will offer much to take your mind off your loss." She darted a glance at the longcase clock that stood just inside the door to the room where refreshments were set forth. How much longer before she could beg leave and depart? She devoutly hoped that St. Aubyn and Mr. Jeffries would spirit Lady Amelia away soon.

"Punch, Miss Hawthorne?" He held out a glass that had been poured by the footman.

She accepted the delicate glass and took dainty sips. The punch would indeed be memorable for its potency, if nothing else. She turned away from the laden table to face the door. Would a footman deter a scoundrel bent on luring a girl who was supposed to be luring him? Or would Mr. Fleming bide his time and select a more suitable spot?

"I do not recall seeing you in Town three years ago."

"I had not come out then." She gave him full marks for having a smooth manner. She waited to see if he would remark on the Torrington marriage, although there really wasn't any reason why he should. One never knew, however, what others had heard—even in the country.

"I am glad I came up for the remainder of *this* Season." He gave her a meaningful look over the top of his glass.

"Are you, really?" Regina wanted to compliment him on his skills. He had very seductive eyes, beguiling and promising much. She felt a stirring within her, and she didn't want to like him in the least. But how dreadful that he could speak thus when his marriage had ended not so terribly long ago.

"How refreshing to meet a young lady with such assurance. Usually young women making their come-out are very shy." His gaze seemed a trifle devious, or was that because she knew ill of him?

"I confess I have my shy moments. You are gifted at putting a person at ease, sir." *Especially if said person is trying to stall for time and will say almost anything to keep you away from the ballroom.*

It seemed that Mr. Fleming had full confidence in his ability to entice young women. Well, with his good looks and elegant dress, not to mention a smoothness of speech, he had that right, Regina guessed. Had she not been aware of his dastardly deed she might have succumbed to his charms, especially if she missed that occasional cunning look in his eyes.

She glanced at the longcase clock again and calculated that sufficient time had passed so she might return to the ballroom with safety. He took the hint.

"Forgive me, Miss Hawthorne, I have kept you too long. Come, I will escort you back to the ballroom."

"My mother will be wondering where I am, sir." She placed the scarcely touched glass on a table to take his arm.

Now, if Pamela were not around to ogle the handsome Mr. Fleming and tumble into love on sight, all would be well. She could wash her hands of the cad and be off. Of a sudden the Hethering ball was not a good place to be as far as she was concerned, in spite of the dash she had cut with the gold gown.

The one thing she found pleasing about Mr. Fleming was that he didn't know about her so-called jilting. He might have a calculating eye, but it appeared to be for a different reason, one that might cause a maiden's heart to flutter if so inclined. "Thank you, sir. Your escort was appreciated," she said politely as she paused before her mother.

"Lady Hawthorne? I vow, I thought it was Miss Hawthorne's sister. Your husband is indeed a fortunate man to have such beauty in his home." He oozed charm and polish.

"Mr. Fleming was so kind as to accompany me to the punch bowl, Mama." Regina sent her mother a look of appeal with the faintest nod toward the door.

"How kind, sir." Lady Hawthorne gazed at Regina with a troubled expression on her face. "I fear we shall have to leave early, my dear. I am still not myself."

Mr. Fleming offered his escort a second time, but was so charmingly refused that he departed with a smile.

"Dreadful man," Regina whispered. "Come, let us leave before he decides to return. Where is Pamela?"

"I trust I shall hear what this is all about when we get home? Here comes Pamela now, with Lord Wrexham."

"Mama, I cannot like that interest."

"Nor do I. We have to be careful, dearest. In our present position an annoyed gentleman can do a lot of harm." She gave Lord Wrexham a smile that revealed nothing of the inner reserve Regina knew she bore.

They made their way out of the ballroom, pausing to chat with Lady Hawthorne's friends, accept an invitation to call, and in general appear casual in their departure.

Mrs. Hethering had revised her opinion of the Hawthornes, it seemed. She begged them to remain and appeared desolate that Lady Hawthorne had a headache.

"I daresay Regina will have a caller or two tomorrow," Mrs. Hethering said with a coy smile. "I saw the way she captivated Mr. Fleming. He is so distinguished and handsome, and has no need of a fortune. Pity his wife died so young. I fancy he now looks for a young lady to replace her." She raised her brows with a significant look at Regina.

The remark was in the height of bad taste. Regina was glad that Mrs. Hethering was not a close friend to her mother. She murmured something soothing, then made a show of assisting her mother down the steps. Papa was as usual at his club, not interested in escorting his wife and daughters to a mere ball.

"Heavens, I am not quite feeble, dearest," Lady Hawthorne whispered with a hint of laughter in her voice.

"What was Mrs. Hethering talking about, Regina?" Pamela inquired. "And why are we leaving so early?"

"It is close to midnight and Mama was getting tired. She is so reluctant to make her infirmity known, but I do not wish her to overdo. How dreadful it would be were Mama to be back in bed."

"No, indeed!" Pamela took her parent's other arm to help her, succeeding in getting in the way. The coach summoned, Regina spent the time waiting on it to turn Pamela's curiosity in other directions.

They passed the time on the ride home with comments on gowns and the music, not to mention the strong punch.

"Charlotte Hethering is famous for her punch. What she doesn't know is that her husband pours in a few bottles of this and that until it is very potent. I am glad you drank very little of it."

Regina chuckled. "It tasted dreadful. I am amazed that anyone can drink it! Though I gather the gentlemen enjoy it."

Once they had entered the house and gained the drawing room, Pamela declared, "I am glad we are home. I am exhausted. I fancy we may have a few callers tomorrow, and I want to look my best." She left Lady Hawthorne and Regina to hurry up the stairs.

"What happened?"

"I offered to keep Mr. Henry Fleming occupied so Lord St. Aubyn could whisk his sister out of the ballroom before she saw him. He is the man who jilted Lady Amelia. It would seem he is now on the prowl for a new wife, as Mrs. Hethering said. I must say, he is remarkably good at concealing any grief he bears." She bowed her head, then added, "I cannot help but think of the grief he caused one I now consider a friend."

"Certainly a sister of a friend, at any rate." Lady Hawthorne thought for a few moments. "I believe things seemed a trifle better this evening. Mrs. Dudley was not around to sow her little snippets of poison. And Lady Sefton invited me to call. That was especially pleasant." She wore a satisfied smile.

"At least you are restored to your proper place." Regina considered the future, then continued, "Even if I do not marry, I believe Pamela will do well. She is pretty and has such natural grace."

"She also has a habit of saying things she ought not and of being willful when it comes to obedience."

"She will outgrow that, I feel certain." Regina patted her mother's thin hands, offering her comfort. She also thought of her own propensity for forthright speech with Lord St. Aubyn and barely refrained from a sigh. Why could she not be as proper as she had been while with Lord Torrington? "Come, let us seek our beds. Perhaps tomorrow will bring something interesting, as Pamela hopes. I mean to be up before Pamela so as to prevent her from slipping out to meet Lord Wrexham."

"Good. I hesitate to outright forbid her, you know. She is just stubborn enough to defy me."

Pamela might be the dearest sister one could desire, but she was also a handful when it came to something she wanted to do.

Bed would be welcome. As she undressed, Regina considered the ball. In spite of the problem with Mr. Fleming, she thought she had ended the evening in a better social position than she had been in before. Perhaps it was merely a matter of attending the events possible and lifting her chin, as Papa said. Having Lady St. Aubyn acknowledge her didn't hurt either. Surely, people must forget in time?

Unless, she reminded herself, they had someone like Mrs. Dudley around. That lady appeared to hold a resentment against Regina for some unknown reason.

Lord St. Aubyn would inform his sister that Mr. Fleming had come to London, most likely to seek out a new wife. How would she react to the news? What a pity that no sooner had they persuaded Lady Amelia that it was safe to reenter Society than that dreadful charmer decided to return.

With very muddled thoughts in her head, of Lord St. Aubyn and Lady Amelia mixed with Mr. Jeffries and a leering Mr. Fleming, Regina fell into a troubled sleep.

When she woke in the morning it was to find Pamela perched at the foot of her bed.

"You do not look well, Regina. Are you all right?"

"Thank you for such concern," Regina said, hoping she didn't sound as ironic as she felt.

"I believe we will have callers today. At any rate, perhaps more interesting ones than in the past weeks. *They* seemed more concerned about possible tidbits of gossip than in pleasant conversation."

"True." Regina accepted her cup of morning chocolate

with a distracted air. If they did receive callers, who might come? Surely Mr. Fleming would not dare show his face—would he?

Motivated by the possibilities the day offered, she gulped the warm drink, then left her bed. "What shall I wear? Let me see—I must have the look of a young lady who appreciates her restoration to the bosom of Society. Something proper, yet with a dash of modishness."

"The periwinkle morning dress would be nice."

Regina smiled. "Indeed."

An hour later the two girls descended to breakfast dressed for whatever the day might bring.

In her heart, Regina longed to see Lord St. Aubyn again, and not merely to know if Lady Amelia had withstood the appalling news without crumpling. Of all the gentlemen with whom she had danced last evening, he alone understood what she had undergone, how she felt. It was so comforting to have someone who understood.

She would admit to nothing more than comfort from him at this point. It would do precious little good to moon over the man. No matter what he might say, she could see that Lady Monceux had some manner of hold on him. Regina might be inexperienced, but she could sense something between them. Until she no longer had that reaction, she would keep firm control of her feelings.

Lord St. Aubyn entered the Hawthorne drawing room before any other caller arrived. He bowed over Lady Hawthorne's hand, then chatted amiably about the preceding evening. Finally, he turned to Regina.

"You will be pleased to know my sister does very well. She would like you to come over to see her if possible."

"I suppose she does not like to go out and about just yet?" Regina asked. Lady Amelia could have come to call with her brother. But perhaps she had a touch of her mother's attitude toward anyone less than an earl and his immediate relatives.

"She was afraid she might encounter someone she

wished to avoid. She believes you are quite eligible for a particular gentleman's attention, you see."

"Good grief," Regina exclaimed in a low voice, hoping that Pamela was not listening.

"May I bring the carriage at half past four of the clock?"

Regina glanced at her mother, who nodded ever so slightly, then replied, "I will be ready then."

He left just as Mr. Jeffries arrived below. Regina stood at the top of the stairs to bid Lord St. Aubyn farewell and watched the two gentlemen hold a low-voiced exchange before the front door.

Rather than have Mr. Jeffries see that she had been watching, Regina hurried back to the drawing room, intent upon reaching the sofa.

"What was all that about?" Pamela rose from her chair and went to peer out of the window. "I see several carriages stopping before the house. What a pity Lord St. Aubyn could remain such a short time."

"Why?" Regina inquired absently, wondering what Lady Amelia would have to say.

"He does lend a touch of elegance to any gathering. I am not such a dunce that I do not know he is considered something of a rake. The only trouble is, I am not certain what a rake is. Mama?"

Exchanging a look with Regina first, Lady Hawthorne considered the matter a few moments. "A rake—and I question that Lord St. Aubyn truly is one—is, according to Mr. Johnson, a man of decadent character and of somewhat loose habits. I personally think the term is applied all too frequently to men who really do not deserve it."

Norton fortunately chose that moment to announce Mr. Jeffries.

Fast on his heels came several other gentlemen with whom Regina and Pamela had danced at the ball. A few brought pretty bouquets.

Lady Hawthorne and Pamela chatted with the others

while Mr. Jeffries managed to isolate Regina just enough so they could not be overheard.

"I thought perhaps you might be willing to go for a drive this afternoon."

"Lord St. Aubyn is coming at half past four of the clock. I am to visit his sister."

"Is that what he said? I think perhaps he wishes to have you to himself." He looked amused.

"He is concerned with his sister, nothing more."

"Mr. Fleming has not shown his face here as yet?"

"I am thankful to say he has not. I should be very surprised if he did." She noted that a few of the other gentlemen looked their way, openly curious. She wanted to end the conversation at once, and so she moved a step away.

"And I should be very surprised if he didn't."

Regina smiled, trying to keep a pleasant expression on her face. What would she do were Henry Fleming to present himself at the Hawthorne residence? She dared not forbid the man. That might undo what little had been accomplished last evening. On the other hand, could she possibly handle a gentleman of his character?

Fortunately, Mr. Jeffries turned his attention to Pamela and Lady Hawthorne. A short time later he was gone, but not before he had persuaded Pamela to drive with him.

"Men are as fickle as women," Regina murmured to her mother as they watched Pamela bid one of her particular callers good-bye. "He asked me to drive with him first. I informed him that I am to see Lady Amelia later this afternoon."

"You are? Did Lord St. Aubyn say how she had taken the news that Mr. Fleming has come to town?"

"I gather I shall learn that later." Regina gave her mother a wry look, then commented on the agreeable behavior of the gentlemen who had called.

Pamela seated herself with a flounce. "I think we ought to be calling as well, Mama."

"We shall, dearest. I was tired today. Perhaps tomorrow. Are you going for a drive with Mr. Jeffries?"

This brought a discussion as to what should be worn, and that lasted until Mrs. Dudley and Miss Carvil came to call.

Regina remained silent and allowed her mother to parry their searching questions. Obviously, Mrs. Dudley had not received an invitation to the ball and was quite put out—particularly when she learned the Hawthornes had attended.

Miss Carvil, on the other hand, wished to discuss the pretty gowns and the lovely music and the scandal of Mrs. Hethering's punch.

Fortunately they had left and Pamela had gone to her room to change for the drive with Mr. Jeffries when the last caller of the afternoon appeared.

"Mr. Henry Fleming," Norton intoned, his manner extremely severe, as it was when he disapproved of something or someone.

"Good afternoon," Lady Hawthorne said politely. Her manner was cool but not frigid.

Regina rose from the chair where she had been chatting about the gowns with Priscilla. "Mr. Fleming! What a surprise."

"Surely you cannot think I would fail to pay my respects to the loveliest ladies at the ball. Fair damsel, do not deny me the consolation of your beauty."

Regina wondered how she was supposed to reply to that remark. She invited him to be seated even as she returned to the simple chair on which she had perched but moments before. Distance seemed a sensible idea.

Lady Hawthorne skillfully held the conversation to matters of general interest. Regina admired her mother's ability to take the reins in her hands, allowing the topics to go only where she wished.

"If I might have a moment, my lady," Mr. Fleming ruthlessly inserted at last. "I wondered if Miss Hawthorne would be so good as to give me the pleasure of her company on a drive tomorrow. My life will not be complete until I am able to know her a little better."

"Gallant words, sir. Regina?"

Exchanging a wordless communication with her mother, Regina nodded. "I would be pleased to accept. Five of the clock?"

"The very time I would have, when all the world and his wife are in the park."

Regina silently resolved to beg the gentleman to take her elsewhere. She rose and was pleased when he did as well, albeit with patent reluctance. "Until then, Mr. Fleming."

She made no comment until they heard the last of his steps on the stairs and the front door closing behind him.

"What shall I do, Mama? I do not think Lord St. Aubyn will be pleased that I drive out with Mr. Fleming."

"And what Lord St. Aubyn thinks is so important?"

Regina nodded, wishing that she might say more.

Lady Hawthorne patted Regina on the shoulder as she passed on her way to the stairs. "I shouldn't worry were I you. What will be, will be."

Once alone, Regina muttered, "And what does that mean, pray tell?"

The clock chimed four and she sped to her room to change. Her heart beating madly and her cheeks blooming a delicate rose, she looked forward to a prosaic drive from the Hawthorne residence to the St. Aubyn town house with far too much enthusiasm.

Chapter Twelve

The St. Aubyn town house was an elegant brick edifice. Upon leaving the carriage they walked up the steps to the grand door, which was painted black with an imposing brass knocker. The butler opened it silently to reveal a huge entryway. The black-and-white marble floor led them along a hall to the stairway that winged up to the first floor. It was far more impressive than the one in the Hawthorne residence. The balusters were exquisitely fashioned of wrought iron in a stylized lily design capped by a mahogany rail. Regina took a surreptitious peek at the ceiling and found what she'd hoped—an utterly gorgeous painting of nymphs and angels. What a pity she was here to chat with Lady Amelia. She would have been more than delighted to inspect the house.

Lord St. Aubyn ushered her up the stairs in silence. He had said little on the way, other than that Amelia looked forward to a talk with Regina. That could mean almost anything.

"Ah, I expect there is something you ought to know." If she didn't tell him, he would learn one way or the other. Better to hear it from her. "Mr. Fleming came to request that I accompany him on a drive in the park. He desires to go to Hyde, but I shall ask that we go elsewhere. I do not wish to drive in Hyde Park merely because it satisfies his wish for the 'world and his wife' to see him there, supposedly with me. I am not comfortable with the idea of driving with him, but I thought perhaps it might please you to have his interest directed away from Lady Amelia."

It was a good thing that they reached the first floor at that point. It gave Regina a chance to catch the expression on Lord St. Aubyn's face. He seemed displeased.

"Be careful. I'd not have you fall into his clutches."

Regina longed to inform him that the only man into whose clutches she wished to fall was he. But a lady could never say such things. The very idea brought heat to her cheeks.

Lord St. Aubyn stared at her, a slow smile crossing his face. The gleam in his dark eyes was disconcerting.

Surely he couldn't suspect that she had grown to admire him—nay, more than that? It wasn't possible for someone to actually read what was in another's mind, was it? The very notion that he might brought even more heat to her face. She was mortified to see her reflection in a looking glass they passed. She was as pink as a peony.

He paused outside a set of doors. "I am not certain what Amelia wishes to discuss. I shall trust your good judgment as to how you deal with her queries."

Faced with the possibility of unpleasant topics, Regina felt her face cool. She was able to enter the drawing room in some degree of calm. Lord St. Aubyn followed her.

She didn't see Lady Amelia at once, for it was an immense room containing a great deal of furniture. Fires blazed merrily in both the fireplaces, lending welcome warmth to the imposing furnishings. The walls were hung with gold silk, the floor covered with exquisite Turkey carpets in muted colors, and light came from tall windows draped in gold. Gold and white predominated and left the senses reeling with the impact. Enormous sideboards of satinwood and mahogany with fanciful legs and gilt trim ranged at the sides of the room. From what she could see, the marble covering their tops was gorgeous. However, Regina thought a few dainty tables would not have come amiss.

"Here I am," Lady Amelia called out from a tall wing chair near the far fireplace. Her slender form almost disappeared from view in the vastness of the chair, never mind that it suited the size of the room.

It proved easier to settle into a conversation with Lady Amelia than Regina had feared. Amelia quickly came to the matter that worried her not a little.

"I was dismayed, to put it mildly, when Jules told me that Mr. Fleming is in town again. Why he had to come at the moment I returned I cannot imagine. Perhaps it is a test of my fortitude."

"Whatever it might be, it is not welcome. Your brother agreed that I should lure Mr. Fleming away from the ballroom so you might be spirited away without seeing him. But I can see where he might fascinate a woman— he is handsome and has a dashing manner."

"Did he fascinate you, Miss Hawthorne?" Lady St. Aubyn said from the doorway.

Regina swiveled on her chair to survey the imposing woman who entered the room. How fitting these surroundings were for her—she did them full justice. "No, ma'am. Mr. Fleming holds no interest for me. I am not a woman who thinks she can reform a man who has done evil in the past."

"Sensible reply." Lady St. Aubyn came to stand not far from the fireplace. The fire had died down to a pleasant glow. It reflected a warmth to her countenance that doubtless deceived one. "My son tells me that you have offered to help Amelia. I must thank you for anything you can do. Mr. Fleming must not be permitted to go unchecked."

"His wife died. There is no reason he cannot wed again," Regina pointed out.

"I understand that you suffered an indignity similar to that which Amelia suffered," her ladyship said, pinning Regina with a sharp gaze.

"If you mean that I had expectations of an offer of marriage and that the gentleman chose to wed another— yes. I well know the embarrassment Lady Amelia has endured. It was not so much that he wed another, it was the gossip that haunted me from the time of the announcement until now."

Lady St. Aubyn merely nodded in comprehension. She still looked remote and unyielding, but about her eyes were little lines of concern. Perhaps she knew a change of heart? Regina sincerely hoped so.

"I have always wondered what prompts these tittle-tattles to grind away at such news." Lord St. Aubyn frowned, crossing a leg while studying his steepled hands. "It is as though they seek to elevate themselves by lowering another."

"What shall we do, if anything? Naturally, I have given instructions that Mr. Fleming shall never be admitted to this house." Lady St. Aubyn surveyed the three assembled in the drawing room. "What else?"

"I wonder if it might not be best were Lady Amelia to simply ignore the man. Surely he will know better than to seek to reestablish a connection with her." Regina looked to Amelia to see how she reacted to this idea and was pleased to see a smile, albeit a wicked little one.

"What a pity I am not the sort to spread malicious rumors. I might be very tempted to let it be known that there is a concern over the cause of his late wife's death," Amelia said.

"Amelia, we know nothing of the circumstances of her death," Lord St. Aubyn stated firmly. "There will be no rumors from this house."

"Shall I attempt to learn of his plans when I ride out with him on the morrow?" Regina shifted on her delicate chair, wishing she might be gone, even though she welcomed time close to his lordship. This was a most unpleasant topic.

"It is always good to know what the enemy plans."

Regina was surprised to hear that sentiment from Lady St. Aubyn. But then, she had been surprised to see that lady speak so kindly to her daughter.

"What do you intend to do regarding your sister's infatuation with Wrexham?" Lord St. Aubyn studied Regina with an expression that revealed nothing of his own thoughts on the matter.

Regina examined the stitching on her gloves with care while searching for a reply. "I know not what to do. I am loath to dwell on what he proffered me."

"May I inquire what Lord Wrexham suggested to you, if you do not mind telling us?"

Regina looked at Lady St. Aubyn first, then to Lady Amelia, who had asked the question. When she revealed the shocking proposition made to her by Lord Wrexham, both women gasped.

"Lord Wrexham did such a thing? That is worse than being jilted!" Lady Amelia cried. "You poor dear, to suffer two such dreadfully unpleasant incidents."

"I am shocked that a gentleman would believe a young woman of your rank would contemplate such a degrading situation." Lady St. Aubyn seemed genuinely horrified.

"My mother felt just as you do, my lady. Evidently his lordship believed I had so sunk in Society's esteem that I would be a prime target for just such a position—if you can call it that. Yet Pamela is so young for her years and so frightfully impetuous that I fear for her reaction were I to reveal the entire truth to her. We decided to say little for the nonce."

"I think the chit ought to be told the whole of it," Lord St. Aubyn declared. "Surely she would see sense." He wore such a fearsome expression that Regina wanted to flee the house. Without a doubt he must feel that she had done something to warrant such a proposition—flirt or lead Wrexham on in some way. Others had voiced such thoughts.

"Jules, you are wrong." Lady Amelia rose from her chair to pace back and forth not far from where her mother stood. "Pamela seems the curious type. She would doubtless find Lord Wrexham fascinating and intriguing—like forbidden fruit."

"I suspect Lady Amelia has the right of it," Regina inserted. "Pamela has always been daring, doubtless coming from being around Cornelius so much. She would likely find it a lark!"

"I should like you to join us, Miss Hawthorne." Lady St. Aubyn issued the invitation in the manner of a command.

Flattered and not a little curious as to the reason for the invitation, Regina nodded. "I would be pleased, my lady."

Lord St. Aubyn looked puzzled but made no comment. Rising, he walked to the window and paused by one of the marble-topped tables. "I shall send notice to her mother."

They were about to sit down at the long mahogany table when Thomas entered the room. "I say, is there a spot for me? I may join you?"

"Of course, you scamp." Lord St. Aubyn gestured to a chair beside him and fixed an eye on a footman. Within minutes a place was set, and Thomas joined in the meal as well as the conversation.

"Saw your sister again this morning," he said to Regina during a lull in the conversation.

"Indeed?" Regina inquired cautiously.

"Why she persists in driving out with Wrexham is more than I can see." Thomas helped himself to cold meat and cheese, unaware of the reaction he stirred in those around the table.

"Perhaps it is time?" Lord St. Aubyn murmured to Regina, who was staring across the table at Thomas with a sinking feeling. How her sister had managed to slip out of the house to go driving with Lord Wrexham was beyond her.

"I do not know . . ." She studied the young man across from her, then spoke. "Pamela is young and foolish, I fear. Perhaps were you to caution her?"

"No good," Thomas replied instantly. "She thinks I am jealous."

"And are you?" Lord St. Aubyn grinned at his younger brother, dispelling some of the gloom that had settled over the table.

"She ain't a bad sort, mind you. Could do worse, begging your pardon, Miss Hawthorne. You see, I like a woman with spirit. She has that. Yet I think she knows what is proper and she has a good background—proper family and all."

"Good grief, Thomas, you have given this a great deal of thought!" Lady Amelia gave her brother a troubled look, then added, "I am surprised you even consider settling down at such a young age."

"Long engagement is the answer." Thomas beamed a smile at them all, but took care not to meet his mother's stern gaze.

"I would agree," her ladyship replied to the amazement of all present.

Regina wondered what had happened to her ladyship that she would even contemplate an alignment between Thomas and Pamela, particularly at his tender age. Then she realized that engagements could be broken, while a marriage is permanent.

"It is one thing to contemplate such a thing, another to make it reality." Lord St. Aubyn paused in his examination of the cheeses offered to study Thomas.

Thomas looked at his brother and winked. "Just watch. *You* might learn a thing or two!"

This thought so overwhelmed the others that the meal was completed in silence.

Regina gladly agreed to join Lady Amelia for a little chat in her room. She decided that the brothers could better discuss whatever Lord St. Aubyn had on his mind with the females of the house out of the way. Lady St. Aubyn evidently felt the same, for she announced her intention to take a nap.

As the men walked down the hall in the opposite direction, Regina heard Lord St. Aubyn ask his brother, "Just how do you propose to support a wife?" Whatever the answer, it was lost as the men turned into a room and the door shut behind them with a decisive snap.

Her mind reeled with the thought of Pamela becoming engaged to Thomas Montegrew.

"Does the thought of your sister getting engaged first bother you?" Lady Amelia urged Regina up the stairs to the second floor and her sitting room, casting concerned glances at her from time to time.

"I am concerned, but for different reasons. I suspect, however, that if anyone might persuade Pamela to behave circumspectly, it would be your brother Thomas. Goodness knows, I have tried and failed." Regina sent a rueful grin to her hostess.

When she later went home, she sought out her mother, wondering what her reaction might be to the information Regina had to offer her. Lady Hawthorne took the news with far more calm than expected.

"You do understand what this means, Mama?"

"Nothing, until it becomes reality," Lady Hawthorne replied, her tranquil face revealing none of her inner thoughts.

"I see what you mean. Thomas Montegrew yet has to court Pamela and be accepted. I'd not give a groat for his chances, knowing that girl so well. I love her dearly, but she is the most exasperating person in the world." Regina wished she knew just how Thomas Montegrew intended to persuade her stubborn sister to marry him. Perhaps the scheme might be reversed on someone else.

The following afternoon Regina dressed with unusual care for her drive with Mr. Fleming. She intended to give him a subtle hint that he might as well drop her and, while she was at it, suggest that he forget about Lady Amelia. She wanted to look her best, and wouldn't admit in her heart that she hoped she might see Lord St. Aubyn while she was out.

Her dusty-blue jaconet-muslin carriage dress she topped with a capelet of sable. The day was pleasant, but the wind could be chilly, and she could see the trees swaying outside her window. She ignored the matching muff, no matter how fashionable. Had she wished to conceal something, the muff would have been ideal, but she had nothing to hide, other than her motives.

Adjusting her neat, narrow-brimmed hat, she fluffed the three plumes attached to the back. They ought to survive a simple carriage drive. Gathering her gloves and reticule, she left her room, feeling as though she went to her doom.

"Very nice, dear," Lady Hawthorne commented when Regina joined her in the drawing room.

Before Regina could reply, Norton appeared to announce Mr. Fleming. She slowly turned to greet him.

"Lady Hawthorne, Miss Hawthorne. 'Tis a lovely day for a drive in the park." He bowed to each, then looked expectantly at Regina.

"Let us not keep your horses waiting, in that event." Regina bade her mother a fond farewell, then went down with Mr. Fleming. What a pity he was so handsome—it made him so difficult to dislike.

He thwarted her plan to ask to drive to a different park by not mentioning where he intended to take her. Rather, he tooled his pair of chestnuts along the busy streets with a careful regard for traffic.

"It is a lovely day," Regina managed at last. How difficult to conduct a conversation with a gentleman one was determined to despise.

"I have missed the City. Although I did a bit of traveling after my wife died. Went to Scotland, tried my hand at angling and hunting."

Regina supposed that was as good a way as any to recover from a death. "You must have felt her loss deeply. I am so sorry."

He checked the horses as they entered the Stanhope Gate to the park. He glanced at her, then said, "I would rather not speak of it."

Well snubbed, and rightly so, she supposed.

She saw her sister at once. She drove with Thomas Montegrew, Lady Amelia, and Mr. Jeffries in a fine carriage drawn by a pair of roans.

"Now I know I am back in Town. To see so many I know is an assurance."

"I'd not expect to renew all your acquaintances, sir.

There is a saying that it is best not to try to recapture what once was." She hoped he would understand that she meant his association with Lady Amelia.

"Is Lady Amelia linked to Mr. Jeffries?"

Regina glanced back at the carriage now behind them. What a brilliant notion. "Indeed, you have the right of it. They are everywhere seen together, and I'd not be surprised at an interesting announcement coming forth before long."

"Who was with Thomas?" He seemed idly curious, and displayed no reaction to her remarks about Lady Amelia and Mr. Jeffries.

"My sister. She and Mr. Montegrew are often a pair." Let him make of that what he would. She was piqued that he exhibited not the slightest reaction to the sight of Lady Amelia with Mr. Jeffries. Why?

Then, as they continued, she spotted Lord St. Aubyn. He was astride a handsome bay. He was also conversing with Lady Monceux, who had halted her carriage at a prominent spot. He perforce was equally visible. Not wishing to let Mr. Fleming know how she felt, she refrained from comment, only clutching her reticule more tightly and looking straight ahead. She didn't wish to see the expression on Lady Monceux's face, nor did she want to learn what Lord St. Aubyn thought.

"Ah, the delightful Lady Monceux. I am told she is a widow now. Is that true?" He seemed mildly interested.

"Indeed, sir." Regina didn't trust herself to make any additional comments regarding the lady.

"And St. Aubyn is captured?" He queried her in a lazy fashion, as though not especially interested.

"I think not," Regina protested. "I cannot imagine Lord St. Aubyn marrying her. That is," she continued awkwardly, "his mother would likely frown on such an alliance."

"I fancy *she* still rules the family." His chuckle was not the least pleasant to the ears.

"Lady St. Aubyn is a good woman. I believe she has the welfare of her children at heart, even if she might seem a trifle stern at times." She thought back to the unexpected understanding that her ladyship had revealed over a number of matters. It had been surprising and rather nice.

"Well, well." He continued past St. Aubyn and Lady Monceux, tipping his hat to her, ignoring St. Aubyn. "You fancy him?"

"Mr. Fleming, you exceed yourself." Regina hoped she didn't blush five shades of pink. She had never dealt with a man who was so direct in his speech. Not that Lord St. Aubyn couldn't be outspoken when he chose. That was different.

"You do." He appeared pleased with that, which puzzled Regina greatly. Why wasn't he upset that Amelia and Mr. Jeffries seemed a pair, but curious in regards to Regina's attitude toward Lord St. Aubyn? It made not the slightest sense.

They continued through the park, pausing here and there so Mr. Fleming might greet particular friends of his. He made a point of introducing her to each person, exhibiting a degree of warmth that Regina thought excessive.

Finally she felt constrained to say something to him. "Sir, I get the feeling that you wish your friends to assume we are beyond friendship." If he could speak plainly, so could she.

"And so we are, Miss Hawthorne. So we are."

He turned them in the direction of her home and said nothing more on any topic. Regina wondered what went on in his mind. Beyond friendship? What would her mother say to that, when Regina had insisted she would attempt to make Mr. Fleming aware he ought not call on her again?

At last they reached the Hawthorne residence. When she made to climb down, seeing that he could not leave his horses and no groom was around, he finally spoke.

"You attend the theater, Miss Hawthorne?"

"At times," she replied guardedly, looking at him with cautious concern.

"I have taken a box and would deem it a privilege were you and your lady mother to join me this Thursday. Supposed to be a fine performance. Miss Pamela could come as well, though I doubt Thomas Montegrew would welcome my company."

"I must speak to my mother, sir. I am not certain what she has planned for the week."

"Almack's on Wednesday, I'll be bound."

"Certainly. It would be foolish not to attend so distinguished an assembly. Do you go?" She strove for as innocent an expression as she might muster.

Had she not been watching she would not have seen that fleeting look of wry chagrin. "No. St. Aubyn will have you to himself that evening. But there are other evenings, and I shall see you then. I intend to pursue you, Miss Hawthorne, so be warned."

"Oh." She swallowed rather hard and fled the carriage as quickly as possible. She paused on the steps to turn back, giving him a questioning look. She might not wish his attentions, but she was a proper lady. "Thank you for a most interesting drive, sir."

"Illuminating, true."

He immediately drove off, leaving Regina to enter the house and seek out her mother.

"How did the drive go, dear?" Lady Hawthorne searched her daughter's face.

"It was not what I expected. He seemed not at all interested in Lady Amelia."

"Thank goodness. But?"

"He invited us to the theater with him. I said I would have to consult you before I could give him an answer. Then just prior to his departure he said he intended to pursue me. Me! I cannot think why."

"You had best report this to Lord St. Aubyn." Lady Hawthorne rose from her chair to enfold her elder daughter in her arms. "Such puzzling creatures men are."

It was not long before Lord St. Aubyn called and was admitted to the drawing room, where Regina still sat in conversation with her mother. Her fur capelet and hat reposed on a chair, and she had curled up on the sofa to mull over the events of the day.

"Well, I saw you with Fleming. You looked tense." St. Aubyn strode across the room to bow before Lady Hawthorne, then took a seat beside Regina. "How did it go?"

Regina sent a beseeching look to her mother. Deciding there was no help forthcoming from her, Regina folded her hands in her lap and debated what to say. "It was a curious drive. He appeared not the least interested in your sister or Thomas—other than to ask who was with him. He queried me on the relationship between Lady Amelia and Mr. Jeffries. I intimated they were more than good friends. It appeared not to bother him. He had a lot of questions."

"Did he, by Jove?"

"He wanted to know if Lady Monceux was truly a widow now."

"That's curious." He studied Regina with a disconcerting gaze, intent and pointed.

"I thought so. And he also asked if you were caught by her." Regina, nervous and not wanting to say more, pressed her hands together.

"Caught by Lady Monceux? Why the devil would he want to know that? Forgive my language, please." He appeared rattled, and that surprised Regina much.

"He is under the impression that I am attracted to you," Regina murmured, painfully aware that she was not sufficiently amused or offhand about this.

"Is he? Nonsense, of course."

Regina thought it handsome of Lord St. Aubyn to be so kind. He could have teased her so easily.

"Indeed so. When I inquired if he would be at Almack's come Wednesday, he looked annoyed and said you would have me all to yourself on that evening. He invited Mother, Pamela, and me to the theater on Thursday. He said he means to pursue me."

"Well, well." Lord St. Aubyn mulled over what she

had reported for some minutes before turning to her. He wore a wicked smile that sent quivers through her.

"What are you thinking, sir?"

"I shall thwart him this time. He'll not entrap you with his wiles."

"He can scarce entrap me, as you put it, since I am aware of his intent and have not the slightest intention of succumbing to him." Regina gave his lordship an indignant look. Really, the man was past understanding, no matter how much she was attracted to him.

"I shall make it clear that I consider you my property."

"You cannot!" Regina was aghast. "I am not some bone to be fought over by two dogs!"

"You call me a dog?" He laughed, but looked as indignant as she had felt moments before.

"If the shoe fits . . ."

"Children, you are forgetting a small matter. Mr. Fleming will want to know about his invitation to the theater. Are we to join him?"

"By all means," Lord St. Aubyn declared. "Only there will be a slight change. Thomas and I will also be there. Thomas can protect Pamela, while I shall hover over Regina. Lady Hawthorne, I entreat you to take the wind out of Fleming's sails. I would wager you are quite good at such a task."

He wore that wicked smile again, and Regina was thankful she was sitting down. Were she standing she'd not have vouched for her knees.

"It's been a long time." Lady Hawthorne gave him an amused smile.

Thomas and Pamela, followed by Lady Amelia and Mr. Jeffries, sauntered into the room at that point, demanding to know how the drive with Mr. Fleming had gone.

Lord St. Aubyn rose. "He declares he will pursue Regina. He does not reckon with me. I'll outfox him."

Lady Hawthorne coughed and took a sip of cool tea.

Regina wondered if Mr. Fleming had any trace of hound in him.

Chapter Thirteen

"I shouldn't have to worry while we are at Almack's." Regina pivoted to give her mother a wary look. "I mean, after all, Mr. Fleming will not attend. He cannot, not having entrée to the assemblies. I am thankful that you have such an unassailable position in Society."

"It would be nice were it transferred to you, my dear. At least I can attempt to help you." Lady Hawthorne settled in the comfortable armchair in Regina's bedroom, contemplating the vision in palest green muslin before her. "At least you are at Almack's. That counts for a great deal, dearest. Think what many young women would give to be in that enviable position."

"But—what about Lord St. Aubyn? Do you think he will really try to 'outfox' Mr. Fleming? I do feel like a bone. How dreadful men are—yet so necessary to our happiness."

"As to being a bone, I shouldn't worry overmuch about that. In time all will be settled. Now, I had best check on Pamela or we will not be ready for Lord St. Aubyn when he comes. I gather Lady Amelia will be with him?" Lady Hawthorne rose from the chair with a questioning expression on her face.

"And Mr. Jeffries as well," Regina answered with a grin. "He has constituted himself as her protector. I would not be the least surprised to find that after a time she will be lost without him. Perhaps she will find her happiness after all. I suspect he has Lord St. Aubyn's support, since they are such good friends. How fortunate that he returned when he did."

Lady Hawthorne smiled and left to find her younger daughter. Shortly, a mild argument could be heard involving the merits of pearls versus a coral necklace. The pearls won, no doubt to Lady Hawthorne's skilled persuasion.

When Regina entered the drawing room minutes later she was surprised to find Lord St. Aubyn awaiting her. She glanced around to find they were quite alone.

"Thomas will be along directly. Lucien and Amelia will meet us at the Assembly rooms, along with my mother."

Regina's eyes widened at this news. "Your mother rarely attends Almack's."

"She wants to lend support to Amelia and encourage Lucien. I was surprised at her remarks when you were with us the other day—she was the most thoughtful I have ever seen her. She approves of you, you know."

"I am pleased." Regina studied her gloves again. It was difficult to know what to say. Never had she felt so tongue-tied.

"I came early so we could plan."

"Plan what?" Regina asked warily, flashing her gaze to his face, in hopes of reading his expression.

He strolled over to her. "Why, how to crush Fleming. He thinks to conquer you with his dashing looks and ready wit. You will show him that he has no power to affect the loveliest woman in London." He took one of her hands to look at the glove she had studied.

"I did not think much of his wit," Regina managed to say, overwhelmed by his calling her the loveliest woman in London. Most likely he meant to bolster her spirits. "I do not believe that telling a woman he intends to pursue her is one bit amusing." Her hand seemed to have a life of its own, remaining in his warm clasp as though it belonged there. Why couldn't she snatch it away?

"Even if he cannot attend Almack's, there are people

he knows who do. I shall hover over you this evening as well as when we attend the theater." He clasped her hand more warmly, and Regina thought she would perish with longing to be his. It was difficult to concentrate on other matters.

"You wish to get revenge on him for his jilting of your sister? Would it not be better to flaunt the growing attachment between Lady Amelia and Mr. Jeffries?"

"That, too. But this is not the first time Fleming and I have challenged one another. We were rivals at school and have been ever since." He spoke reluctantly, as though he hadn't wished to reveal that intelligence to her.

Regina absorbed that news slowly. Did he seek her out merely to best his rival? But then she considered his sister, jilted by the man who had been a longtime rival. Of course he would want satisfaction. How complex the situation was. "The girl he married. Was she someone in whom you had an interest?"

Lord St. Aubyn chuckled at her hesitant query. "No. For once he ended up with a young woman I cared not the slightest about—I believe she trapped him. At least that was what I heard."

The chance for any additional discussion about thwarting Mr. Fleming was lost when Pamela and Lady Hawthorne entered the room, to be shortly joined by Thomas. Pamela received his generous compliments on her appearance with blushing grace. They left at once.

At Almack's they quickly found themselves surrounded by friends. Lady St. Aubyn greeted Lady Hawthorne with flattering graciousness. When Mr. Jeffries and Lady Amelia welcomed Regina and the others, it was observed that this was the select group of the evening, to be emulated and sought after.

Pamela found that she was much in demand, to her delight. If Thomas Montegrew stood smugly at the periphery of the dance floor with the air of one who has had some say in her partners, she apparently failed to see it. She flashed a dazzling smile at him whenever her current partner returned her to his side. He stood close to Lady Hawthorne, true, so it might appear that she came to her mother. An intent observer would soon realize where Thomas ranked in favor.

"Pamela flirts quite dreadfully, Mama," Regina murmured between sets.

"That is quite all right, dear. Thomas has things well in control. I fancy he always will."

Regina took another look at him and was compelled to agree. When he stepped up to dance with Pamela, the look he gave her other partners made it quite clear where they stood as far as he was concerned.

"Admiring my brother?" Lord St. Aubyn said in barely heard tones.

"His methods are not to be faulted. Does this skill with people come naturally to your family? Your mother, Lady Amelia, not to mention you, all seem to do well at it." Regina caught his fleeting frown and recalled that Amelia had not done well on one occasion. "I'm sorry, that was ill-spoken of me. How are we coming on this evening?"

She studied the dark brown eyes that met her gaze, searching them for something—she wasn't certain what.

"Do you mean have we created talk? I believe we have. You are reckoned to be an incomparable now, you know," he said with a heart-melting grin. "I have heard it from any number of beaux and gallants this evening. That pale green thing you are wearing sets off your hair to perfection."

"Then you might say my problem is solved." She saved his comment on her gown to savor later.

"Not entirely. There is still the matter of Wrexham. I should like to teach him a lesson he won't forget. That any man would think to offer you a slip on the shoulder is incomprehensible. A man might ardently desire you, but a gentleman knows the proper limits."

Regina glanced about them, hoping no one could overhear this amazing conversation. She wondered if *he* longed for her. She wasn't certain precisely what all that involved, but it sounded delightful. A stir at the entry brought her gaze around that way.

"He has just arrived," she observed. "I cannot like that he seeks out Pamela so often. I wish your brother might persuade her to neglect that interest."

Lord St. Aubyn turned, brushing against Regina's arm as he did. He picked up his quizzing glass, an item he had recently acquired, and inspected Lord Wrexham as though he were an unknown species of weed.

"Oh, very good, sir," Regina murmured with approval. It was such a beautiful setdown and wonderful to be so public. If only her sister would pay attention to what others seemed to think of Lord Wrexham!

The sensations caused by Lord St. Aubyn's closeness she prudently ignored. He might look at her with that wicked gleam in his eyes and turn her bones to jelly, but she suspected it was all in aid of his "plan" and so to be disregarded. Or at the very least put to the back of her mind for consideration later.

"I believe this is our dance, Regina," Lord St. Aubyn said clearly for anyone who was within ten feet of them to hear.

"You ought not use my given name and you know it," she whispered as he led her forth to where the dancers formed new sets.

"Wrexham was passing us," he replied calmly, then turned to greet Pamela and Thomas when they combined to make a set. "I want him to realize that he has been quite cut out, missed the best to be had."

Regina discounted the nonsense uttered by Lord St. Aubyn. But she did wonder if Lord Wrexham were a friend to Mr. Fleming. It would be interesting to find out. If he were a friend, would he report regarding the attention paid to Regina by his old rival?

There were so many things to consider—who was a friend of whom, who was in and who was out of favor with the cream of Society. In the event that Thomas and Pamela did make a match of it, Regina might retire to the country with a measure of satisfaction. Although there was the foolishness that Lord St. Aubyn had said about her being an incomparable now. She gave leave to doubt that very much. How could she be elevated to such a peak when she had been virtually ostracized by Society not long ago?

Was such the power St. Aubyn possessed, then? How fortunate that he was the one who had found her in the park that day when her spirits had been so low. She hadn't believed he could restore her. But now that he had, what next? Would he trifle with her, not meaning to, but amusing himself for a time?

The intricacies of the dance required more attention than she had paid them, and she was compelled to put aside her mental wanderings until later.

"I am pleased to see we have you with us again." Lord St. Aubyn gave her a somewhat mocking smile as he took her hand in the pattern of the dance. "What a blessing it is that you can perform these patterns without thoughts. It is certain that yours were elsewhere."

There was a hint of question in his words. When next they met, she said, "I have much to mull over, my lord." She fluttered her lashes at him as she had seen other women do when they flirted.

"Minx," he murmured.

He had left her to fetch some lemonade when Lord Wrexham accosted her, requesting a dance. What to do! Could she possibly convince him to leave Pamela alone? That little widgeon did not know the difficulties into which she might plunge herself did she continue to flirt with the man.

"I await some lemonade," she said at last. "It would not be proper to leave here."

"St. Aubyn dancing attendance on you, is he?" His laugh sounded bitter to her ears.

Regina plucked at a riband dangling from the neck of her gown. What a pity the deep green trifle offered no help in finding an answer.

"You have insulted me in a way no lady of gentle birth should ever know. How can you think I would wish to dance with you, have any contact with you in the least?" Brave words, indeed. She ignored his apology, feeling it false.

"Because you worry about your precious sister. I fascinate her, you know. She thinks me wicked and dashing. If you truly want me to leave her alone, you will have to persuade me."

Regina gasped. "You cad!" she whispered. "I want nothing to do with you. If the patronesses knew what manner of man you are, you would be banned from here. You can forget my meeting you for any reason."

"But you will. Here comes your protector. Or is he? We shall see." He bowed, then left her.

"Why was Wrexham talking to you just now?"

"He first requested a dance. When I said I awaited you, he threatened that unless *I* persuade him to leave Pamela alone he will do something dire. Just what he intends to do he did not say, but he insists that I *must* meet him. I do not know what to do." The last words were uttered more to herself than to her escort. "He is determined that I must be the one to *persuade* him. And how I am to do that I cannot imagine!"

"I've no doubt he has something all thought out. Since you refused his first offer he might take it into his head to force the issue."

Regina studied Lord St. Aubyn's grim visage, reflecting on his words. "You do not mean . . . ?"

"Oh, but I do. You must take great care from this moment forth. Never go out of the house unless you have adequate protection. That means a man, my dear. Your sister or a maid will not do."

"I will not yield to his threats. Nor will I be content to hide in the house."

"How fierce you look, but I doubt you are a match for him when it comes to force."

Regina firmed her mouth and narrowed her eyes. "I shall carry a pipe with me—a lovely length of iron."

"And start a new style? Shall you paint it to match

your pelisse? Have one in each color, perchance? Shall we soon see Society ladies all armed thus?"

"You mock me." She flashed him a look of pure annoyance. "I shall think of something, you may be certain."

"I shall inform your mother that you have a threat against you. She knows what was contemplated."

Regina turned her face away so it would seem they spoke of trivial matters. It would not do to appear to be deep in serious conversation. "Yes, she knows and worries about Lord Wrexham, particularly as pertains to Pamela. I doubt she thinks I am in any danger. And no doubt Thomas will see to Pamela."

"She still should know."

"I shall take care, sir, and I thank you for your concern." Suddenly the image of Lady Monceux as she had leaned out of her carriage to flirt with Lord St. Aubyn returned. What was it she had said—that St. Aubyn often helped lame dogs over a stile? That had rankled when uttered weeks ago, and it still did. Was he so intent upon granting his assistance that he would say and do almost anything? What should she believe and consider so much fustian?

"Regina . . ."

Whatever he had been about to say was lost when Thomas and Pamela joined them, requesting that they join them for another dance. There was no way one could refuse without questions being asked. Regina wanted no raised brows tonight. She was certain there would be plenty come the evening they attended the theater.

On the way home from Almack's Lady Hawthorne patted Regina's hand. "I think the worst is over, my dear. There is so much to discuss that your little jilting is out of date. There is nothing so dreary as old news, much talked about and done to death."

"I trust you are right, Mama."

"Well, I had an agreeable time this evening, and I look forward to the theater. Thomas said he would be there

at my elbow to protect me from any unwanted suitors."
Pamela gave a happy bounce on her seat. This was uttered with such enormous satisfaction that Regina
couldn't refrain from a soft chuckle.

"Lord St. Aubyn will be with you," Pamela said with
a puckered brow. "I cannot see how you can have two
escorts. Mama, you go with us. Who shall it be?"

"I suggest we allow the gentlemen to settle that
matter."

Annoyed though she might be, Regina did not leave
the house for the next two days without adequate protection. Perhaps Lord St. Aubyn had been overly concerned, but she was not about to take any chances.
Ignoring Pamela's plaintive queries, she took the carriage
and a footman when she went shopping to select the
proper slippers for her new gown and more gloves. She
had an idea for a clever wisp of an evening hat as well.

Of course there was no one about to kidnap her. She
was sure of that. On the other hand, she was sufficiently
leery of Lord Wrexham to take ample precautions. Perhaps it was those Gothic novels Pamela loved to read
and relate to her that prompted the feeling. It was the
look-over-the-shoulder sort of thing occasioned by just
that, plus the realization that it could be real.

By the day they were to attend the theater she felt
comfortable with her defense. When Pamela persisted in
knowing why they dragged along an extra footman, Regina simply murmured something about it being the latest thing to do, and Pamela subsided. She might have
still been puzzled, but she knew better than to question
her sister on a matter of what was up to the minute.

When Mr. Fleming arrived at the Hawthorne residence, he found Lady Hawthorne, Pamela, and Regina
waiting for him in the drawing room. Regina wore a new
gown of green spangled gauze, not too unlike the one
she had seen on Lady Monceux, except that Regina's
was more discreetly styled and had a hint of blue in the

green. It reminded her of the sea on a sunlit day. Her tiny hat was composed of bluish-green ribands that looked a trifle like seaweed if one studied them closely.

Pamela curtsied, pink silk roses in her hair and her simple white muslin flowing about her in pleasing folds.

Lady Hawthorne rose from the sofa to greet him, regal in her deep blue gown of sarcenet.

The sight of three gorgeously arrayed women apparently surprised him. He blinked, then bowed deeply. "I am indeed honored to escort such charming ladies this evening. It will be an evening to remember." If he gave Regina a significant look, she ignored it.

Regina exchanged looks with her mother, hoping that all would go well and that it would, as he put it, be an evening to remember. He possessed an elegant carriage, worthy of a duchess at the very least. Well, a handsome man might feel the need for an equally handsome equipage.

She found it difficult to maintain a calm exterior, threatened as it was from two directions. The danger from Mr. Fleming was not as serious as that from Lord Wrexham, but it was something with which she must deal. How fortunate she had friends who would help.

The theater lobby thronged with patrons intent upon reaching their places. Regina accepted Mr. Fleming's arm, more to guard against any danger than from a desire for intimacy. Of course he assumed that she had decided not to oppose his courting, or whatever he called his pursuit. He beamed a fatuous smile at her, as though she had already succumbed to his charms. What a pity he seemed so nice, because he could have been truly nice—had he not been so odious.

They had nearly reached his box when Thomas and Lord St. Aubyn stepped forward from the crowd to greet Fleming, nodding to the women.

"You are outnumbered, old friend," Lord St. Aubyn said most jovially. "I believe we must come to your aid. Recall, I always did in the past." He bestowed a grin on his old school enemy that should have warned him what would happen next. Before he could say a word, Mr. Fleming found Lord St. Aubyn arm in arm with Regina and Thomas Montegrew gathering Pamela to his side.

Lady Hawthorne offered a wry smile. "It would seem you must lead the way, Mr. Fleming."

Too poised and far too much the man of the Town to cause a scene, Mr. Fleming shot a look of loathing at his nemesis, then gallantly offered his arm to Lady Hawthorne. "My lady."

Regina could not help but be glad that things were working out so well. Now, if only the evening would continue in the same vein, it might even prove to be fun.

Once they were settled on the chairs in the box, she dared to glance at those assembled in the theater. She spotted Mrs. Dudley with Priscilla Carvil on the far side, the elder gossip busy scanning the boxes with her glasses.

Then she looked beyond them and had to smile in chagrin, for Lady Monceux was wearing her green spangled gauze tonight as well. Regina dwelt upon the sight, feeling that her own gown was by far the more becoming. But then, she never wished to worry about falling out of her gown. To her, the extremely low neckline was more suited to women who were vulgar. The thought of Lady Monceux being vulgar was enough to warm her heart. Of course, she would never say a word, though one had to take comfort where one might. To be deemed vulgar was about the worst thing that could be said of a lady.

Her gaze shifted to the man with Lady Monceux. Lord Wrexham? How interesting.

"I see you are curious as to who is present this evening," Lord St. Aubyn murmured in her ear.

"You undoubtedly see the same couple I see. That is a most intriguing pair. Do you not agree? Would that he would transfer his request to her!" Regina had felt his breath stir the curl she had allowed to fall close to her ear, and she found it strangely appealing.

"You do more justice to the green spangles than Lady Monceux does. How came you to select that particular fabric?"

"I admired it on her, but this color is not quite the same—there is a hint of blue in mine. How quaint that we should both wear our spangled gowns the same evening. I do hope I shall have the opportunity to greet her," Regina concluded with relish. She was younger and more proper, and there were times when propriety worked to one's advantage. She didn't like Lady Monceux in the least. If it weren't for a strong desire to offer a blindingly sweet smile to the woman, she would cut her dead.

The play was virtually ignored, what with all that went on in the audience, not to mention the machinations that occurred in the Fleming box.

Mr. Fleming took the chair on the other side of Regina's, which sat almost touching Lord St. Aubyn's. He leaned over to inquire as to her comfort, suggesting that St. Aubyn might like to fetch her some lemonade.

"I understand you are rather good at that sort of thing," he concluded with a wily grin.

Regina realized he must be sufficiently close to Lord Wrexham for that tidbit to be relayed. She gave Lord St. Aubyn a significant look before returning her gaze to the stage.

"Fleming, you cannot think I could tear myself away from this breathtaking guest you have with you this evening? Old man, you underestimate me—as usual."

Mr. Fleming took a deep breath, most likely a very annoyed one, and slipped his arm over the back of Regina's chair. That ruse might have worked had Lady Hawthorne not dropped her reticule and begged his help in locating it in the dimly lit box. Being the perfect host must have played havoc with Mr. Fleming's good nature. His face grew a trifle red, and his handsome mouth thinned as if in resolution.

At last the reticule was found, thanks bestowed, and then it was the intermission.

Regina exchanged a wordless look of thanks with Lord St. Aubyn before asking her mother if she desired a breath of air.

"No, dear, I am quite happy to sit here. Dear Mr. Fleming is so attentive to my every need." She smiled and patted the gentleman on his hand with her fan.

Dear Mr. Fleming looked as though he might explode.

"If you wish to stroll in the corridor a bit, I should be happy to escort you, Miss Hawthorne," Lord St. Aubyn declared. He suited his words to actions and within a twinkling assisted Regina out of her chair and to the door of the box.

Once outside, Regina succumbed to a fit of giggles. "I am sorry, sir, I never giggle. You must admit that your old school chum will likely never be the same again. I had no idea that my mother could be so devious."

"I pray that you are right about Fleming." He turned his gaze from Regina's mirthful face to note who approached them, and his expression altered to one of extreme politeness.

"Lady Monceux, how lovely to see you again," Regina gushed. "I declare we are almost twins! How clever of you to dare a lower neckline." Regina smiled, hoping she quite put Lady Monceux in a fury. "I fear I am a trifle too young, or perhaps too proper, although I know it is done," she concluded hesitantly.

"You little . . ." Lady Monceux gathered her wits and smiled in return, a strained stretch of painted lips.

Well, Regina decided, perhaps she needed the paint to cover a pallor that came from staying inside too much. "You are well, my lady?" Regina tried to convey a deep concern for one who appeared unwell.

"I am extremely well. I must congratulate you on your choice of color. With your hair, you must find it a trial to select colors that are, shall we say, flattering?"

The two men gazed at each other with that helpless expression men wear when women are being bitingly sarcastic.

"I have not the least trouble." Regina bestowed a delighted look on her adversary. "Madame Clotilde is such a marvelous help, always showing me what is exactly appropriate." Since none of Lady Monceux's gowns bore the elegant touch of a premier mantua-maker, Regina felt safe in mentioning the woman's name. Although she had to admit the lady usually appeared in gorgeous creations, even if a trifle daring.

"So I see."

Her manners and rearing came to the fore, and Regina felt guilty for being such a dreadful snipe. Perhaps there was a reason that Lady Monceux behaved as she did. "You do look lovely, my lady." She curtsied politely.

Having delivered what proved to be a most telling score, Regina exerted a slight pressure on Lord St. Aubyn's arm. "Perhaps we should return, my lord."

"By all means. Lady Monceux. Wrexham." He bowed correctly to both. He then escorted Regina back to Mr. Fleming's box with a firm clasp of her arm.

"If you want to start a conflagration, remind me not to assist by handing you tinder. I thought your red hair would take flame."

Regina sobered and stared at him in concern. "Lady Monceux angered me." It was a poor excuse, but the best she could think of at the moment.

"She is older than you, and not as lovely. You must forgive a woman who is past her prime."

"You seem to find her fascinating enough." Regina could have kicked herself for uttering the thought that had popped into her head. Of course he found the older woman more interesting than a mere spinster. A widow with assets that were not limited to her bank account could beguile quite easily.

"I shall forget you said that."

She stared into those dark eyes and devoutly hoped he would.

Chapter Fourteen

"Mama, I was utterly beastly. I cannot believe I was so rude. Lord St. Aubyn will likely never speak to me again!"

"He will probably consider your red hair. I know I do."

"Lady Monceux referred to it," Regina said, plumping herself on the sofa next to her mother, who was also her dearest confidante. She couldn't tell her everything, of course, but she was a great comfort at times like this.

"What should I do?"

"You cannot invite her to call. It simply would not be done." Lady Hawthorne avoided meeting Regina's gaze.

"Why can I not invite her?" Regina ceased pleating the skirt of her green muslin day dress to study her mother's suddenly pink face. "What is it about Lady Monceux that prevents her from attending Almack's or being invited to tea here?"

"It is nothing more than hearsay, and I refuse to tear a reputation to shreds. You know how dreadful that can be." Lady Hawthorne seemed very ill at ease.

"It must be something unsavory, then. I have heard snippets about the conduct of some widows. And she is a widow. Is that the situation?"

Her mother said nothing, but looked increasingly uncomfortable.

"She is some gentleman's mistress? St. Aubyn's?" She thought a few minutes, then added, "It would fit the little hints and lapses I have noticed—and ignored." As close as she might be to her mother, Regina guessed there were some matters she would not talk about.

"Now, dear, we must not leap to conclusions. Just because he has been seen in her company quite a bit and he used to take her to the opera and for drives in the park is no reason to make assumptions."

"He does not take her to the opera or for drives now?"

"Not as far as I know." Lady Hawthorne rose from the sofa and went to the window to stare down at the street. "Mr. Fleming is below. It seems he is intent upon his pursuit of you. What do you plan to do about him?"

"Oh, dear. What a pity he is such a handsome wretch. It is most awkward for me. St. Aubyn talks nonsense about escorting me everywhere, thwarting Mr. Fleming. Yet, were Mr. Fleming sincere . . ."

"You cannot forget that he jilted Lady Amelia." Lady Hawthorne turned from the window to give her daughter a reproving look.

"No, I cannot, of course. I merely think it is a pity that such a handsome, eligible gentleman should be such a frightful wretch."

"True, true. But then, there must be other eligible gentlemen to be found." Lady Hawthorne gave her daughter a hopeful look.

"So—what do I do about him?" Regina was not to be drawn into a discussion of eligible men, of which Lord St. Aubyn would top the list. The memory of those dark brown and exceedingly cold eyes still smote her heart. How *could* she have been so stupid! To pass her rudeness off as jealousy was no excuse. She hadn't even known about his connection to Lady Monceux at that time. Although—she *had* suspected something and had simply wished not to admit it.

Norton paused at the door, looking at Regina with a disapproving eye, likely because she had an afternoon caller before the accepted time. "Mr. Henry Fleming."

"Please show him up, Norton."

Mr. Fleming appeared to be somewhat under the weather. He did not look his best.

"Ladies. I trust you are recovered from the delights of the theater." He bowed to Regina, then turned to Lady Hawthorne next to the window and bowed to her. He offered a small bouquet of spring flowers to Lady Hawthorne.

Regina wondered what delights he had sampled after leaving them. "It was a pleasant evening, sir."

Lady Hawthorne sniffed the flowers, then rang for a maid. One appeared promptly and bore the flowery offering away to be put into water. Her ladyship sank gracefully onto the sofa, offering Mr. Fleming a polite smile. "Indeed, sir, most agreeable."

Mr. Fleming was skilled at saying small nothings, the sort of talk one indulged in when calling. It was surprising that he had not lost his touch while off in the countryside.

Regina exchanged a glance with her mother when he had sat with them for about fifteen difficult minutes.

"I hope Miss Hawthorne will do me the honor of taking a turn about the park this afternoon."

"Sorry," Lord St. Aubyn said from the doorway and not sounding the least regretful, "Regina is going with several of us to a picnic. Is that not right, my dear?"

Scathing words burned on her lips. How dare he again use her first name? And what picnic? It was the first she had heard of it. She opened her mouth to denounce the scheme when she realized it would be a wonderful excuse not to go driving with Mr. Fleming. Perhaps that was Lord St. Aubyn's intent?

"True, there is a picnic, and very shortly. All I need to do is don my spencer and fetch my reticule and bonnet. Lady Amelia and Mr. Jeffries are joining us, are they not?" She smiled sweetly at Lord. St. Aubyn.

"Certainly. I saw Pamela as I entered the house, and she has agreed to go with Thomas." He made an ironic bow to his rival. "Sorry, old man. I will not wish you better luck next time. Rather, I suggest you look to greener pastures."

Possibly deciding that he would try again later, Mr. Fleming gathered his tattered poise and made a very good exit, all things considered.

Once she heard the front door close, Regina turned on his lordship with a dangerous eye. "A picnic, pray tell?" Why did she have to fall in love with such a man? At first he thought to help her *like some lame dog,* and now she was a tool to best his old rival. She decided she had endured more humiliating trials than should fall her lot.

"In the rush of our departure from the theater last evening I quite forgot to tell you about the scheme. My sister would like to have a picnic, and I thought we ought to join her. We will go to my home—a short drive on a lovely spring day."

"A picnic," Regina repeated. She would have sworn it was something he had made up on the spur of the moment to thwart Mr. Fleming.

"Now, put on your spencer and do whatever else you must do. That's a good girl."

"For two pins— I do not believe you planned this last evening." Regina rose to face him, hands clenched at her side.

He looked at her mother. "Hair about to flame, would you say?"

"I fear so. Surprises are not always accepted as gracefully as one might wish." Lady Hawthorne made a shooing motion to Regina, then said, "Urge Pamela to hurry, will you, dear? You know how she can dawdle."

Knowing when she was beaten, Regina curtsied properly, then marched out of the room in quite justified ire. She paused at Pamela's door to request that her sister hurry, only to find her dressed and ready to depart.

"You are dressed to go! When did you learn of a picnic?" Regina demanded.

"I bumped into Lord St. Aubyn at the foot of the stairs and he told me. I think it prodigiously wonderful.

He and Lady Amelia have a lovely home and gardens. It will be far better than ending up in some cow pasture." She wrinkled her nose in distaste. "I'll wait for you below."

Dazed, Regina went to put on her dark-green velvet spencer and locate her matching velvet reticule. The reflection in her looking glass as she adjusted her chip straw bonnet looked quite as confused as she felt. Had the world gone mad?

With hesitant footsteps she returned to the drawing room. There'd be no help from anyone in clarifying the muddle. Clearly, her mother sided with Lord St. Aubyn on anything he chose to do. Pamela looked happy, but then she now enjoyed Thomas's company regardless of the circumstances.

All Regina could think of was her parting with his lordship last evening and the coldness in his eyes. She took heart that it was no longer there. But what was? Whatever, there was nothing lover-like present now.

"Ah, ready, I see, and looking exceedingly charming. Lady Hawthorne, you have done yourself proud with these young ladies."

"I like to think so, my lord." She crossed to give Pamela a hug, then turned to meet Regina's confused eyes. "I know you will have a pleasant day. I doubt the rain your father predicted will occur."

Regina gave her a hug, then left with Lord St. Aubyn and Pamela, feeling as though she had wandered into one of her bewildering dreams, when things seemed so real, yet weren't.

"I understand they are laying odds at the clubs as to who will catch you—Fleming or me. What do you think?" St. Aubyn sank back against the squabs, studying Regina while rubbing his chin.

"I think you are mad. And what is this about odds? Betting on me?" Regina closed her eyes in dismay. "I wonder if I ought to simply sail off to America."

"Regina!" Pamela gently touched her arm. "Think how this has turned all attention from your jilting. Why,

I doubt there is anyone who even recalls it. From what I have heard, the gossips are all atwitter about the challenge between Mr. Fleming and Lord St. Aubyn. They wonder who will succeed."

"Betting *and* gossips. Dear sir—is there anything else you have planned for me that I do not know about? I should like to be prepared. It is so awkward not to know what is going on." Regina bestowed a sweet smile on the man she adored—the man who also happened to be her nemesis. It was truly amazing what love would tolerate.

"Oh, yes, but I will not tell you about it now. Time enough later on."

Regina fumed in silence.

They paused before the stately St. Aubyn town house to pick up Thomas. He plopped himself beside his brother with a jaunty air. "Everything taken care of, Jules, just like you asked."

Regina was about to inquire what that might be, then at the slow shake of Lord St. Aubyn's head she didn't say a word.

"Very wise, Regina."

She satisfied her longing to snap a reply with a mere fulminating look.

"Such a lovely day," Pamela chirped.

"It will rain later. Papa said so, and he is rarely wrong."

Regina gave his lordship a demure look. Picnic, bah! Never mind that she longed for his company, thought a picnic a marvelous idea, and wondered what offerings his cook might conjure up for them.

"We can always go into the house. That is why going to our home is better than a pasture."

"I told you so," Pamela said with great virtuousness.

Regina gave her sister a nudge with the hope it would silence her, then sat with her thoughts the remainder of the way while Lord St. Aubyn and Thomas debated the merits of two horses running in some race.

She thought they would never get there.

Lady Amelia and Mr. Jeffries met them when the carriage arrived at the St. Aubyn country home. It must be delightful to have the prospects offered by the country and yet be only a short drive from the city.

"How nice that you could all join us," Lady Amelia said with great composure.

Regina raised her brows and bit back a grin. She turned to Lord St. Aubyn. "You certainly have your family well trained."

"Yours would do the same for you, no doubt?" He was odiously smug.

She considered the matter a few moments. "I'm not so sure of Cornelius. He is wretchedly independent."

"Red hair too?"

"Now that you mention it, it is a sort of mahogany. Pamela is the one who takes after Papa with his brown hair. Cornelius and I are more like Mother. Her hair is mostly gray now, so it's hard to tell what it once was." She accepted his arm, relishing his closeness as they strolled along to a path that led to the rear of the house.

"Family faces are always interesting. Should you like to take a look at our long gallery, you would discover that I resemble a great number of my ancestors. Such a useful trait if ever there might be a question."

Even Regina had heard of the questionable parentage of a number of the Melbourne offspring, gossip being what it was. Although upon looking back, she was reluctant to believe anything spread about by the tittle-tattlers. She prudently avoided making any comment regarding that remark.

"If it does rain I should like to see the pictures," Pamela said with her boundless enthusiasm.

"That is a promise, Miss Pamela."

The earl was all suave politeness. For a few moments Regina wondered what it might be like to be a countess, particularly Lady St. Aubyn. The mind boggled at the notion, and she soon gave it up. How could one anticipate what one had not the slightest knowledge of? Her parents seemed to have an agreeable marriage, and she supposed there could not be so vast a disparity between a baron and an earl. Money, prestige, perhaps land. Although her father had invested wisely in land and other interests, so they had no worries.

They reached the gentle slope that ran down to the artificial lake to find a table set out, complete with a marvelous repast awaiting them. Regina was impressed.

"We can eat now or later, as you please. Perhaps you would like a stroll in the garden first?"

Everyone seemed to look at Regina, as though she was some manner of fireworks about to go off.

"I should like that very much. I enjoy gardens, and I am not quite hungry yet."

"An honest reply. Very well, we shall walk first, eat later. The rest of you may do as you please." St. Aubyn led Regina toward a hedge, behind which they found the garden in magnificent bloom.

"I was hoping to be able to speak with you privately," Regina forced herself to admit. "I feel utterly dreadful about what I said and did last evening. Can you ever forgive me?"

"And is that important?" His gentle query gave her hope.

"Yes. I have to live with myself, you see. I was simply so angry. She . . ." Words failed her. It wouldn't do to let him know that she had tumbled into love with him and resented Lady Monceux's obvious familiarity. "Lady Monceux deserves an apology as well, but I daresay I will not see her in private."

"True. She generally spends her time with older women."

Jules had no idea what gossip might have been relayed to Regina about Beatrice. He'd wanted to protect her from the tittle-tattle so beloved of the Society madams. Yet it seemed as though he'd plunged her into the fray again with Henry Fleming. He ought to have known that Fleming would leap to a challenge like the beautiful redhead whom Jules found interesting. And Fleming ought to know that if Jules cared for her, he wouldn't let Fleming win. And Jules did care. Very much.

They strolled through the first of the gardens; from there they inspected the herbaceous border, and then the fine arrangement of roses. In spite of her stern demeanor, his mother greatly admired roses, and the gardens displayed an excellent selection. It had been Jules who thought of having gardens devoted to various colors. There were the yellow, the pink, and lastly, the white. It was a challenge for the gardener to find the proper plants, something he did with the aid of the catalogs Jules ordered.

"This is very lovely. I've never seen anything remotely like it." Regina bent to sniff one of the yellow roses, an early one that he particularly liked. "Although you really ought to have a blue garden as well."

Jules glanced up to note that clouds had gathered to the west, dark and menacing. "I believe your father may have had the right of it after all. Look at those clouds." He took the opportunity to tuck her arm more firmly close to him and then turned back toward the house.

Before they reached the tables, rain began to fall. He virtually carried her up to the shelter of the rear entry to the house. "There, little damage done."

But the rain had dampened her gown, allowing it to cling enticingly to her figure. Jules thought he had better get her inside and dry before he betrayed his attraction more than he had already. He wanted to kiss her and never let her go. He couldn't imagine what she might do in the event that he gave way to his impulse. Probably bash him over the head with that pipe she had threatened to carry with her.

"Something amuses you?"

"Only that you were right, my dear. Come—let us go into the house. I don't want you chilled."

The footman held the door open, averting his eyes from the appealing picture she presented.

"There you are!" Amelia cried with obvious relief.

Did she think he intended to sweep Regina off to the remote gazebo to dally with her? Not that he wouldn't enjoy it. But he knew better, however difficult it might be to stifle his longings.

"You had the food brought inside?" He glanced at the footman, who nodded.

"I had them take it to the conservatory." Amelia gestured in that direction. "That will be almost like eating outside and very much like a picnic."

"I am glad my sister has so much common sense." He turned to Regina. "If you would like to dry off, Amelia will show you where you can go."

The two young women disappeared while Thomas, Pamela, and Jules wandered off to the conservatory.

Here the viewer found ample space to roam under tall trees from tropical countries. The perfumes of various flowers scented the air, along with the aroma of damp earth. Jules took note of what was blooming and resolved to ask the gardener to cut off a few of the exotic blooms for his guests. He inspected the table that had been set up, approving what his sister had arranged.

He doubted if Henry Fleming could begin to think of something so diabolically clever. After all, Henry didn't have the cooperation of a sister and brother. On the opposite end of the conservatory, he noted Thomas pointing out an unusual tree to Pamela. The delightful peagoose looked more enchanted with Thomas than with the tree. Well and good. It would keep her away from Wrexham. What the man's scheme was, Jules couldn't figure, but he didn't trust him an inch.

In a lovely bedroom on the first floor Regina surveyed her image in the cheval glass with dismay. "I look rather damp—to put it mildly. What your brother must have thought!"

"I shouldn't worry too much about Jules. He is the best of brothers, you know. I venture to say he will make an excellent husband." Lady Amelia handed Regina one of the towels the maid had brought.

Regina's heart sank to her toes. "He intends to marry soon?"

"I do not know for certain, but I'd not be surprised.

He has hinted." Lady Amelia chuckled. "He is ever one given to surprises. Like this picnic. Was there ever such a delightful picnic? It is nice for Lucien and me to have a chance to visit away from Society and the eyes of all those gossips."

Regina agreed, all the while wondering whom Lord St. Aubyn intended to marry. Surely not Lady Monceux! Yet there was obviously something between them.

They returned to the ground floor, then passed through a succession of rooms to the conservatory. It was like entering another world—a very green and foreign world.

"Enchanting!" Regina craned her neck to view the tall, strange trees such as she had never seen before. She strolled along the graveled path, admiring exotic flowers and rare greenery. Lady Amelia slipped away to find Lucien Jeffries. They seemed to have reached an understanding, and Regina was glad for her. How good that someone could find deserved happiness.

Overhead, rain beat a gentle tattoo on the glass. At the far end of the conservatory Regina saw Lord St. Aubyn standing apart from the others, waiting for her.

"All right and proper?" At her nod, he offered his hand, which she promptly accepted. "There are a few plants I would show you, and then we shall eat."

What joy to be in his company. But in the back of her mind the knowledge that he intended to marry soon haunted her. It was inevitable that she would slip. "Your sister said you plan to marry before too long. Is that right?"

"Yes, I hope to marry before too long."

That was all. He said nothing more, and she had been too forward as it was to ask him who the bride was to be. To make matters worse, he seemed to be highly amused, and his eyes laughed at her.

"How nice. I hope you will be happy." Such stupid words, ones she did not feel in the least like uttering. It wasn't done for a lady to be so bold as to inquire into the personal life of a gentleman as she had done already. She dared not probe further.

"I believe I shall." He said nothing more, and that was the end of the subject.

She viewed the plants with well-mannered enthusiasm while pondering ways to find out who this bride would be. By the time he escorted her to the table she was no wiser, nor had she thought of a means to find out. She simply could not ask and risk a snub.

"Come, let us eat. I think the others are already there. You know, Lady Monceux has never viewed this room, although she enjoys flowers very much—or so she says." He urged her to a chair drawn out from the table.

Regina paused briefly before taking a seat. Could he actually be contemplating a marriage with Lady Monceux? Why else would he bring up her name at this time, just after talking about his hoped-for marriage? Horrors!

The delectable food might have been mush for all she tasted of it. Her heart had lodged permanently in her slippers and nothing appealed to her in the least. When Lady Amelia cleared her throat, Regina happily set down her fork.

"Lucien will place the proper item in the papers, but I want to reveal this now. We have an announcement to make to you, our dear friends—and relatives. He has asked me to marry him and I have accepted. And he promises me that we can live at his home in the country. I need never endure another Season." Her eyes sparkled. When her brothers applauded, she beamed with delight.

"Until it is time for our daughters to make their come-out," Lucien added, with a fond look at his love.

Lady Amelia blushed prettily. "Well, I am pleased to beat both of my dear brothers to the altar. I'll wager you thought I never would."

Jules grinned. "I knew you had plenty of sense. You merely needed the right one to make you happy."

Regina smiled and laughed and applauded the engagement, admiring the pretty sapphire ring, all the while wondering who the earl's "right one" was.

At last the meal concluded. If anyone noticed that Regina had done little more than push food around her plate and nibble a bit of fruit, no one said anything.

The rain ceased drumming on the roof, and the earl suggested they stroll about outside again.

"Very well." Regina decided she might as well go. After all, she might have a chance to change his mind. She could flirt—maybe. She would never want him to laugh at her, and she had the uncomfortable feeling that he had done just that on a number of occasions already.

"You approve Amelia's engagement?" Lord St. Aubyn inquired as they walked down a path.

"Of course," Regina said at once. "After such a dreadful experience as being jilted, she must welcome the love of a fine man. I'll wager they have a quiet wedding, and very soon."

"Lucien would never jilt her, if that is what worries you. You would like a quiet wedding? After being jilted, that is." He sounded very offhand and certainly not particularly interested.

Regina doubted that she would marry, although she knew her mother nursed high hopes. "I fancy I would—with just the closest of friends and family. A simple gown, a few flowers, a kind groom. I'd not care for the ostentation of the Torrington wedding we saw." She managed to smile as though she'd made a joke.

"No—I imagine you'd not wish to be reminded of that."

"It has long ceased to bother me, you know," she earnestly assured him. "When I saw the love on his face as he looked at Katherine I knew they belonged together. He must have had his reasons for squiring me about, but they had nothing to do with marriage."

Whatever Lord St. Aubyn thought of this confession was not to be known, for Pamela and Thomas marched up to them at that moment.

"Thomas refuses to take me on the lake. He insists it

might rain again." Pamela folded her arms before her and had that obstinate expression she wore when determined.

"If Papa said it would rain today, he meant it. You do not know but what another shower may come this way." Regina gave her dear sister a reproachful look, then met Thomas's rueful expression with a smile. "Thomas is right, love. Best to remain in the gardens. They are very lovely. Have you seen the roses?"

Diverted, for she loved flowers, Pamela permitted Thomas to cart her off to the rose garden.

Like all good things, the picnic came to an end. After being presented with bouquets of exotic flowers, the young ladies were all popped into the carriage, then joined by the gentlemen. The conversation dealt with the coming wedding, which would be a quiet one, as Regina had guessed.

"You both will come, will you not? And I intend to go to Madame Clotilde for my gown. Perhaps you would like to come with me, Regina? You can help me select the design. I'll wager it will not be long before you are looking for your own."

Regina murmured something noncommittal in reply, but agreed to go with Lady Amelia whenever she chose.

"Won't the gossips have fun with this bit of news!" Lady Amelia said with glee.

"It is always a joy to best them. I doubt that even Mrs. Dudley suspected a thing." Regina reflected on the occasions when Amelia and Lucien had been in public and decided they were few. Indeed, the tattlers would be amazed. "It will be a nine-day wonder!"

"At least they are not wagering on who will marry you," Pamela said, sounding grumpy.

"No. Who is being wagered about?"

"I doubt anyone is interested, Amelia," the earl inserted suddenly.

The carriage hit a bump, dislodging Regina's bonnet when she jostled Pamela. A bit of confusion, then all was set straight once more.

"I wish to know. It is dreadful to be so behind in what is going on in Society, and I can see that you know who it is, dear brother." Amelia gave him a narrow look, which he returned in kind, startling her.

Thomas answered. "They are betting who will get Regina's hand in marriage—Jules or Henry Fleming."

"Good grief!" Amelia turned to face Regina. "You couldn't accept Mr. Fleming!"

"No, that will never be!" She'd not wed the other, either. He intended to marry someone else.

Chapter Fifteen

"I appear destined to be food for the gossips." Regina paced the width of the drawing room, then turned to pace the other direction. "I cannot believe anyone would be so foolish as to bet on my possible marriage. I will not marry either of them!"

"Be thankful Lord Wrexham is not included in the betting." Her mother's comment dropped into the silence of the room with all the effect of an explosion.

Regina stopped dead to give her mother a horrified look. "I would prefer not to be the object of any betting at all—whether it be Mr. Fleming, Lord St. Aubyn, *or* Lord Wrexham. I believe Lord St. Aubyn did not wish me to know anything about it. He most likely feared I would explode."

"Well, dearest, you do on occasion have a temper. I expect it has to do with your hair, although I cannot see how we can blame every loss of temper on that."

Lord Hawthorne entered the drawing room wearing a frown on his elderly face. "What is this I hear at the club? My daughter the subject of a wager?"

"So it is true? I had naught to do with it, Papa." She compressed her lips, wishing she could fly away. "The gossips are having a fine time, I gather."

"It might interest you to know that St. Aubyn is the odds-on favored candidate for your hand. I approve of him, if that is true. Fine chap."

Regina shot her father a scathing look, although she stood with hands neatly clasped and her back stiff. Papa so rarely made an appearance, she had no desire to quarrel with him when he did. "That is well and good, but his sister told me he plans to wed, and he has said nothing to me. I fear the betting book is a deception. Perhaps he wishes to conceal his true plans."

Her father paused in the act of retreating to his library to give her a beetle-browed stare. "St. Aubyn had nothing to do with the bet being entered in the book." He gave her a long look, then left the room.

"I fear Papa is displeased," Regina said, turning to meet her mother's eyes.

"Well, we shall see if anyone comments when they come to call this afternoon. Mrs. Dudley is bound to come around, not to mention a number of others. Would that we might deny her!"

"Oh, Mama, she would really create a calamity in that case. We had best try to divert her attention to something else. Perhaps Lady Amelia's wedding to come. She said it would offer the gossips something to chew on for a bit."

"I wonder if Lord St. Aubyn will appreciate your efforts in that direction?"

"Oh, bother Lord St. Aubyn. Were it not for him, I'd not be in this pickle." Regina gave her mother a defiant look, compressing her mouth in annoyance. Never did she want anyone, least of all her dear mama, to know the extent of her love for Lord St. Aubyn. She would die an old maid. How could she marry another man when she loved Lord St. Aubyn?

"He only tried to help, dear," her mother reminded her. "And recall, the original dilemma occurred when Lord Torrington led you to have expectations that vanished when he wed Miss Talbot. Just think, you might still be the object of pity you were then."

A considering look settled on Regina's face for a time before she spoke. "I truly do not know which is worse." At least she had not loved Lord Torrington.

"You had best remind Pamela that we are likely to have callers following luncheon. I suspect it is something she would as soon forego."

"Indeed, Mama. I believe I shall change into a very demure dress. It would never do to look like a temptress." Regina marched up to her room, debating which of her gowns looked the most suitable for a spinsterish governess sort of woman.

Mrs. Dudley was among the first of the callers.

Regina had often wondered why they were referred to as morning calls when the people came around three of the clock. When Norton announced several gentlemen whom Regina scarcely knew, she guessed that the following hour or so would be busy.

The rich and gossipy widow, Mrs. Dudley, was about to depart when Lord Wrexham was announced. The widow sank down on her chair. Although custom and manners said that she ought to leave after a brief time, her nose quivered with the possibility of new tittle-tattle to spread.

His lordship bowed to Lady Hawthorne, then took a stance by the fireplace close to Regina. She had barely refrained from dashing out the door when she saw him, and now she was pinned in place by his attentive gaze and the curiosity of the entire clutch of callers.

"Miss Hawthorne, I am most fortunate to find you at home today. I thought certain you would be driving with either Fleming or St. Aubyn."

"I cannot think why you might assume such a thing, Lord Wrexham." Regina smiled, a mere stretch of her lips. She made no effort to speak quietly. She wanted the others, particularly Mrs. Dudley, to know that the stupid bet had no substance. Too, those silly young men should learn that she was not inclined to matrimony with either Fleming or St. Aubyn. Not that she wouldn't marry Lord St. Aubyn in a heartbeat. But he wasn't likely to ask her!

"I trust you will agree to taking a drive with me— since you seem to be inclined to go driving these days." It was a pity his lordship extended his invitation in a

ringing voice that probably could be heard all the way
to the front door.

You could almost hear the room hold a collective
breath.

"Or perhaps Miss Pamela would grace my carriage this
afternoon?" His eyes flickered from Regina to Pamela,
perched on her chair, her eyes as large as saucers.

Regina knew a threat when she heard one. She met
her mother's gaze, then looked at Pamela, sitting as docile as a ewe lamb. Her eyes sparkled—likely at the
thought of driving out with so dashing a gentleman.
Thomas simply couldn't begin to compete with Lord
Wrexham when it came to being fashionable. Fortunately, Pamela wouldn't dare to put herself forward,
leaving Regina to figure a way out of her predicament.

If only the other callers would leave! She found it
difficult to deal with Lord Wrexham when so many eyes
were upon her. This was one time she doubted that
Mama could interject some clever remark to resolve the
matter. No, Regina would have to think of some manner
of refusing Lord Wrexham's request without angering
him or creating more tattle. It was providentially close
to the end of the customary time for calling, which was
helpful. Wouldn't a number of these people go if she
stalled long enough to let them see she had no intention
of satisfying their curiosity?

A stir at the door turned all eyes as one to see who
dared to interrupt the most interesting request from Lord
Wrexham—a request that Miss Hawthorne found difficult to answer.

It proved to be Lady Monceux! Regina rose, thankful
for the diversion, but she wondered what on earth
brought the striking widow to the Hawthorne drawing
room. She wore a stunning yellow silk pelisse adorned
with black silk frogs and bands of black at the hem. Her
broad-brimmed hat of yellow silk, trimmed with black
plumes, was the very latest in fashion. She was very stylish and dashing.

Regina suspected that in comparison her prim gown

gave the impression of a prudish spinster. But was that not what she had intended?

Perhaps—if the others would but depart—Regina might have a chance to apologize for her rudeness at the theater.

"Good afternoon, my lady," the widow said with the utmost grace, nodding first to Lady Hawthorne. She smiled at Regina. She then swept a haughty, dismissive gaze around the room as though ordering them all to disappear. Several ladies rose and made diplomatic departures, as did the disappointed gentlemen who'd had no chance to find out which way Miss Hawthorne leaned in the matrimonial betting contest. Mrs. Dudley, apparently realizing that she had overstayed her time, left with visible reluctance.

"Lord Wrexham, I am indeed surprised to find you here." Lady Monceux gave him a mocking smile before taking Regina's arm to lead her to a dainty settee a short distance away from the fireplace where he reclined against the mantelpiece. The fashionable skintight breeches currently in vogue did not allow ample room in which to be comfortable while sitting. Hence, men often stood in a graceful post against a fireplace mantel, as Wrexham did now.

He appeared a trifle disconcerted, but he did not alter his position. His eyes narrowed at Lady Monceux's comment. "I have been here before. You have not."

Regina thought he wore the expression of a cat about to pounce on a particularly delectable mouse.

No one saw fit to remark on his statement. Somehow Regina found herself cozily seated with a woman who had good cause to dislike her.

Lady Monceux studied Pamela, then turned her gaze to Regina. "I had not realized how much alike you two are, although Miss Pamela has brown hair. She is the same height, and I would venture to say you wear the same size of gown. Did I guess right?" She gave a delighted smile, as though she had been terribly clever.

"Actually, I am just a trifle taller than Pamela," Regina said, "but as you observed, we are alike in many ways." Regina flashed a warm look at her sister. They were without a doubt closer than many sisters.

"I would wager one of you could pass for the other." Her trill of laughter brought a smile to Regina, one quickly doused when she caught sight of the expression on Pamela's face.

"Well, it is fortunate that neither of us would contemplate doing such a thing. Is that not right, Pamela?"

Pamela chewed at her lower lip a few moments, then nodded. "As you say, Regina."

Lady Monceux took the conversation into her capable hands, not permitting other than mild agreement with her words to come forth from the others. Several minutes passed in pleasant conversation, if anything so one-sided might be called that.

When she rose, Regina did as well. The opportunity had not come to beg forgiveness for the rude words spoken at the theater. Of course it was due to jealousy, she realized that. But still, she would feel better were the words offered.

"Wrexham, give me a ride home," Lady Monceux sweetly demanded. "I dismissed the hackney when I came here. Perhaps you would summon your man—and mind you wait. I shall be down directly."

To his credit, Lord Wrexham did not argue with the lady, nor did he repeat his request for Regina to go driving with him, to her relief. He rose, bowed, and made a creditable leave-taking.

"Oh," the widow paused before she made what was likely to be her departure. "You go to the Rothman ball this evening, I imagine." At Regina's reluctant nod, Lady Monceux gave a girlish giggle that caused both Pamela and Regina to widen their eyes. "Pamela ought to wear the green gauze gown. I think it would be great fun. Promise me you will! I shall wear mine. With her brown hair she might almost be *my* sister. I do not have a sister."

These final words had been said with such pathos that

Regina truly wondered if the lady was quite right in her mind. Perhaps she enjoyed being dramatic. Her choice of garments leaned in that direction. And widows were allowed more leeway in their behavior, so she had observed.

"If Regina will permit me, I would love to wear that green gauze gown, my lady." Pamela's eyes sparkled.

"Good." She was out the door in a whirl of yellow silk, the black plumes on her hat flouncing in the breeze created by her rush.

"That has to be the oddest caller we have had in some time. I did not know that you were so well acquainted with Lady Monceux, Regina." Lady Hawthorne studied her daughter with shrewd eyes that made Regina feel uncomfortable. Her mother on occasion could see more than one would wish.

"I do not. Know her well, that is. I cannot imagine what brought her here today."

"Well, she wants me to wear the green gauze gown this evening, and I, for one, am thrilled." Pamela left the room humming a gay tune and bouncing a little.

Following silently, Regina was surprised to see the first footman hand Pamela a folded bit of paper. A message? From whom? Pamela knew none of the gentlemen who had flocked here earlier and left so reluctantly. Perhaps it had come from Lord Wrexham? He would have had time to jot a line or two, most likely inviting Pamela to slip out for a drive with him later.

The stubborn girl knew how dangerous Lord Wrexham was, yet she thought he would be different with her. Foolish one. As to the green gauze, Regina decided she would let Pamela wear it merely to discover what was afoot. That something was going on she had little doubt.

Should she relate her hunch to Lord St. Aubyn? That was hard to say. If he turned up at the Rothman ball, she might pass along the quizzical turn of events, providing that it didn't stir more gossip, that is. Let those silly fools who would bet on a marriage lose every penny.

*   *   *

The Hawthorne family was not in the least in strait-ened circumstances. On the other hand, Lord Hawthorne did not believe that a girl could wear a gown once, then set it aside, especially if it chanced to be expensive. The gown of gold gauze with the pattern of gold leaves had been just such a gown.

If Pamela wore the green, then Regina felt obliged to wear the gold again and just hope that no one remarked on it. It would do her hopes of finding a husband little good if she was thought to be impoverished.

When the family departed for the Rothman ball there were mixed expressions by the various members. Lord Hawthorne deigned to attend, commenting that he could count on a few good partners for cards at the Rothman do. Lady Hawthorne, obviously pleased that her spouse decided to join them, offered no complaint regarding his plans.

Regina stewed on her comfortable plush cushion. Her sister looked too satisfied with herself. She beamed smiles at one and all, preening a bit, smoothing the deli-cate fabric of the green gauze with obvious delight.

"Your gold gown truly is lovely."

Regina wondered what prompted Pamela to offer the compliment. Not that she was unwilling to say nice things—she merely didn't do so often.

"And as Lady Monceux fancied, you look very nice in that green. Does she truly think you and she will look like sisters? There must be ten years between you." Regina wondered what actually was in the lady's mind. She'd not sent a message to St. Aubyn, as Pamela had not left the house once all the callers had gone. Regina had made a point of lingering in the hall, leaving her door open, and in general keeping an eye on her sister's doings. Nothing strange had occurred.

It took some time for the coachman to maneuver the carriage up to the entrance of the Rothman home. A red carpet had been laid down to protect delicate slippers and gowns. There were a few urchins and others standing about to gawk at the beautifully garbed guests.

Lord Hawthorne collected his ladies to escort them inside, then once they had greeted their host and hostess he disappeared in the direction of the card room.

"Did Papa ever dance?" Regina wondered, not for the first time.

"Goodness, yes. He is wonderfully light on his feet and capable of dong a fine minuet should he choose. He does not like these fast dances they have nowadays. Nothing, he insists, can match the elegance of a minuet."

Regina made no comment, for she thought the minuet a fading fancy, even though St. Aubyn said he could show her otherwise. On the other hand, the waltz was a trifle daring. She knew how to waltz, for everyone attended waltzing parties on occasional mornings to practice the breathtaking dance. She could not forget the pleasure of being in St. Aubyn's arms.

There was no sign of Lord Wrexham, to Regina's enormous relief. Lady Monceux bustled forward to greet them all as though there had been no rude words, no past cold shoulders.

"My dear Pamela, how lovely you look. We do seem a bit like sisters, do we not?" Her smile seemed gleeful to Regina's intent gaze.

It was amazing how much they did look alike, given the difference in ages. Although Lady Monceux had darker hair, she had styled it something like Pamela always did. Her slender figure said much for her willpower when it came to sweets. She looked more like Pamela than Regina did.

"Well, dear girl, do not do anything I wouldn't do." She patted Pamela on the cheek, then drifted off to the opposite end of the ballroom, far from the door.

"Mama, what was all that about?" Regina covered her face with her fan, hoping Pamela would not overhear her words, although it was unlikely that she would, given the general noise of the throng of people.

"I cannot imagine. However, I'd not be surprised if we find out before the night is over." At Regina's quizzical look, she shrugged. "I have this feeling, you see."

Thomas presented himself as a partner for Pamela, praising her appearance enough to please her. They went off to join a set just forming.

Regina was happy enough to sit by her mother, knowing that Mr. Fleming was unlikely to attend this select event. Then a familiar figure wound his way through the guests, causing Regina's heart to perform a happy jig.

"Lady Hawthorne, allow me to spirit your lovely daughter away. I would have a partner, and she is the best I know." Lord St. Aubyn bowed, offering his hand to Regina. His eyes gleamed with amusement and something else she couldn't identify.

"How could I possibly refuse such a courteous invitation?" Regina rose, giving him her hand while wondering whether she ought to tell him of her disturbing premonition.

"I like your mother," he said while leading Regina away to join a set of dancers.

"So do I. She is very special. Your mother is charming." Regina hoped her comment on his mother was sufficiently kind. That lady had unbent considerably since Amelia had become engaged. She seemed quite human now.

"I have not seen you for a few days."

"I noticed."

"With that dratted bet, by keeping my distance I hoped to thwart a small amount of the gossip and speculation. Your father was not pleased regarding the wager. Fleming tried to speak to him, and your father walked past him as though he wasn't there."

"Oh, dear, he cut him? Did many people see?"

"Not too many. You were frowning before. Is there a problem?" They parted in the movement of the dance before she might answer. When he took her hand once again, he continued their conversation. "And I was surprised to see your sister wearing that green gown of yours. Not that the gold thing you are wearing isn't superb on you. You are a golden goddess."

Delighted by his praises, Regina felt completely able to confide her troubles to him.

"Well, you will likely think it silly." She related the events of the afternoon, ending with the folded paper that had been slipped to her sister in such a secretive manner. "And she has said not one word about the note. I hoped she might reveal the contents to me. It seems that it was *very* confidential."

"It's dashed odd that Lady Monceux suggested Pamela wear that gown this evening. I wonder why?"

"Mama said she intends to watch and wait."

"Wrexham!" Lord St. Aubyn caught sight of the man that Regina had just seen enter the ballroom. "I'd not thought he would attend something so tame as the Rothman ball. This is a surprise."

"I was upset when he came to call today. He may have apologized, but I still do not trust him. I have tried to avoid him since . . ." Regina frowned while attempting to find an adequate word to politely describe what he'd proposed.

"I can well imagine you have. I am glad you are not avoiding me." He swept her away from Wrexham's view, nicely keeping her so that she was not easily visible.

She thought it kind of Lord St. Aubyn to be so considerate of her fears. When her gaze met his, Regina hoped her eyes would not reveal the depth of her feeling for him. She could make no reply that wouldn't disclose too much, so she remained silent for the moment. Then she asked, "What do you think?"

"It is a definite muddle. I think your mother has the best idea. We shall keep our eyes open. Where is Pamela?"

"With your brother. Lady Monceux is at the far end of the room, I believe. It is like a drama."

"I always thought Beatrice had a flair for the dramatic. I wonder what is up her sleeve."

"Besides her arm?"

"Dreadful, my girl." He flashed a grin at her to allow she had made a witticism. The dance at long last ended, and he walked along with her to where her mother sat visiting with Lady St. Aubyn. Not far away Amelia walked with Lucien Jeffries. Lady St. Aubyn was holding forth on something of interest, given her mother's intent expression.

"I trust they can be wed before old Lord Quellan goes aloft. He has taken a turn for the worse, and Lucien must let the servant know his whereabouts at all times."

"Since Amelia and Lucien want a quiet wedding, would it make a great deal of difference?" Lady Hawthorne inquired.

Lady St. Aubyn gave her old school friend a look of respect. "Perhaps not. Surely everyone who matters would understand."

Regina turned to Lord St. Aubyn. "I gather Lord Quellan is much worse, with no hope of getting well?"

"Lucien will be a viscount before long, which will help his cause with my mother, I am certain. Not that she minds Amelia marrying him. She is glad that her only daughter will not be a spinster."

"I suppose mothers do worry about that," Regina said, reflecting that her mother had good cause to fret.

"Thomas informed Mother that he intends to marry Pamela. Has he asked her?" Lord St. Aubyn moved along toward the shadowed recess behind their parents' seats.

"Not that she has said to me! Do you suppose that he sent her that note and she is expecting a proposal from him?" Regina glanced at her sister, standing with Thomas and still in some disagreement. What could they possibly find to argue about for so long?

Lord St. Aubyn also looked at his brother and Pamela. "I doubt it. He has a ways to go before he will be able to convince her."

"They cannot seem to get along. Why must they squabble?"

"I've observed that some couples do that sort of thing. You must admit it reveals a kind of familiarity."

"Not something I should like." Regina gave her sister

a puzzled look. There was an excitement about her that she would wager had nothing to do with the dancing or with Thomas.

"Come, I hear the strains of a waltz. Join me, Regina?"

"Just keep me away from Lord Wrexham. I see he is talking to some friends. Could we dance at this end of the room? Away from him?"

"My pleasure, I assure you. I have no reason to admire him, and I fully approve your concern."

Regina relished the feeling of being in Lord St. Aubyn's arms, with no reproach possible from anyone. To waltz with just anyone would never do. But she found being in his arms irresistible and gave herself up to the charm of the dance. They waltzed in silence for a time.

"What happened to Pamela? She is not with Thomas, and I cannot see her anywhere." Lord St. Aubyn spoiled Regina's blissful dance with his urgent query.

"I cannot see from my height. Where did you see them last?"

"She isn't with Thomas, for he is talking to Mother." Regina thought of the odd look in Pamela's eyes. "Something is afoot, I just know it."

He waltzed her over to the far end of the room, where Beatrice, Lady Monceux had last been seen. She was not to be found either. Further searching revealed that Lord Wrexham appeared to have left.

"This is no mere coincidence! I think we must investigate."

Regina didn't object when Lord St. Aubyn led her from the dance floor, although she regretted her lost waltz with him. "Do you think we will find out anything? I mean, just because we cannot see Pamela, or Lady Monceux, or Lord Wrexham is no reason to suspect foul play. But then again, perhaps it is, considering that visit today and the suspicious message, not to mention that peculiar expression Pamela wore not long ago."

"I wonder what Lady Monceux had in mind when she

suggested that Pamela wear your green gown. There had to be a reason."

They walked quickly along the halls, examining each and every room as they went. People were found, but not the ones they sought.

"I had no idea that so many assignations were arranged during balls," Regina whispered after peeping into another room that held an amorous couple. Lord St. Aubyn shut the door with care not to make a sound.

"It is one place that is public, and yet privacy can be found. For instance, I could whisk you into this recess and do this." He bestowed a highly satisfactory kiss on her most willing lips. "No one saw us, and we are as safe from censure as though we were in church."

Safe, as in not being compelled to marry her when he didn't wish it. Regina felt ten kinds of fool for permitting the kiss. Never mind she had longed for such. She had encouraged him, so she could scarce scold him. She decided it was best to ignore the entire matter for the moment. She could dwell on that kiss later.

"Perhaps we had best seek help," St. Aubyn said. "I shall ask one of the footmen if he has seen a lady in a green gauze dress."

Regina refrained from reminding him that two women wore such dresses.

At last they found a footman on duty near a side entrance to the house. "Indeed, milord. A lady as you describe left here a bit ago with a fine gentleman. She had on a cloak with a hood, but I could see that green stuff peeking out from under."

"Pamela! That foolish girl, to run off with Lord Wrexham merely because she quarreled with your brother. That must be the case. I can think of no other man who fascinates her as he does."

"Yes, I'm told the wicked are often beguiling to the innocent. Come, we must go after them."

Recalling his kiss and what he had said afterward, Regina was not too inclined to go along with him. "What about Lady Monceux? She also wore green gauze."

"She would have no reason to sneak off with Wrexham. She could ask him to take her for a drive anytime she wished." St. Aubyn impatiently tugged Regina's hand.

"I believe I *had* better go with you. I cannot allow Pamela to be compromised to *such* a man!"

Chapter Sixteen

Thomas stepped into the hall, hurrying toward them with urgent steps. "Have you seen Pamela? We were to have the next dance, and I cannot find her. Her mother has not seen her either."

St. Aubyn looked at Regina. "No, but we intend to hunt for her—we have a clue. You search the house; it is possible she might be around here—somewhere." He turned to request that his carriage be brought around immediately.

"Have you learned something? I demand to go with you." Thomas glared at his brother, taking another step closer.

"No, please. You investigate this house. 'Tis best we spread ourselves about." Lord St. Aubyn was dismissive and calm.

Thomas did not seem very convinced, but accustomed to listening to his elder brother, he nodded with obvious reluctance and left them.

Regina watched Thomas disappear, then clutched Lord St. Aubyn's arm. A thought had occurred to her. "Jules, I really doubt I should go with you. Amelia told me you are to be married. I feel certain your future wife would not approve my haring off with you, even to search for Pamela."

Lord St. Aubyn searched her face, quite what for, she didn't know. His slow smile cut to her heart. "To be sure, I am planning to wed, and soon. My future wife would not in the least mind your going with me."

"She must be extremely forbearing. If I were to marry

you I'd not tolerate another woman in your company, no matter what." Her composure was hard won. How did a woman who loved a gentleman bear to share him with others?

"That is nice to know, but you have no need to concern yourself." He stepped forward to the door to see his carriage coming along the narrow lane from the mews. Once he escorted her from the house, they waited briefly.

That was a snub if she had ever heard one. Well, she would be as silent as a fish if he wanted no conversation.

The footman assisted her into the carriage while Lord St. Aubyn spoke with his coachman. Within minutes he joined Regina in the carriage and they set off.

Forgetting her decision to remain silent, Regina asked the question that had been burning on her tongue. "Do you have some notion where he has taken her?"

"He needn't go far, you know. All he has to do is find a reasonably close house. He lives on the edge of the city, not too far from here, as it happens. I want to try there first."

Regina wondered what Lord Wrexham hoped to gain by absconding with her sister. He had originally sought Regina by infamous means. Now he was being equally villainous, taking a young girl from her family and friends! "He is an utter cad," she pronounced with sudden vehemence.

"I'll not argue with you on that score. Did you never find him appealing—before you tangled with Torrington?"

Regina thought a minute, then gave a careful reply. "All young women are brought up to consider each eligible gentleman they meet as a possible husband. It is the way we are taught. Of course I wondered what he might be like. I must say that I never at any time wished to marry him. But he was considered, along with a great many others."

"Ah, then you have contemplated me as well?"

He queried her with an absentminded manner that

made her think he might have his mind elsewhere, but she had learned enough about him to know that if he asked a question, he expected an answer. What to say? She had dug her hole well and good. Now, how to extricate herself from her own stupidity. She could scarcely tell him she dreamed of him, longed to be his wife. "You *are* eligible, my lord," she said at last in a dry voice.

"Hoist on my own petard." His chuckle was brief.

"What do we do when we get to this house?" She thought it best to change the subject. The carriage racketed along the dark streets, lit by an occasional flambeau in front of a house and a half moon above. She would have been utterly terrified had she not been so worried about her sister.

"I believe we are about there. Leave everything to me." The carriage turned a corner into a quiet street.

"If you think I'll remain in the carriage, you may think again. I shall be right behind you." She gathered the folds of her golden skirt and inched forward on the seat.

"I figured you would."

The carriage slowed to a halt before a neat and somewhat elegant house. The street appeared decent, with smart, proper houses of solid brick. "A reputable area?"

"Oh, indeed. He has no need to pinch pennies. Come, we shall be very quiet. No need to warn him his enemies approach. He has not been here long, I suspect. My coachman said his vehicle left shortly before we did."

"Then he will have had no chance to . . ." Regina felt the remainder of that sentence best unuttered.

"I feel your sister will be unharmed."

His words comforted, yet Regina wanted to push him to action. "Hurry."

"Careful, careful." His whisper barely reached her as she left the carriage to join him before the front door, neatly spruce and painted black. At least, it appeared black. In the dark many colors could have seemed that, and there were no flambeaux to light the area.

Lord St. Aubyn tried the door. It was unlocked. "How

odd." He gave Regina a frowning look, then he opened the door and they slid inside as quiet as mice.

Light glimmered from the first floor. Taking her hand in his, St. Aubyn led the way, stealthily climbing the steps without a sound. There was a squeak or two that were apparently unnoticed by those upstairs.

Regina's heart pounded so hard that she was certain St. Aubyn must hear it. Never in her wildest dreams had she imagined she would *ever* enter a strange house in such a manner. "Fright" did not begin to describe her fears. "Terrified" came a trifle closer.

As they neared the drawing room voices could be heard in argument.

"That does not sound the least like Pamela." Regina's whisper pierced the silence of the hall.

St. Aubyn nodded, frowning. "Could we have made a mistake?" He considered that for a moment, then shook his head. He stepped forward to grasp the doorknob, opening the door with sudden force.

"Lady Monceux!" Regina cried in a very small voice.

"Here, what's the meaning of this? Cannot a man be private in his own home?" Lord Wrexham advanced on Lord St. Aubyn with determined steps.

"Sorry, old fellow. We obviously are under some misunderstanding. I apologize if we have interrupted a rendezvous." Lord St. Aubyn stepped back, looking from Lady Monceux to Wrexham.

Regina observed that Lady Monceux did not scream for their protection, nor did she have the expression of one furious with her abduction. If she was indeed abducted. As a matter of fact, she looked enormously pleased with herself.

"But where is Pamela?" St. Aubyn demanded. "She has disappeared, and we thought since you were also missing that you had taken her away."

"I thought I had her," Wrexham admitted, with a wry glance at Lady Monceux.

"But he didn't." Lady Monceux chuckled. "I see I must share my scheme with you. I suspected that Miles was about to abduct Pamela in order to get you to follow after her, Regina. He does not like being thwarted, and you had so cleverly put him in his place. He thought to lure you here by using her. He left a clear trail, and all the coachmen saw his carriage depart. I suspect he intended to send her home, quite unharmed, once he had you in his clutches. Such a poor villain he is, not to make certain of his quarry."

"You wore the green gown." He was obviously angry, his voice harsh. He reached out to touch the glittery green gauze, so like Regina's gown that Pamela had worn.

"Of course. I hoped Pamela would agree to wear the green gown—as she did. It was a simple matter. I merely locked her in one of those many little rooms, knowing that some servant would open the door sooner or later, while I took her place. Dim light, the right gown, and the cloak he so conveniently plopped over my head did the rest."

"Upon my word!" Regina didn't know whether to congratulate Lady Monceux or feel sorry for Lord Wrexham.

"As to why I did this?" Lady Monceux continued. "Do not bestow any chivalrous ideals upon me, my dear. I have no great love for your silly sister. I decided Miles would suit me very well as a husband. How much easier could I persuade him than to have someone find us in a most compromising situation? Which you so obligingly did." She dipped a little curtsy, a teasing smile curving her lips.

"I could almost feel sorry for you, old man, were it not that you deserve such a fate." Lord St. Aubyn shook his head in derision.

"We shall wed, then travel, I believe. When we eventually return we will be old married folk, and no one will have the slightest interest in us." Lady Monceux clapped her hands with what appeared to be delight.

"Clever, indeed, my lady," St. Aubyn said in admiring accents.

"If you will excuse us, old friend, I have a few matters

to discuss with my future *wife*." Lord Wrexham gestured to the door, making it clear that their presence was unwanted and quite unnecessary.

"Do not worry about me," Lady Monceux cried. "I can take care of myself. Besides, Miles and I are two of a kind, and he knows it. We will do quite well together." She whirled about, the green gauze sparkling in the light of the few candles that had been lit.

Regina wondered, rather unkindly, if either of them was ever given to helping lame dogs over a stile. She doubted it. They were most certainly two of a kind, as Lady Monceux had said.

Lord St. Aubyn hurried her down the stairs and out to the carriage. He ushered Regina inside, then spoke briefly to his coachman. When he joined her, he remained silent for the ride back to the Rothman ball.

Regina was thankful for his silence. She wanted to mull over a few things—like if he'd had no intention of wedding Lady Monceux, who had been the most visible candidate for his wife—whom did he propose to marry?

Regina had nurtured hopes, but they were strongly colored by her wishes and not to be trusted in the least. So, which of the beautiful Society women had he been seen with of late? Or was it some delicate creature he had found in the country, one who had not made her come-out or who preferred the rural life?

"I am sorry, my lord. I hope you did not think to marry Lady Monceux."

"Have no fear. I didn't." He didn't elaborate on that, so she was none the wiser as to his chosen wife. "I thank you for your concern, however."

When they reached the same side door they had left not so terribly long before, Lord St. Aubyn escorted her inside and along the hall. He tried one door after another with no success, always with Regina in tow like a child's toy to be dragged behind him.

"Perhaps someone has released her. Could we not wander through the ballroom? See if one of the footmen let her out, as Lady Monceux hoped? Or perhaps your brother found her?" Regina tugged at his sleeve, with the intention of heading in the opposite direction.

He spun around, and proved to be far closer to her than she had anticipated. He wore the strangest expression as he gazed down at her. Regina took a step back from him.

"Ah, no. We have gone too far for retreat." He reached out one capable hand to capture her chin, then drew her closer. In moments Regina was well and truly kissed, most expertly, too. She had always heard that a rake was accomplished in this skill, and what she had heard paled next to the reality.

She had closed her eyes, drifting off to a pleasant dream where he would ask her to be his wife. How rudely she was awakened. He released her, allowed her to take a step away from him. Then he spoke, and not to say what she hoped to hear.

"Come, we shall find my brother. He may have news for us." Taking her by a hand, he pulled her along behind him like a piece of baggage.

It was a blow to discover that he appeared not the slightest affected by what to her was a wondrous kiss. Regina stumbled on the ballroom threshold, and he righted her with a hand that seemed impatient.

"There he is, on the far side." Still tugging her behind him, although she had in vain tried to free herself, he forged a path through those who lingered along the side of the room.

"I should like to see my mother," she managed to say when she was able to catch her breath.

"In due time. We want to settle the matter of your sister first." He drew up before his brother. "Thomas, did you find her?"

"No. You had no luck either, I gather?"

"Not in locating Pamela." Lord St. Aubyn gave his brother an odd little smile. "We found other game, however. Did you try any of the small rooms? She is locked in one of them. Unless a footman has released her, she must still be there. Unfortunately, I do not know which room it is."

Thomas didn't waste words asking silly questions, like "How do you know?" He turned on his heel and went to the other side of the house. Lord St. Aubyn again tugged Regina after him.

Really, she thought, this was most ridiculous. Was she to follow willy-nilly wherever he went? Of course, were they wed, she would go along with him to the ends of the earth. She doubted it would be necessary, his interests being what they were. But her heart was his—not that he appeared to want it. In one way she longed to know the identity of this woman that he would marry. And then, perhaps not. She would learn eventually, and by then she expected to be off in the country.

Partway down the hall Thomas found a door that had the key dangling from the lock. He quickly inserted it and threw open the door.

Regina judged that opening doors like that must run in the family.

"Regina!" Pamela cried. "I knew you would eventually find me."

"It was Thomas who spotted the key, love." Regina enfolded her sister in a loving hug, and then held her away to observe on her cheeks the pathways made by a few tears.

"How did you come to be in here alone?" Regina guessed how it must have been, but she wanted to hear her sister's explanation.

"I received a message to be here at an appointed time. I came, only to have the door quickly shut behind me. When I heard the lock click into place I was so frightened."

"The note was from . . . ?" Regina suspected it wasn't Lady Monceux.

Pamela looked down at her meekly folded hands and said in a very small voice, "Lord Wrexham."

"Lord, Pamela, how could you be such a widgeon?" Thomas declared in disgust.

"I believe Pamela ought to see her mother," Lord St. Aubyn declared in no uncertain terms.

Thomas looked as though he would object. One glance at his brother's determined face stilled his tongue.

Freed of Lord St. Aubyn's firm clasp, Regina took her sister in hand and within minutes had located her mother. She paused, looking at his lordship with a brave gaze. "Thank you, my lord. Even if we did not find her where you feared, you tried. I guess you *do* help lame dogs over stiles."

Leaving Jules totally puzzled as to her meaning, Regina Hawthorne joined her mother, with her sister at her side. Judging from Lady Hawthorne's expression, Pamela was not to be let off easily. And that was to the good. She had caused a great deal of trouble this evening, not that Wrexham didn't deserve his fate. He was welcome to Beatrice. Jules suspected she could cause trouble if things didn't go her way.

Henry Fleming came into view, and Jules soon waylaid him. He guided him off to the far side of the room.

"Do not challenge me, St. Aubyn. I have given up all interest in Miss Hawthorne." Mr. Fleming backed away a few steps, warding off Jules with a hand and a grin.

"Then you had an interest in her?" Jules rubbed his chin, attempting to appear nonchalant and totally ignoring the curious stares from others close by.

"Well, I heard how Torrington had squired her about, that everyone figured he would marry her. All a hum, of course. A good friend of his said that he had used Miss Hawthorne as a ruse, that he'd been madly besotted with Katherine Talbot all along. Made me curious to know what manner of woman Regina Hawthorne could be." Fleming gave Jules one of those smirks that he so hated.

"Yes, she handled her jilting better than my sister did." Jules gave Fleming a narrow look that sent the man scurrying in the opposite direction. Jules hoped Fleming got a shrew for his next wife. He certainly deserved some punishment for the grief he had caused.

So—Torrington had deliberately used Regina to bring

Miss Talbot to his arms. In Jules's estimation it was a despicable deception. Had Torrington no conception of what damage he would do to Regina Hawthorne? Apparently not. No gentleman would knowingly so use a lady. The knowledge plunged Torrington to the very bottom in Jules's estimation.

The knowledge that Fleming let drop cleared away a mystery that had puzzled Jules, not that it would have made any difference in the long run, he knew. But he liked to have all his loose ends tidied up. He sought the card room, where he suspected Lord Hawthorne would be found.

His conversation with that shrewd gentleman didn't take long. Jules believed in being concise and to the point. The matter was concluded in a highly satisfactory manner to both, judging from the pleased expression on Hawthorne's face.

Jules then sauntered over to the Hawthorne ladies sitting in a cluster. Pamela looked exceedingly chastened. He bowed before Regina. "May I have the pleasure of the next dance, Miss Hawthorne?"

She turned to her mother, seeking permission. That readily granted, she rose, smoothing out her skirts and looking nervous unless he missed his guess.

"I haven't bitten anyone recently," he murmured wickedly. It was meant to torment her, but she rose to his teasing so beautifully.

"I did not think you had, my lord." Frost could have formed on her words.

"Why are you nervous?" He looked forward to provoking her some more. She was such a delightful baggage.

"Who said I was?" She tilted her chin, challenging him with her eyes.

"Forgive me. Appearances can be so deceptive." He was glad the dance proved to be a waltz, for it meant he was able to hold her close in his arms, ignoring the required distance. He also paid no attention to the rebuke he saw in her eyes. Holding her close seemed a necessary thing.

"I must agree with you there." She looked away from him then, a sad expression flitting across her face. It had been so brief that had he not been watching her intently, he would have completely missed it. Torrington had deceived her. Perhaps that was what made her wary?

"Not all men deceive." He whirled her about, skillfully avoiding another couple without taking his gaze from her face.

"Perhaps not. But I think they may give a girl the wrong impression without realizing it." She closed her eyes a moment, as though dizzy.

"Are you all right?" He began to move toward the side of the room, concerned with her sudden paleness.

"I am well, thank you."

He noticed she said "well" and not "fine." There was a subtle distinction. He wondered if he was mistaken in her interest in him. Had she merely looked to him as one to help her? He recalled her earlier words of his helping lame dogs over a stile and frowned.

"You think of me as a helpful person, perhaps? Someone who might come to the aid of one in distress, as I did you?"

"Yes." Her reply was abrupt and almost stoic.

He was disturbed. This wasn't working out quite as he had expected. He had thought he would waltz her away, tease her into a delightful mood, and propose. She didn't sound the least delighted, and her mood was shocking.

"Why do you think I wanted to help you?"

"Because of Lady Amelia. I reminded you of her." The blue eyes raised to his had that smoky haze in them; he remembered it well.

"And so you did. But there was more to it than that, you know." This time he had captured her attention. He couldn't mistake the curiosity in her eyes, nor the lack of resistance as he waltzed her to the edge of the floor, then off toward the door.

"We do not need to look for anyone, my lord."

"You called me Jules earlier." He smiled at her.

"That is a wicked smile, and you know that I was in a panic." Yet she did not resist him when he led her into the hallway.

"Do you mean I shall have to put you in a panic to persuade you to use my given name for the rest of my life?"

"No. That is, I may not know you that long." She was being terribly prudent, he could see that. And precious, as well.

"How long do you think you may know me, in that event?" It was wicked to bedevil her so. On the other hand, she deserved it.

"How can I know?" She shrugged and slipped away from his light clasp to cross the room they had entered.

"I know." He followed her to stand immediately behind her slim form.

"Do you? How very clever, my lord." She turned to face him, studying him with a narrow gaze. "You said there was another reason for helping me. What was it?"

"Jules. Say Jules; you will not leave this room until you do."

Her eyes lit with some inner smile. Did she at last suspect he was serious? "I would like to know, sirrah."

"Jules."

"Jules," she repeated obediently, but still reserved.

"I think I fell in love with you then, that first day, and it grew each time I saw you. It was a hopeless case in no time at all." He had laid himself wide open and was at her mercy.

"How nice, Jules." Her smile had a mischievous tilt to it, and he wondered what she would do or say next.

"Good, you learn very quickly. And if I say you will remain in my arms, you will?"

"No." She tilted her head, and he wondered if she had the slightest idea how seductive her smile was.

"Ah, my dear, but I have you in my power." He sobered, then continued. "And I will not leave you, nor desert you, nor ever cease caring for you as long as I live."

She stepped forward into his open arms, holding her face up to his, giving him the most trusting of looks. "I accept that lovely declaration, whatever it means." She raised her hands to place them on either side of his face, then kissed him ever so gently.

Jules was stunned. Whatever he had expected, it wasn't this. He placed his hands over hers. "It means, my love, that I am asking you to marry me."

"You should have said so. It would have saved so much time and effort."

"Minx. Say you will."

"You will. I will. That makes it unanimous, I believe."

This time she didn't have to do a thing. Jules saw to that.

"I feel well and truly kissed," she murmured when at last released.

"I should hope so. And that is just the beginning."

"Oh, good. Kiss me again."